Rie se

W9-BBV-993

MAY   2023

THE
TIP
LINE

THE
TIP
LINE

A Novel

VANESSA CUTI

CROOKED
LANE

NEW YORK

This is a work of fiction. All of the names, characters, organizations, places and events portrayed in this novel are either products of the author's imagination or are used fictitiously. Any resemblance to real or actual events, locales, or persons, living or dead, is entirely coincidental.

Copyright © 2023 by Vanessa Cuti

All rights reserved.

Published in the United States by Crooked Lane Books, an imprint of The Quick Brown Fox & Company LLC.

Crooked Lane Books and its logo are trademarks of The Quick Brown Fox & Company LLC.

Library of Congress Catalog-in-Publication data available upon request.

ISBN (hardcover): 978-1-63910-264-8
ISBN (ebook): 978-1-63910-265-5

Cover design by Heather VenHuizen

Printed in the United States.

www.crookedlanebooks.com

Crooked Lane Books
34 West 27th St., 10th Floor
New York, NY 10001

First Edition: April 2023

10 9 8 7 6 5 4 3 2 1

For my father.
And for all those who have ever been missing.

CHAPTER ONE

I just wanted to get married. Start my life like anyone else. I was thirty, single. Drinking wine every night while I swiped my way through online dating sites. I was between jobs. It sounds better when I say it that way. I was between jobs in that I had just left one and I hadn't yet found another. I was renting a cottage at the back of an estate. It was private and had its own driveway, but still. Part of the agreement was that I had to pick up the mail and the newspaper for the owner of the big house and walk it up to the porch. There was a box marked "Mail" just in case I forgot this one task, in case I got all the way there and was wondering what I had come for. He called it The Big House, the owner did. He slapped around in slippers and met me at the door sometimes. He was in his fifties and married to a much younger woman, and I saw her leave for yoga some mornings. And sometimes I saw her milling around their large yard, her hands behind her back, looking for a project, something to start in on. Her life seemed to me to be easy and very straightforward. If you have a life like that, you cannot in good conscience complain.

My two best girlfriends were well into their first pregnancies, posting photos of their stretched bellies and their husbands leaning over to kiss these bellies or leaning back and sticking their own bellies out, pretending to be pregnant too. "Beer," they wrote on themselves with marker, with an arrow pointing down. How could you not roll your eyes. They posted photos of shoes: wife shoes, husband shoes, baby shoes. In blue! In pink! Pictures of nurseries. Giraffes and trains and rocking chairs positioned in golden afternoon sun, cushions so deep you could imagine the plush coming up around your hips while you sat for hours and watched your child breathe. Look at that. Beautiful. I could hear their voices, see their heads shaking in unison at me while they bit their bottom lips in turn: *You have to be open minded, Virginia, not so picky. What you think is important now totally changes, and your priorities become so different. Looks don't matter, money doesn't matter, you just need someone who loves you as a person, someone who makes you happy.* Yes, right. Open mind. We hardly spoke anymore, what with their priorities happening all around them, but if we did talk, this is what they would have said to me. Like they were sitting me down.

This is why. All of these things. This is why I had to take the job at the police department. I just wasn't on track. Or I was on track, but it was the wrong one. A little behind on my life plan, as my mother would sometimes say. She said, *Just a little behind, that's all.* She said, *This job will be the perfect place for you to meet a nice man.* She said, *Like shooting fish in a barrel.* I am not the type of person to think in terms of a life plan, but I was not in an ideal situation, and I knew it. And here it was: A way to meet people and put myself out there and find a nice man. Or at that point, any man, really. A man who could turn into a husband, a house, kids, on and on. I was trying to make things right.

*　*　*

I had this idea that there would be a perceptible beginning. It was just this sense. While driving there on my first day, I figured I would walk into the building, and things would be immediately changed. That the front door was some sort of portal to an *after* and everything else a *before*.

The whole way there and for days prior: A thump thump of nerves in my stomach, a cat's twitching tail, the catalyst of a new chemistry. My new chemistry. *Here I am,* it said, spelled out in slowly moving, mixed-up letters and then sliding into place, like on a screen at the beginning of a movie. And there I was, ready for everything, grown, new, happy, capable.

I was early so I sat there, AM radio on low, blowing on my coffee. Preparing. I was wearing a new gray suit, a pale blue button-up blouse, and new black leather pumps. I had a decent overcoat, a gift from my parents. I had washed my hair, blow-dried it, parted it in the center, and tucked it behind my ears. I tried to detach from myself, to see myself objectively as a stranger would see me. I closed my eyes and cleared my throat, ridding myself of my opinion, and then I opened my eyes. Like I could catch a glimpse if I did it quickly enough. The cloak of a ghost. Something elusive. But what I saw: I looked like a child's idea of a grown-up. A bank teller or a receptionist from a photograph in a brochure or an illustration on an exam. Mousy and simple and boring. This wouldn't work. I tried to run my hand through my hair, part it on the side so it fell a little loose. And then, what a disaster. It stuck out, away from the side of my head, a puff above my ear. I shook my head and saw a woman on the phone in the car next to me, watching. She didn't look away when our eyes met. I just left it.

There was nothing ceremonial as I got out of the car and crossed the parking lot. It was too cold. The wind slit open the front of my coat and then lifted the flaps of it, one at a time. Then it went into the buttonholes, into the places between the buttons, touching. My fingertips and face felt numb by the time I made it across. There were tears in my eyes.

I held the front door open for a uniformed officer behind me, and then—I don't know—I got nervous. I got nervous back then in the presence of police. I got nervous and dropped my purse and banged my head on the door handle going down to pick up the things that had fallen out: A lip gloss, a small hairbrush, and a compact mirror from which the top half had broken off. The mirror was the worst part. It would have been less embarrassing had a used tampon fallen out, or a sheaf of condoms, or some deep, dark medication bottle. People would see the mirror and understand that I cared about what I looked like and that still, all I could come up with was this. This fake grown-up.

"Jesus, are you all right?" the cop said, stooping down. He was young, earnest, clean-shaven to the point of shining.

"I'm fine," I said. My head throbbed. I could feel the push of blood there, trying to shape itself into a bump. It must have been something in the way I said *fine*, he must have seen how red my face was, that I was sweating, really disturbed by the whole thing. He must have heard my heart going nuts, because he stood up and backed away and just said, *Okay* as he left. What a story that could have been for grandchildren. What an adorable story. A meet cute for a newspaper piece on our fiftieth anniversary. And I had ruined it. Not a surprise.

Inside, I felt my new chemistry shift. The small spark, which I had finally lit against the wind, was flickering, fixing to go out. *Do not stop,* I wanted to say. *Please, let's try again.* I was superstitious—still am. I don't like to start things off wrong; it sets the stage for everything to come. I considered going out to the car and then coming back in, a do-over. But I stood up and brushed off my front, as though I had fallen in the dirt. I imagined the wiping clean of a blackboard, a towel on a window, a net cutting through the muck that scummed the top of a swimming pool. Visualize. Imagine. Around me, people moved about, waited on line for pistol licenses, walked in and out of the restroom. I heard the toilet flush and gurgle. I smelled a hundred perfumes. I was fine, fine. I was ready again. No one seemed to be watching. No one had seen. The chemicals started back up. I sat down, crossed my legs at the ankle like a lady. I touched the softness where I had hit my head and imagined that if I pressed hard enough I could poke a finger clean through.

* * *

We got started right away. My commanding officer, as they say—Lieutenant Donovan—brought me up the stairs and through a maze of halls and to a room. *Welcome aboard,* he said when he shut the door behind him. He was a ship captain, then: gray haired, weathered in a pleasant way. I imagined him in a dripping raincoat. Then in a cowboy hat, sun beating down. Then as a young cop walking his beat, swinging a baton and whistling as kids rigged a hydrant open behind him. No, he was a ship's captain. I was certain he smoked. That he was unmarried. Either divorced or a life-long bachelor. I could picture his home: untouched cutlery and china, a leather recliner with a blanket on its arm, an ashtray on a side table. He sat down behind what was going to be my computer and began pecking at buttons, hunching.

"Not really work for a nice girl like yourself," he said without looking up. "I hope you don't leave us too soon." He tapped a final key with a flourish and leaned back in my chair. My chair.

"No," I said and tried to make my voice sound disappointed that he had even thought that. "No, not at all. I'm happy to be here."

"That's just fine," he said like a person in an old movie. Then he looked up at me. "Well, let's go over a few of the most important things. I hate to say it but I can't really sit here and train you all day. So you're going to be winging a bit of it."

I was to answer an anonymous tip line. It was secure, no caller ID, unrecorded. I was to ask each caller a series of questions from a sheet of paper taped to the desk:

Thanks for calling our tip line, this is (say your name). What information would you like to provide? Can you give me a physical description? Vehicle description, if applicable? License plate? Time of activity? Do you know if the subject has weapons, a dog, an active warrant? Address?

   ***Don't push too hard, don't waste time with the irate or unstable. Get useful info and then move on.

I was to input the information into a program and then send it to the appropriate command. He pointed to the phone, on its own small table next to the desk. An old-style phone, bright red plastic with a curly cord and push buttons. It sat still and quiet as a relic, a decoration. It needed a spotlight or a museum placard with its provenance. I couldn't picture it ringing.

I was surprised, kind of. The job description had said heavy phones, light typing, administrative float pool, related tasks as assigned by supervisor(s). The one interview I went on had been with Lieutenant Donovan and another man in plainclothes, and neither of them mentioned the tip aspect of it. The public-facing part. The description had made it sound numbing and doable. The perfect place. I'd sit at a desk and lean forward over a stack of papers, make eyes at whichever single guys walked through, chat one up, dating, engagement, the end.

"It's not brain surgery," Donovan said. "You seem sharp enough; you'll do fine." I felt myself blush at this, this near compliment. "Any emergencies, tell them to call 911. You can't deal with that bullshit from here. You'll get crazies, psychics, all of it. It's a free call, remember. Talk to them, hang up on them—I don't care. However you'd like to handle it. You'll find the majority of the calls are about drugs. 'My neighbor's selling weed,' 'my kid found a crack pipe in the street'—whatever. Take the info, send it over to narcotics. Everything else, send to whichever squad, okay?" He gestured to a faded paper pinned to the wall, with squad phone numbers in each of the precincts and then a list of specialized squads at the bottom. "What else, what else?" he said. He leaned his head on the back of the chair and looked up at the ceiling. "Oh," he said and sat forward.

"We just issued an alert on an old case. Unsolved homicide from the nineties. I don't expect anything useful, but who the hell knows anymore. You get anything on it, great—send it through. But they usually want their tips walked down to them. Big shots, over there in Homicide." He made a face, just short of rolling his eyes. "Fax machine isn't good enough for them. You'll have to bring it over on a platter."

"Okay," I said. I was thinking of the windowsill, of putting a small plant there. A stack of books, brass bookends. How about a clock for my desk? One of those little heavy ones. A green, glass-shaded lamp with a pull chain. I would tell my parents I had an office. I would take a picture of my keyboard and my morning coffee and send it to the girls. I'd let an inch of the computer screen in, something official-seeming. Something important.

"You know where they are? Homicide? Anyone walk you around yet? Down to the right, then a right. It can get confusing, so just ask if you get lost. One of the other secretaries will help you." We both looked at the door like we were waiting for someone to walk in. "Actually, out at that other desk right there," he said and pointed, "is Evelyn. She knows everything. More than most of us. She would love to help you out. You know what—hold on a sec, hold on." He huffed himself up, walked out. Came back a minute later with his hand on the shoulder of a woman.

"This," he said, waving his free hand in front of her, "is Evelyn. Evelyn, this is Virginia. Our new tip line person."

"I've been here for thirty years," she said without a hello. "I did paperwork for some of these boys when they were coming in from the academy. So if you need any help with anything, sweetheart, you just tell me."

"I will, definitely," I said. "Thank you."

I saw her look around.

"Why don't you jazz this place up, make it your own?" she said. "You're in here all by yourself, you might as well. Some candy, some decorations. Holiday decorations. People are so festive around here."

"That's a good idea," I said and nodded. Like I was imagining blinking Christmas lights, a tiny tree.

"Great, great," Donovan said and clapped his hands together. "Perfect. I have to get going, though, so how about any questions."

They were both looking at me, waiting.

"Nope," I said. "I don't think so."

"So smile," he said, his thumbs in his belt loops. "It's not going to be so bad."

"Of course not," I said and I smiled and smiled and smiled.

*　　*　　*

So many of them told me to smile. When I saw them in the parking lot, in the hallways: *Smile.* Like they'd die if they couldn't find a girl showing her teeth. *Smile, it's not that bad,* they said. *Oh, really?* I wanted to answer back. *How do you know?* But I smiled instead, I did. I bit my bottom lip into the smile, couldn't help it, and I looked down, and I felt my cheeks get pink under the weight of their eyes. I knew that they watched me pass, sized up my body and my hair, but my body mostly, and then snapped their attention away and said the same thing to the next one of us who walked by.

They were dashing in their uniforms, you had to admit. The patrol guys in dark blues, higher ranks in white shirts, all their brass twinkling, shining like teeth in the fluorescent lights of the place. Detectives in suits, plainclothes in stubble and jeans with just the tips of their shields showing, just the tops of their guns showing.

They meant no harm. It was true—they were just being friendly.

CHAPTER TWO

"Hello, thank you for calling Suffolk County Crime Line, this is Virginia. What information would you like to provide today?"

"Yeah, look, that guy in the picture you just put out?"

"Sure, sir. What can you tell us?"

"Is this call recorded?"

"No, sir. Completely anonymous. No caller ID, and we are not recording."

"The guy was kind of a dick. I mean, forgive me, rest his soul and all, but no one liked him. You guys know that, right? He was getting into a ton of fights. He was in a dart league. Sucked at darts, by the way. He gave some guy a concussion once after a game. That's the kind of person we're talking about. Cops were there. It should be in the records. But they had bad blood between them. There was bad blood with him and a bunch of people."

"Name?"

"I thought you just said I didn't have to say who I am?"

"Sir, I apologize. I meant the first name of the man who was injured in the altercation."

"Oh, so you have an attitude on you now? I'm not smart enough for you?"

"Sir, all I'd like to do is get your information to the right place so that it can help the investigators."

"You are a prissy little bitch. You know that?"

Click.

*   *   *

Of course I got lost walking it down. This on my third day of work. I made a right, then another quick right, just like Donovan said. Only I wound up in a quiet dead end that opened onto another suite of offices. "Chief of Department," the plaque on the door said. I heard the secretaries chatting inside. They had Christmas lights on the main door, silver tinsel, character cutouts. An elaborate door—one of the most elaborate, I'd say.

"Excuse me," I said, leaning in. "Hello?"

Three women stopped talking and turned to me, silent.

"Hello," I said again. "It's just that I'm new? And I'm trying to find the Homicide office? I think I'm lost." I shook my head at myself: How silly of you, you silly girl, what are we going to do with you?

"Oh, sure, hon," one said. She rolled her chair back. "Let me show you." She came toward me, curls bouncing, wiping her hands together. I heard a voice from deeper inside the office, then, and I saw the other two women straighten their backs and look at their screens, fingernails poised over their keys, like their tapping had stopped mid-thought. But it was that voice that had snapped them into action.

"Catherine," I heard the voice say, boom, and one of the women jumped out of her chair, sending it rolling out behind her. She nearly ran to that voice.

"This place is a maze," the woman helping me said, whispering, as she got closer. "Come."

She walked me to Homicide and left me at the closed door.

"You'll get it eventually," she said and turned back toward her office. Then she stopped and looked back to me. "Hon, you'll have to knock for them. They're the only people in this place who keep their door shut."

"Thank you," I said, my hand already raised to knock. I waited until I couldn't see her anymore before I did it. I was self-conscious about everything. I used my top knuckle, the knocking one, and I gave it an authoritative but polite tap. I heard the sound my knocking made as it traveled through the wood. I waited. Nothing. Knock again. Wait. Wait. Wait. Walk back to my desk and try again later? Call them? Ask them when I could come back? Make an appointment to come back. Arrange a meeting for a drop-off. Ask them to come down to me. Ask Lieutenant Donovan to call, ask him to come up and bring it over for me, please. I wanted Donovan to do it.

The door opened, and the man who opened it was not opening it because I knocked. He was on his way out.

"Hi," I said. "I'm new over at the tip line. I just wanted to bring you this tip I took this morning." I held it up to prove it. I nodded. I looked at him like he was grading me. That's how he made me feel.

"What's that?" he said. He was shrugging his arm into a suit jacket. "Where?"

"The tip line?" I said. "Down the hall?"

"Oh, that's still here? I wasn't sure we still had that, even," he said and stopped moving for a second, long enough to look me up and down. "Civilians in there now, I guess." He put a folder in his front teeth and shrugged the other arm into the other sleeve and then fixed his cuffs. "Go ahead in. Someone will take it from you." He held the door open for me, and I went in under his arm.

Three of them, that I could see. All wearing dark suits, white shirts, red or blue ties. One stood at a file cabinet, and the other two sat on opposite sides of a desk. No secretary. They did not look up when the door shut behind me.

I stood there, looking. I could say, *Hello, excuse me.* A usual and orthodox greeting. They are just people, Virginia, and this is just their job. You are not afraid of the postman. You're not afraid to talk to the chef at a restaurant or to a kindergarten teacher. Go ahead. I took another step in, hoping my shoes would make enough noise that the men would hear me and turn. Nothing. There was paper everywhere. Stacks of it on shelves along the walls. Piles of files and folders on the desks. Desks made unusable by paper. A phone rang somewhere, deep in an office. I imagined it covered in paper.

"You going to come in here, or you want us to come to you?" one said.

"Yes," I said. "Hello." I walked toward the desk, though it had been the one at the file cabinet who spoke, I think. "Right, sorry." I felt myself turning red. "I'm new and I'm not exactly sure of procedure. Lieutenant Donovan said I should walk these over."

"Oh, thank God," one of the seated ones said, motioning his chin to the paper in my hand. "Here's the information we've been waiting for." He looked mean. Bald with a round face, his shirt collar tight around his thick neck. "Pack it up, guys." Then he looked back at whatever papers were in front of him. I disappeared.

"Ignore him," the man across from him said. "He just wants his nap and his blankie. He doesn't mean to be rude." He waved me over. "You can leave it here." He pointed to a pile of paper in front of him and then rolled his chair to a computer. "Thanks," he said, but he was already looking at something else.

I let myself out.

I had sweat through my shirt. I felt it at my lower back and under my arms. I thought to go to the bathroom and dry myself off, but I had already been away from the phone for so long. When I got back to my desk, I cracked the window and breathed into the cold air that came in. I imagined the men down the hall. They were talking about me. Laughing. They had seen my sweat rings and the pull in my tights and my stray eyebrow hairs not yet long enough to catch with a tweezer. I imagined these laughs: friendly, easy. Big smiles like blackjack dealers and car salesmen. And then they were on to the next thing. They were done with me.

Deep breaths. I smoothed my shirt, smoothed my skirt. I sat straight in my chair, hands on my keyboard. I waited for the phone to ring.

CHAPTER THREE

Friday, the last day of my first week, was significant in two ways. In the morning, Donovan stopped in to check on me. It was the first I had seen of him all week. I had tinseled my door and put a small bowl of chocolates out on my desk, the way Evelyn had suggested. I watched as he noticed. He took a candy before he even spoke. He nodded as he chewed.

"How are you holding up?" he said, balling foil between two fingers. His teeth were lined in the brown of softened chocolate. I smelled the sugar coming off him. "Everything okay?" He tilted his chin down when he asked this and looked upward at me. I think he was convinced I was delicate.

"Great," I said. Though it came out so loud I swore I saw him back away. So I leaned forward, my palms on the desk like a grade-school teacher. I thought I should start wearing knee-length skirts, pleated. With little sweater sets. It seemed like the right place for them. I steadied my voice, calm. "Everything is great," I said again. He had come to reprimand me, had heard about my encounter with Homicide, heard I hadn't been reverent enough, or too strange or too quiet or too rude. He'd heard about the caller who had information on this—an actual unsolved *homicide*, for God's sake—and I had botched it, ruined it, angered the caller who could have given me everything, had I not been so stupid. I rushed to preempt him. "I'm still trying to get the hang of it. I feel like I forget something important every time. And then I wish I could call them back and ask what I forgot, just so I'll have all the information. Has anyone said anything about the tips? Have they made any arrests on anything?"

He slapped his thigh and sat down. Laughed like I had said something outrageous. He took his time, finished with his chocolate. I saw him wipe his tongue across his teeth behind closed lips.

"Sit a minute with me," he said. I did. "These tips," he said, folding his hands. He stopped and then started again. "So, we used to have cops answering the phone, taking the tips. Then a new county exec comes in, says we have to cut back, we can't pay cops to sit here all day, all night, over-time, the like. The salaries are too high to begin with, these resources are being wasted. He wants to say he got them all back on the street, see? Doing *real* police work again. So he had us bring in a civilian." He slapped his hands onto his armrests, raised a hand to point at me. "That's you."

"Right," I said. "That makes sense." Nodding, closing my eyes to agree. I had no idea if it made sense.

"And the thing with these tips, you'll see. Hundreds of them. Thousands. They take a while. We can't just have our guys go busting doors down based on anonymous tips that could be from anyone. We can't just take one caller's word for it. Could be one of the loonies in the bin, you know? You had any of them yet?"

"I think so," I said. "Maybe."

"Right. So. Like I say, takes time. Months, if we're lucky. Most of them go nowhere. Probably they're just sitting in piles around every precinct in this county, sorry to say. Everyone is too busy. We're stretched too thin everywhere."

"Sure," I said. "Okay."

"But look, you're doing a great job," he said and smiled. His teeth were clean of chocolate. "We're happy to have you here. And don't be afraid to get up, stretch your legs, use the restroom, take your lunch break. Evelyn tells me you don't leave the room. You're not chained to this desk, right? If someone has a tip and you miss the call, they'll call back. And if they don't?" He shrugged and then let his hands fall onto his thighs. "You're not responsible for solving any crimes from here. So don't worry about it too much." He stood up and looked out the window above my head, eyes slits against the light coming in. He nodded slowly, and I expected it: wisdom, a bit of history, anecdotes, inside information, some guidance. "One for the road," he said and took another candy. "Have a good weekend."

* * *

So that day at lunch, I did take my time. I ate at my desk, but then I took the phone off the hook and luxuriated in the walk to the bathroom. Listened to my feet on the floor, the sounds coming from around me. I did more lip gloss, re-parted my hair, straightened out the neck of my sweater. I checked my teeth, stared at myself in the mirror.

Fix this, Laura would have said as she pointed at the corner of my mouth, a blip of lip gloss collecting there. She'd have the other hand on her bump, rubbing. *Too much, you hussy. Try subtle for once?*

I mean really, Rebecca would have said, coming out from under a haze of hair spray, radio going on behind her. Her pregnant body just rubbing up against Laura's pregnant body. Their unborn babies, best girlfriends already. *Our girl is trying to go big right out of the gate.* So I fixed it, tip of my finger, all gone.

But I was settling in. You could see it. The look of the lights on my skin was no longer so unusual. I belonged. I was starting to belong.

I walked the long way back, passing offices I'd never seen, smiling in at the secretaries. I would become comfortable here. Eventually, I would know the number of steps from my desk to the bathroom. I would have a preferred stall. On lunch breaks I would power-walk laps with Evelyn and the women from the front desk and from records, little weights Velcro-strapped to our ankles. I would chip in for the coffee fund and the water cooler fund and for ice cream cakes, and offer to take responsibility for getting people on our floor to sign birthday cards and I would attend HQ happy hours at the bar down the road, one every month, always on a Friday—I'd seen the flyers—and there I would smooth my fingers down the side of my drink, pooling moisture onto the table, and smile with the rest of the women and make eyes at the men, I guess, I guess that's what they did, what I would do, whichever men, and wait until one struck my—

I side-stepped in time, but I had to jump a bit, and my shoulder hit him. He was walking backward out of an office and had just yelled something back into it.

"Oh, excuse me," he said. He put his hand to his neck, onto the knot of his tie. With his other hand he touched my shoulder as he went to move around me. "I'm so sorry. I didn't know you'd be right there," he said. Which was obvious. Of course he didn't—it was the most expected thing anyone could say, but it was also completely accurate too. I just shook my head. I meant for this gesture to say, *It's fine, no problem—don't be silly.* He did a little smile with his eyes, and a half nod and then kept going down the hall when I couldn't manage to say anything out loud. I walked three or four lengths behind him until I got to my door.

He was probably about five feet eleven, dark hair long enough for the ends to start to curl up, thirty-five to forty years old. He was wearing a dark gray suit, a white shirt, red tie. An unbuttoned hooded parka on top of that. I could say confidently that he was not a smoker, that he wore a common enough though unobtrusive cologne, that he was chewing fruity gum. I could feel his pulse through the palm of his hand when he touched me. This is how close we had been.

In that one moment I knew something was there. Just the way I felt, I guess. The way his hand felt on me. Sometimes just the sense of a certain person nearby changes you. I wasn't racked by it, but it was there. A twinge. A tiny thing, a diamond chip. And this is not crazy. This is not obsessive or desperate. Some things you can just sense.

Despite all of my awkwardness and my strangeness, it's not that I was unlikable. I am fine in social situations. I keep everything that's dark and odd quiet, leashed in a corner, gnawing a rawhide and smacking its tail on the ground. I drink socially. I present well. I am five feet five, average weight or just below. Mousy brown hair, like I said, but decent hair. Thick and long and well cut. Someone once said my eyes are the color of the sea, but that only happened once because my eyes are gray, really. So maybe only a very cold ocean or maybe the ocean only under a cloudy white sky.

My mother was worried about my being alone. She said I was *pulled in* and *walled up* and *closed off* and, frequently, *remote*. Whenever she said these things, I imagined a fortress, bricks shimmering in southern sunlight, machine guns lining its top perimeter, wind swirling sand. And in the far distance, a civilization busy building homes and birthing children and fetching water from a gurgling brook while a lush jungle gave them shade.

It's true I'd had trouble with men. I had dated plenty of them, sure. I'd fucked them all. After one good date and after one mediocre date and a few times after one terrible date. I'd like to say that I always had to be compelled, that there always had to be a reason. But for a while it was hard to figure out what that reason was.

My first year of college, I dated an artist. He was only one year ahead of me, from the same midsize town, but he seemed worldly and famous. He went by his middle name. The looks he gave made me nervous. They made me cross and uncross my legs. An eyebrow thing, an edge-of-the-lip thing. Hard to explain. I was afraid to call him too much. It took eighteen months until he let me meet his parents. Once he asked me to roll naked in paint and then press my body on a blank canvas, making shapes. He asked me to pose for photographs where he showed only close-ups of the dip of my abdomen or the curve of my calf. He cheated on me greedily. Left his phone open to messages I shouldn't have seen. Let me meet him on nights that other women were meeting him. Asked me to shower with him despite bite marks and hickeys that weren't from me. He knew I wouldn't say anything, and he was right. *I think,* he said, drying himself off, *that it's important we are honest with each other.* And did I love this about him? Maybe I did. Maybe I loved not knowing what I would find next. Maybe I loved the idea of trying to catch someone and make him my own. Maybe I wanted to see what I was capable of.

I thought of what our future life could be like. Living in a bungalow, both with well-washed white T-shirts and ripped jeans. Clean silverware. A warm floor, canvases stacked and rolled, old cans filled with dried paint and soaking brushes. The tang of turpentine. Somewhere in the middle of the country where it's flat and open and scrub grows along the border of your vision for miles around. Maybe Arizona so we didn't get cold. Our children would be dark haired and wispy, take after their father, not a note of me to be found. We were together for years, and I thought I would never be over him.

When I was twenty-three, still in my parents' home, still finding thongs stuffed in the cases of the artist's pillows and the cracks of his couch, and still convinced his lips were slicked with the wet of another woman, I met a man at the bank. A *man*. He was forty-one and divorced, no children, hair graying already, God bless him. He was behind me in line and his phone rang, and when I turned around, he shot his cuffs to pick it up but smiled at me before he said hello to whomever. He asked me out when he finished his call. Who does that? But you bet I said yes. He drove a late-model sports car with a manual transmission and drove it recklessly. He took me to a sex shop after dinner on our first date. This is who he was. A charge. A darkness. A death wish. It's the way he went through life. Like a bullet or a bird of prey. A tipsy canoe on the stillest, deepest river. A hurtling car on the pit straight.

He brought chocolates for my mother when he came to meet my parents. And I think she was charmed, by the brand of them and by the old-world gesture and by the cut of his sports coat. My father hated him. Hated the way he backed into the driveway, hated the way he took up so much space in the room, and hated his boom of a laugh. He hated him because he knew—in a way that men know, I guess, in some secret language of men—that this man was fucking his daughter in a very specific fashion. Hated him because she was still so young. Too young to be fucked, or at least too young to be fucked in the depraved ways preferred by this man.

With this man, my future life would be in a renovated cape in a neighborhood by the bay. He'd get me a matching sedan, automatic transmission, four doors for the sake of the child seat. He'd smile, eyes untouched, when he patted my pregnant belly, and then smile, eyes crinkling, when the belly was gone. When I was back. True joy to him, this body. We broke up when I was twenty-six, marriage on the brain, talking too much about *commitment* and *our future together,* afraid that I was going to lose him, and then what do you know—he was gone. But here's the thing: it was the darkness about him, the darkness hidden and protected by his well-cut suits, his smile at valets, at waiters. I liked that most. It scratched an itch. Lit a match. Set me on a quest.

After him, nothing special. Men through friends, mutual acquaintances, bookstore, bar, online—nothing special. Boring, boring, boring. There was always something I'd find wrong. Very bad hands or lots of body hair or too old, too young, no job, not technically divorced, or too controlling or too gentle or too emotional. Because I was always trying to find that little place of darkness in a man. So that when we were quiet, lying in bed, just before or just after, our little darknesses matched up, spots of rot covered by blood by muscle by skin and then by our artificial scents, nice nice, cherry on top. Those spots—ticking constantly like quartz within us—would be carefully contained, encapsulated, by all of the rest of the virtue surrounding them. We were normal people, good people, and we would keep each other's dark spots from growing, from taking over. This is what relationships were for. What marriages were for.

Honestly, I only wanted to stop looking. I could not understand why it was so hard.

And so, here we are. The police department.

*   *   *

That weekend, I wondered about him: the man in the parka from work. Here and there, I mean. At the supermarket, I saw, from behind, a man with the same coat and a little warm jolt came up near my throat. Turn down an aisle, stay behind him, say hello, what. But then he stopped to look at a display of stacked pasta boxes, and it wasn't him at all. This man, this man in the parka from work, I thought, he's married. Has to be. I tried hard and thought I could remember seeing his ring. Figured it was inscribed inside. *Eternity with you* or something. *Our eternity. Our love is forever.* He had a kid. Only one. He was tired, that was why we collided. He was up all night with the child, a baby, a newborn. I saw the circles under his eyes, didn't I? His wife. His wife was a looker, I'll admit it. Not blonde. Too obvious. I had her brunette, tall and large boned, with a handsome face. *Striking,* people said. She was having a hard time with the baby weight. But he loved it on her, this extra weight. He said he could have handfuls of her now, more of her; there was more of the woman he loved, and what could be better than that? Even though they hadn't slept together since the baby. She said she was still healing.

*   *   *

That weekend, I brought my laundry to my parents', and when I was almost done, when the dryer had only ten minutes left on the very last load, they finally asked. My mother asked, but my father was standing right next to her and it was clear they had come up with it together, that they had discussed it beforehand. I will say, they had shown some restraint in waiting.

"Well?" she said. We were in the kitchen, the news on in the background. The news was always on then. "How's the job?" She was trying to lean on the island behind her, her elbows moving to find it. She wanted this position to say: relaxed, cool, no pressure in this question. She had to turn around and resituate herself, and then she leaned back, satisfied finally.

"It's . . ." I said. And watched the anchor. I nodded slowly so I looked like I was thinking.

The sound was muted, but I could tell it was something grave. Shaky aerial footage from a midwestern state. Looked like a strip mall, big parking lot. Then a police sketch of a man. Then back to the crime scene tape. A bystander in an interview, tears streaming down her face. Call me, I thought to myself. I'm miles and miles away, but you never know. Ma'am, call me and tell me what you saw, which way he fled, and I will help you. I'm here to help. That's who I was then, who I had become already. Intent on helping.

"Have you met any nice people?" my mother said. Nice people. The sketch with the mustache was gone. Tape gone.

And then the first thing that came into my head was him, the man from the hallway at work. I was almost surprised by it, the way it popped up. The way it cleared everything else out. This news. This thing. Nascent. Secret. A bud, a shoot, an idea. All mine.

I ignored her question.

"It's good," I said and nodded, looking at her now. "It's, you know, a job. A chance to be productive. So."

"It's still brand new," my mother said. "Give it a few weeks, settle in. You'll be fine." I could feel the shoulder pat in her words, but she didn't move to come near me. "Make any friends yet?" She managed to keep all innuendo out. She was really trying.

"Everyone is great," I said. "Everyone wants to help out."

"You'll find people," she said. "You always wind up making friends eventually. Don't worry." But the way she said *eventually* did make me worry.

So when the dryer dinged from the basement, I jumped up, ran down, ran up, my warm bundle losing socks, shirts. I had to nurture it, this bud growing, going through me. Alone. They asked me to stay for dinner, but I was already on the porch, into my car, down the street. I was already at home in my bed, blankets around my ankles and thinking of him: me pressed against him, his mouth near my ear, the heat of his hands, my back against one of the brick-lined hallways at headquarters; my back against the door of my car, his car; my back against an ancient Roman pillar; against an airplane seat; against a palm tree, the sand and the water, aqua, and the sun high and shining on us.

Already counting the minutes until Monday.

CHAPTER FOUR

A gift, really. Something easy in my life. This is how I knew we would be perfect. That things were happening. Around lunchtime on Monday, he was standing in the doorway of the very same office, shouting in at whom I figured was the very same person. Clockwork, a sitcom. I went slowly this time, looking. He had a shield on his belt, and I saw the bump of his gun under the flap of his suit coat. No ring after all. But none of them wore rings. This didn't mean a thing. I saw his handsome wife roll her eyes at me. *You fell for the no ring bit? You can have him,* she said. Detective, I guessed. I made myself so slow. So, so slow. I was warm just looking at him. The coat. The one I had been in, in a town's worth of places, imagining. I could smell it, I could feel the fur on my face. He was gesturing at someone, and I knew his hands already. I knew the nick from a can on a camping trip at eight years old, right there between thumb and index. I knew the edge of the tattoo that curled up from his sleeve at the wrist, stopped just shy of his palm. I knew the tick of his good watch, a gift from his father when he graduated the academy years back, a cop family, the lot of them. The warmth of his neck, the one curl, hair too long, his smile when he scratched his temple and said, *I really need a cut.* And then I was past him, and he was still yelling into the office, laughing at something, involved with something else, totally unaware.

And that's it.

I had worn a better outfit. I had worn black tights and a black pencil skirt and a sweater set for good measure. My hair, mascara, everything. And for what? For nothing. I went back to my office, stood there looking out the window and scanning the landscape slowly, my arms folded at my chest, like an oil baron surveying. I could have said hello, at least. *Oh, hello. Hi. Heeeey there. Let's not crash this time. Here, I'll give you some room.* Then moved in a wide berth around him, exaggerating. Or spun my back to him like we were squeezing by each other, *ha ha, look out,* my hair flying in that second, it was long enough, we were close enough for it to land on his shoulder. I could have dropped something. I could have said hello to one of the secretaries, pretended to look at Christmas cards.

I watched patrol cars coming and going in the parking lot below, watched people leaving in pairs and groups for lunch, their hands held up against the wind, trying to shield themselves.

I sat down and leaned my head forward, rubbing the back of my neck. Stupid. I should have done something.

Just tell me one thing. Laura—it was Laura—one eyebrow up, smallest shake of her head. *A sweater set? Explain the thought process behind this choice.* I could almost hear her.

"Virginia, is it?" I looked up. It was him. Enchantment. Pixie dust.

"Hello," I said and nearly winced at the formality. I smiled to soften it.

"Tough to find you all the way back here," he said. "But that's why they made me a detective." He tapped his temple with his pointer. I saw him look around, at the bowl of chocolates, at my jacket hanging on a hook by the window, at the red phone. Then he came closer. "Charles Ford," he said and leaned forward to shake. "Charlie." Nice hands. Not a problem there. "I wanted to come down here and see who was behind the new paperwork." He smiled. "And a civilian, no less. Unbelievable." He faked outrage, shake of his head. "I'm down in Homicide," he said and gave a quick look behind him, indicating.

He was still wearing his coat and to watch him in it—to watch him gesture and nod and raise his eyebrows as if asking permission when he took a chocolate—it was like seeing something of mine. And his hair, I had felt that hair, let it fall through my fingers, tucked it behind his ears, felt its softness in my lap. I imagined him winking at me, the crinkle at the corners of his eyes. I knew him already.

"So, listen, how about I make things easier for you from now on, and I'll come and pick up these tips? Then you don't have to walk them over, right? Deal with those guys?" He said *tips* like it was in quotes. He had eaten three chocolates. I thought to refill the dish. I thought to remember to refill the dish later, after he left. "This way no one'll give you a hard time."

"Sure, okay. If that works," I said. But that's not what I meant. I had a habit of saying things incorrectly. Of saying the right things but in the wrong way. I had habits. I stood up. Because he was going to leave and I didn't want him to misunderstand me, to be on the wrong foot already, and I also wanted him to see me before he left. Properly. The whole of me. Regardless of the sweater set, a poor choice, what I should have known was a poor choice. So I came around the side of my desk and leaned on it. And he did look. I did see him look. "I guess I didn't make the best impression on your coworkers," I said. He waved his hand, dismissing it.

"Don't worry about them. I know how they can be," he said. He narrowed his eyes and seemed to notice something. "How did you wind up here, by the way?"

"I just responded to a posting," I said. "And then Lieutenant Donovan called me and had me come in. The job sounded interesting."

"Interesting, definitely. But you don't look like you belong here, is what I mean," he said.

"Oh yeah? Where do I look like I belong?" That's it, there it is, you can do this.

"I meant it as a compliment," he said. He scratched the back of his neck. "And you know exactly what I meant."

"Well, thanks, I guess," I said. "When you put it like that." I made it playful, put a smile in there, a little tease.

"Keep up the good work," he said as he was leaving. "I'll see you tomorrow. Stay out of trouble in the meantime."

And this is the way I met Detective Charlie Ford, Homicide Section, Suffolk County Police Department. This is the way our relationship began. Oh, the days we would have. The days at the beginning when we drank too much and passed forks between us from plates of carbonara and cleaned the cream sauce from each other's faces with fingertips. Then we licked them. When my innards zinged from the sound of his voice in the hall, or his name on my phone, or the way he looked at me over a cup of coffee. When I made him wait. And wait. And behaved like a woman I didn't even know, making him wait like this, making myself wait like this. When it became too much—painful, this waiting—and he would recoil even just seeing my hands come close to him. When all I wanted to do was let him. This is how I found my husband at the police department, exactly as I had intended, exactly as I had set out to do. We married in a modest ceremony. An inexpensive dress, simple flowers, a basic plan that included a cake, and we did not opt to upgrade. But we did go to Greece for a honeymoon. He had relatives there. Distant, distant relatives. Distant as the horizon across all that sea. Too much sea. And when it was time, I got pregnant, and he touched me with reverence, with respect. He fetched me things from the kitchen at all hours. He stayed by my head in the delivery room but was energetic and sincere and sweet in his coaching and in his exaltation. We had two children. Even now they astonish me. I look at them with awe. Charlie Ford, I love you, I loved you from the first moment, and then everything else followed, just like it was supposed to, just like that, the end.

CHAPTER FIVE

He came in the next morning at 9:10 with two cups of coffee and slid one across my desk, gently as an offering.

"We don't have any lids. There's a trail of coffee on the floor all the way from our office." He gestured to the coffees with his chin. "But I wanted to stop in before we went out on the road, in case I didn't get back before you left for the day," he said.

Was I warm? I was warm. Flushing. Trying to think of the cold outside. The banks of snow turned dirty ice at the side of the road. I tried to think of going out there and putting bricks of it on my wrists and the back of my neck, of lying in it facedown, slowing my breathing. Just trying to cool down. He was wearing a navy suit, thick material that looked like wool, another red tie but different than the one from the day before, a white shirt, no coat. No coat.

"How nice," I said. I pressed my wrists against the cool of the desk, visualizing. "Thank you." I was trying to seem calm, ordinary, calm. I took a sip then. I was at work, drinking this coffee that this man brought me, and I was calm and ordinary. That's all. "No coat today," I said. And that was a little weird, maybe. Kind of a strange observation. I should have nodded and kept drinking, said something else. Just a regular observant person, maybe being a little flirtatious, no law against that. But then I thought about what I had said, how I had said it. How I had imagined that coat and the smell of it and the weight of whatever was in its pockets: a radio, handcuffs, paperwork, car keys, mints in twisted cellophane. And that had come out, that was all over what I had said—that I was thinking of this, that I had thought so much about him and his coat already and now he would know it—and I put the cup down. My hand put my cup on my desk, I saw it. Tried to, anyway. But it hit the edge of a notepad and the whole thing went over. "Oh," I said, watching it go. Into my lap—the gray skirt—a little pond between my thighs. Splashes up onto the silk of my blouse. It dripped from the desk in a thin but steady stream onto the floor. "Shit," I said and finally, finally stood up.

And there he was, gone and then back already with rolls of paper towel, making fists of it as he came toward me. No hesitation in him. Someone who moves, acts, does. He came right around the back of my desk. He uprighted the cup and then started on the spill and then, gentlemanly, handed me a handful to do my own front with. I think I was expecting him to do that too. To pat me gently, up and down. To be tentative, hands as light and quick as a tailor.

"Jesus," I said. "Typical."

"You're fine," he said, finishing. "You're good." He was bent over, stuffing a wad of paper onto the spill on the floor. The back of his neck looked soft and smooth. A freckle behind his ear. The edge of his hairline neat. Down there, on his knee like that. Look, I can't say I didn't think of what it would be like, his proposing. Of course the thought crossed my mind. And when he stood up, he was very close. It was wool, his suit. Navy wool. Good suit. With a faint, thin white stripe. His teeth were very straight.

"My fault for no top," he said. He leaned around me and threw the towels at the trash can and they went in, of course. "I didn't know how clumsy you were." He winked at this.

I had serious questions then about the power of my perfume. Its sillage and strength. Was he getting any of it, and if so, was it too much? Could he see the line of my tights through my skirt or the place where my bra straps met the skin of my back? My face. My pores. The scar at the very edge of my mouth, one quarter of the size of a pencil eraser.

"Well, we've got to get going," he said. He walked behind me and stood at the door, leaning one hip on its frame. "There are bad guys who need catching." He straightened his tie, smoothing down its whole length in the V between thumb and index finger.

"Right," I said. "Thanks again for the coffee." I picked up the empty cup then—I'm not sure why. To indicate my thanks maybe—who knows? Then I threw it away.

"I'll be back tomorrow," he said. "But no more coffee for you." He pointed a finger at me, wagged it. He laughed and left.

In the outer office, someone called to him. "What's up, Ford? What're you doing all the way down here with the likes of us?"

"Police work," Charlie Ford said back, and I heard the smile in his voice. I heard it, I swear to you I heard it.

Then the roll of a chair and Evelyn came in. She stood in the doorway and waited a few counts before she spoke.

"Isn't he adorable?" she said. "Single, too, in case that's an option for you. I don't know." She looked down at her hands.

"I am," I said. "Single, I mean. He seems very nice."

"The sweetest. Could not be sweeter. May I?" She pointed to the chair. When she sat, she looked around again. "Good for you with the candies. You'll feel at home soon enough. It's always hard starting something new, I know." She nodded along, still smiling. "You're such a pretty girl," she said. "They're going to eat you up in here."

"Oh," I said. "Thank you. Everyone has been so nice so far. I'm very lucky. Happy, I mean. To be here."

"I think he just went through a breakup, Detective Ford. Girlfriend, not wife."

"Okay, great," I said. "Not great. That's not what I meant."

"I know, honey, I know what you meant." A phone rang in the hall. "I have to get that. But you come and see me. Because whatever you need to know," she said, "I know it."

* * *

Charlie Ford. Single. Recent breakup. Kismet. I thought to call my mother. To say, *I think I met someone* or *I've met someone.* There's this guy at work, he brought me coffee. Or, no. He brings me coffee every morning when he visits. Make it habitual. He's a detective. I'd say the word *detective* in italics. Homicide detective, actually, I would say then. Like I was just remembering. I wanted to twirl a phone cord around my arm and lie back in my chair like important people in offices did. Or like a teenager in a movie. A canopy bed, the rain on the window, a notebook open to unfinished homework. I wanted to wave away any person who came to my door, just one slow sweep of my hand. Mouth the word *later.*

I would not call my mother, I decided. She would give me advice. She would say to play hard to get, to roll my eyes at things he said and act offended and *out of reach*. This was her methodology. *I held your father off until* he *was the one who was talking about marriage. That's how you do it. You have to remember that you have something that they want.* No, not my mother. My two girlfriends? I could text them: *You will not believe this guy I met.* Because in high school these are the things we lived for. We convened, between periods, three faces pressed into the nook of a locker, reading the tea leaves of what some boy had said in passing, thrown over his shoulder, something like *hey*. Back then something like *hey* had a world inside its three letters. It throbbed with possibility. It gave us something to get dressed for, made a chill rip up our spines when he—my he, our he, any he— passed too closely in the halls or sat nearer than usual at a lunch table or waited for the late bus, not far from where we waited for the late bus, and even mumbled some curse and we nodded in commiseration, violently, desperately nodded, but kept silent. I hear you, I agree with you, you and I think the same way, we are the same and we belong together, we thought along in our heads.

But now I could expect to hear back from them hours later or the next day: *So happy for u! I want to call and talk. Maybe tonight after Rich is asleep.* Angry face. Tired face. Heart. *XO.* Almost the exact same message from both of them, though the other one's husband was named Dan.

CHAPTER SIX

It happened a lot more quickly than I thought. He brought me coffee again the next day and sat, legs stretched out and crossed at the ankle. No coat, no keys, no papers. His pose said *nothing but time*.

"I have nothing going on today, finally," he said and took a sip. "What's exciting down here at the tip line?" I looked at him for a second and thought: This was all supposed to happen. That I took this job. That I had been wayward and flailing beforehand. That I took this job and smacked into him in the hallway and got that tip and walked it down and acted like an idiot to those other detectives and because of that, because of that *he* was tasked to come find me, handle the civilian, take the tips back himself. I felt goodness coming from him, this stranger. I felt potential and kindness radiating. I liked his socks, dress socks with bright red race cars on them. I liked the way he cocked his head at me, waiting. I liked the way his hand wrapped his cup, his thumb moving up and down its side.

"Exciting?" I said, repeating. "Not a lot, really. I mean, the excitement kind of wore off after the first thirty people called saying, 'My neighbor is a drug lord.'" He laughed.

"You're telling me," he said. Then he leaned back, like he was watching a play. Ready to listen. "So what about you? What's your story?"

"Well," I said and looked down at my desk so I could try to stave off the flush that I felt coming. "My story. Well, that's interesting." I tapped my fingers on the keyboard, thinking. I knew I was red already; I was trying to buy time before I looked back up.

"Oh, by the way," he said, saving me, "you'll notice I changed my mind about you and the coffee. But I did manage to find you a lid." He pointed with his cup to my cup, and I wanted to thank him with my eyes for that small consideration. But I was still too red and couldn't yet look up. I deep-breathed one, deep-breathed two. Okay, okay. Good. Go.

"I see this," I said, looking at him again. He was smiling. Nothing big, no teeth. Just a mouth-closed smile. Amused by me. "I'm so pleased you have faith in my ability to be a civilized human." I took a sip, doing fine, just fine. "I promise you won't have to clean up any of my messes today." And then I smiled back. And it did something to him, it must have. It changed something.

"Hey, you want to take a walk? Are you allowed away from here for a few?"

Yes, of course, yes. But then I imagined my heels getting stuck in the packed snow, the salted sidewalks, the sand, teeth chattering while we tried to make conversation. Dumbed by cold. I must have glanced toward the window.

"Not outside," he said and half rolled his eyes like we had known each other for years. Like he was used to my hijinks, my mishaps. Oh, Virginia. "The food truck's here. The breakfast truck. Are you hungry?"

"Breakfast truck," I said. "I had no idea."

"You're still an outsider," he said. "We have to let you in on these things bit by bit."

So yes, as I said. Of course. We walked to a back hallway, a back staircase, a back door. And there, its quilted aluminum glinting in the sun, stood the breakfast truck. A secret. This building, so much bigger than I had imagined. Its offices and hallways and parking lots endless and labyrinthine and full of a million things I had yet to find out. I waited while he went out, watched his suit coat blow open in the wind. Watched him walk back, a foil-wrapped package in each hand.

"I didn't ask what you wanted because they only have one thing," he said. And the cold air came off of him like wind. Like a breeze. "We can sit in my office for a minute. Everyone else is out on something. Then you can get back to your calls. Sound good?"

"Sounds good," I said and followed him back up the stairs. Sounds perfect.

Bacon, egg, and cheese. He was a neat eater, held a napkin balled in one hand. Did not have any smears on his fingertips or lips. He did not speak with his mouth full. My mother would love that. She really would. He had gone to college, started as a bio major with the idea of premed, and then switched, just like that, to criminal justice. And now here he was. He asked about me too. He was very polite. He was polite but he did tease me. Teased me within reason. Flirtatious, definitely. Mentioned, in passing, so briefly, a dog he had had with an ex. Didn't really bat an eye about it. That was it for his romantic history.

"You'll have to come out on the road with us one day," he said. "Nothing really exciting happens in here." He nodded at the paper behind him. The walls of books.

I'd love to, I thought to say. But how canned. How fake. No one talks like that. That'd be awesome. No, I didn't use that word. Awesome was the word of a cheerleader, a yoga teacher, someone happy and excited. Maybe that was me now, though. Maybe it was who I was becoming. Sounds good, I could say, again. To everything he asked, from now on, from this day forward, to everything he would ever ask me. Sounds good.

"Definitely," I said. It was all I could muster.

And then he just said it: There was a happy hour on Friday, dive place just down the road, I should go, or not, he didn't know what I was up to or into (and at this his foot shook, just a bit, just for a sec), but some of the guys from his team were going to go, the girls from the front desk, a lot of the people from HQ usually went. It was a good way to meet people, you know, out in a natural habitat, away from here. He made the shape of a box with his hands then, napkin still balled, miming the walls of the building.

"Thought I'd throw it out there," he said. He took a sip of coffee. Cool. Very cool. "See if you had any interest."

"Ahh," I said and looked into the far corner of the room, trying to remember. Looking like I was trying to remember. I was trying to remember nothing because I knew the only thing happening on Friday was dinner at my parents' house or wine alone in my bed, like any other Friday. "Yeah, I think I can do that." Still looking at the corner. Still looking. Then back at him. I'm sure he knew what I was doing. This man, his job watching people for lies, tells. But I did what I could. "No, I think," I said. "I think that will work."

Nothing from him. No change, no visible excitement or surprise.

"Cool," he said.

"I should get back," I said. "Donovan will wonder why no crimes are being solved." I raised an eyebrow at him.

I walked to my office slowly. Luxuriating. My lungs swollen and warm. My heart going. This is a real beginning, I thought. This is what it feels like. Here we go.

*   *   *

I didn't want to. I went back and forth. I didn't want to and then I did. I just wanted to say it out loud, so I did tell my mother. That evening. I also texted the girls, together, a group text. Something we did rarely. For big things like the deaths and the affairs of people we went to high school with.

"He can't take you on a proper date?" my mother said. She was sitting in the living room with my father. I heard the TV. I heard almost nothing but the TV.

"I can hardly hear you. Can you move to the kitchen? Also, can you please not say anything? Dad doesn't need to know about this just yet. There's nothing to know about, really, even," I said, correcting myself. "I just can't hear anything you're saying." I was on my bathroom counter, close up to the mirror. That little scar. Wrinkles, already, at the corners of my eyes and along the sides of my mouth. Right deeper than left. They were so slight, hardly visible, but they were there. I could see them.

"Oh, honey, stop. He's not listening to me. He doesn't hear a thing I say. I'm just asking you why he can't ask you out to dinner," she said, and I heard movement in her voice.

She was up, walking. I saw her flick on the kitchen light, pull out a chair, sit. I saw her reach for a magazine, heard the pages riffle through her fingers. "Or for coffee, even."

"No," I said. A groan. "Mom, stop. It's fine. It's not like that anymore. No one goes out to dinner. No one asks another person out to dinner. This is what people do now." I had recently found a small patch of grays on my right temple. Just a few, fewer than a dozen. I had been plucking them. I plucked them again, phone to my other ear. Let them drop into the sink, a little pile. She was silent. Not because of our conversation. She was reading.

"Well," she said after a while. After longer than polite. "What are you going to wear?"

My friends asked the same thing. They were on West Coast time, both of them, so it was around dinner out there, and I could tell they were harried and busy by the lag in their response times and by their half-assed responses. After all, they were making meals, aprons taut around their middles. They were pivoting from stove to sink, disappearing into the steam as they cleaned hot pots and roasting pans. Their husbands, feet up, TV blaring from another room.

Awesome I love it yes, Laura finally wrote back. *Are you excited tell us more abt him.*

OMG V so happy what are you going to wear, Rebecca wrote. And for a minute I could hear them again. Their East Coast accents warmed by the LA sun. Their voices changing maybe, just a touch, slowing to West Coast time, easy and full and satisfied. I could feel their palms on my forearms, on my shoulders. We used to touch each other so much and not even think of it. It was like touching our own arms, our own earlobes, necks, to tighten a piece of jewelry. To fix a clasp we couldn't see. It was so nice to have them back. Even just like that.

I have no idea and I have no clothes. What do you think? I have to stay professional, I wrote back, from the bathroom counter, still inspecting myself.

But it was hours later when Laura finally answered, and all she said was *Don't stress about clothes see if you even really like him first.* I didn't see it until the next morning when I woke up. But regardless, I already knew.

CHAPTER SEVEN

Charlie sat and patted the seat next to him and motioned me to come from the other side of the bar. I had been looking around, putting on the act of checking the place out. But I saw him the second he came in. I nodded at him, a half nod, and excused myself from the women I had been listening to. Men, work, weight talk. The walk over, the walk over. I was light, smiling, my hair moving behind me, down my back, my sweater smooth, tucked at the waist, fresh and scented just right with my best perfume. It was slo-mo. It was everything in the place stopped under a spell, a bell jar. It was only the music left on the jukebox: Buddy Holly, Guns N' Roses, David Bowie. No, at that moment, it was something instrumental. Something no one had the words to and could ruin by singing along. He clapped a hand on my back, gentle, when I got there. Patted me, more like. Raised his eyebrows, amazed that I came. He pulled out the chair for me, shooed away the guys from his squad, and leaned forward to hear me when I started to speak. So close. The heat from him, the pulse in his artery, even. I could see it. A lock of his hair brushed the edge of my mouth, and I breathed him in.

No, not quite right, I don't think.

Maybe this.

Charlie pulled up right at 4:59 PM, right outside my office window. I watched him wait there for one full sweep of the second hand around the wall clock, and then I took my coat and clicked off the lights and floated down the stairs, a ball-gown ballooning under me, opera gloves to my elbows. He got out to open the car door for me, and in that light—the high-pressure sodium bulb and the heavy dusk of a North-eastern winter, overcast, no moon—his dark suit was a tux and his hair was slicked and neat, and he was a prince or a spy, and I almost cried when he said *my lady* and opened the door of his take-home Taurus for me. I almost asked him for a handkerchief to blot my eyes.

Not yet. Keep going.

We didn't even make it to the place. He came to my office, 4:59 PM, doors closing all over the rest of the building as people left. He knocked, though the door was open, knuck-les on the metal jamb. Then he let himself in and closed the door behind him. To anyone else, it was just another door closing. OT, evening shift, maintenance, late-night meeting, brass bitching, another emergency. I was still sitting, still going through the motions: closing up, shutting down, put-ting my special pens away. I knew what it looked like. It was preoccupied, it was tired, it was work weary, hair messed, shirt warm with wear and body creased. *Oh, hey,* one of us said, or both at the same time. *Oh.* Oh, when he came to me, walked to me—finally, finally—saying something about how happy hour could wait because he had been waiting for this, *this*, thinking about it for days. He had imagined it from the second we first spoke—no, nope, before that. When we crashed. In the hall. Since then. He had smelled me on his sleeve that afternoon, had brought his arm to his face a hundred times, trying to catch it. He had asked around, then looked up my name in the database, found my age, car make and model, home address, no violations, no brushes with the law, minor crash a year before, not my fault. Oh, closer, when I felt his hand on my chin and my cheek, oh, okay, yes, of course. Desk? Desk chair? Up against the wall? I was wearing a skirt, tights are tights, we took care of that. Did you know that certain bodies fit together better than others? You can tell from the very first second. Did you know that once you know this, you will never want it to stop? That, I mean, that you had to figure.

There were dozens of these. These were just a few.

* * *

But Friday. Friday, Friday, Friday. I woke with hope. I woke knowing that Friday was a special day for me, always had been. A thread pulled me awake, moments before the alarm. And it was metallic, this thread, woven from something thin but strong, and I want to say that's what a superstition looks like. Or an instinct. A thin but strong thread nestled inside the softest parts of you, webbed over with flesh, but charged. In and of itself. I was pulled awake by this, before the alarm. But I was awake, fully. I washed my body like I was preparing for prayer. Cupped my hands and let the water fall over me, rinsed my mouth, soaped every fold, every follicle. Watched the used water fall away, circle the drain, bringing with it everything I didn't want. I could see the molecules of grime, of history. Of *before*. Watched them go. Goodbye.

I couldn't go too big. I couldn't go over the top with something that said I was trying too hard and had given the

day, the evening, any special gravity. Any as of yet unde-
served gravity. So, I could do nice, but not too nice. Subtle.
I bartered. I could blowout my hair, but then I had to wear
the lower heels. I could do the lightest, faintest, most barely
there smoky eye, but then no lip at all and also a button-
down shirt instead of the tighter sweater. There were rules,
after all. So I had everything laid out on my bed. And then
I sort of just walked in front of them, turned my back, and
when I turned around again, saw a sweater, one I had worn
already, and a pair of pants, of all things. Nothing special at
all. But they stood out to me, as though lit from behind.

In the mirror, before I left, I looked at my face. I had aged
well, after all. I could say it. Aside from the grays and the
minor wrinkles near my eyes, I looked young for my age.
My hair was smooth, bouncy, the slightest wave. Pushed half
behind my back and half in front of my shoulders. I had opted
for no smoke on the eye, palest pink lip, the higher heels.

That's it. Go.

* * *

He didn't come in at 9:00, 9:10, 9:15. Something jagged and
shiny, a hundred little points, balled itself up and started
to rub at the bottom of my lungs and made things hot and
strange in there. I cracked a window. I thought of pacing.
I stood up. Sat down. At 10:19, I heard a man in the outer
office growl *Ford*, lots of "R" in there, and then I heard the
slap of two palms together, and I breathed completely for
the first time that morning. By the time he got to me, I had
calmed myself and was typing meaningless sentences into
an open document: *Let's see what today is today is friday my
birthday is in september my mother's birthday is in april I like*

*the summer the summer here is magnificent we are so lucky
do you like to boat it is too cold now to boat no one boats in
december.*

I looked up.

"For you," he said and leaned forward to put the coffee
on my desk. He didn't sit. Why didn't he sit? He was wearing
his coat. He was on his way out. He lifted his cup to drink
and drank long, like he was trying to finish it in one go.
"Overslept this morning. I'm shot."

"Late night?" I said. I pulled my cup to me and blew on
it through the hole in the cap, though the coffees he brought
were never very hot.

"Here till two. Bunch of useless shit. Too boring for me
to even tell you about."

"You poor guy," I said. Here was a choice. How forward
could I go with it, really? I saw a tiny roller coaster, a car at
the top of its wooden hill. Teetering. A bit of wind, a change
in the clouds, a bird too close. I ticked it with my fingernail.
"Better have another cup," I said. "Big happy hour tonight."
I looked back at my hands immediately after. I had no idea
what I was doing. I heard the wheels click, then rush down
the wooden track. Whee! Whee.

"That's right," he said, like I had just reminded him. In
a movie he would've snapped his fingers with the realization. "It's okay. We're going out on the road now, and I'll get
myself some proper coffee. I'll be in fine shape for later—
don't you worry."

Are we meeting there? Are we meeting downstairs,
going together? Should I be there at five? Five thirty? Later?
When are you getting there? Are you going with other people? Should I find other people to go with too?

"I'll stop in again before later and we can figure something out," he said and swirled his cup and then finally finished it. He came toward my desk. Reached his arm out. "Can you toss this for me?" And of course our fingertips touched when I took it. Of course they did. I'd love to say I felt an exchange there, when we made contact. Something intoxicating and unusual. Wild, indescribable, dangerous. I didn't. I liked it, though. It was very nice. It was nice.

"See you in a bit," he said. I watched his back, his walk as he left. Buoyant, on a mission. I listened to him whistle when he got out into the hall.

CHAPTER EIGHT

Three PM. Watching the clock. Counting down. Two hours left.

"Suffolk County Crime Line, this is Virginia."

An inhale, a sniff. Music in the background. A laugh track. Daytime TV. One of those judge shows. A soap.

"Hello?" I said. I had no space for this—I was all taken up. I was waiting. I was waiting and ready for something so much more important than this. This would be about a dog's constant barking. Illegal fireworks at all hours. A wrong number, if I was really lucky. Someone wanting to be transferred to Legal.

A shift, scratching against the phone. I was just about to hang up. Donovan told me, don't waste your time, just hang up and move on.

"Hello?" A woman. Young. Tired or crying. "Hi, I have to. Hold on." Movement as she got up, a door closing, then silence wherever she was. "Sorry," she said. More human now. Cleared throat, smoothed out. Legs crossed at the ankle and sitting up straight. "I have to report something," she said. Came out quick and easy. Almost a little bored sounding, a bit casual. I pictured her looking at her nails.

"Okay," I said, taking my notepad. "What kind of information would you like to provide?" I ran my pen in circles. Started a leaf, then a vine down the side, caught it on one of the blue lines like a trellis, a hanging garden in the margin. I made a rose, then a few. Would make pebbled paths through them, half circles, an English garden, charming, the birds, dipping through sunset, a pond, a manor, that sunset. Waiting.

"This is not good," she said finally. "I shouldn't be saying this. I shouldn't have called you. This is so fucked." She exhaled then, and I wondered when she had lit the cigarette. I hadn't heard the whir of the wheel in a lighter, the crack of a match. I hadn't heard her suck the cigarette to life. I could have missed so many other things.

"I understand. But it's okay. Go on," I said. I was already getting good at coaxing. I knew what to do with my voice, how to use it. I knew the tone to take. It was friendly and feminine but with an undercurrent of certainty, of authority, even. An undercurrent strong enough to pull you, to bring you deeper, to get your feet caught in the sand to the ankles, to the knees.

"I'll tell you, but you have to keep me out of it. You don't see my number, right? It doesn't come up? I blocked it. I had to." It was then that I knew. It was not a narcotics call, some idiot selling weed at a street corner near a bus stop, dear God, save our children. It was not crack, crack pipes, crack rocks, cocaine, eight balls, E. Or tiny dime bags of heroin empty or not, found on the pavement, in your son's room, on school grounds, in a locker—the horror. It was not fentanyl mis-prescribed by the crooked practitioner who pockets the cash and then writes the script and then turns his back when they come back for another—or wind up dead, which is usually the case. This was something else, and I knew it then and I was scared already. I was scared. "You have to tell them that there are dead girls out near Gilgo Beach. They're not even buried. Just lying in all the weeds and bushes and shit out there off Ocean Parkway. Thrown away. Dumped like garbage."

A snake of cold got me right away, born and shaped of my own intestines, and it licked and hissed its way around. Going slowly. Checking every crevice. I had to keep the girl on the phone, that I knew. I shook. I was shaking when I started to talk again. I tried to hide it.

"Okay, ma'am. Where is this exactly?" I knew the beach, sure. Everyone on the island knew the area. But it was not a small place. I waited. That was it. You can't ask for too much at once. That's when they hang up or freak out. I had learned this much. It was delicate. But I was fine and calm. I was drunk on the sound of my voice. Could not believe it was me.

A noise like a small animal. She might have been crying. I wanted to wait to ma'am her again. I wanted her to come back to me. My snake hissed, bid its time. Coiled and ready. I could have thrown up.

"On the beach," she said. "In the bushes. Somewhere on that stretch. But they're out there like trash. It's fucked up. You need to do something. This guy needs to get caught."

"What guy? Who is it?" I said, not waiting. I upped the undercurrent, tried to make her wade in a bit more. I felt like if I kept going, I could get closer. I saw something there, glimmering. "Do you know who the girls are? Any of their names? How they got there?"

"Please don't do this," she said. It was a whine. Begging me. "That's all I can say," she said and ended the call and that was it.

I was sweating. I was sweating in my perfect sweater, down my back, into the waistband of my pants. My perfume was blooming off me. Each beat of my pulse brought up a huge, unwieldy flower of it, so hot and sweet I seemed to be rotting from the inside out. Fuck.

I looked at the phone for a minute, probably less, and then I typed out everything and saved it into the program and printed out the tip and took the paper out of the printer, still warm, and out of my office and out of the outer office and down the hall, toward Homicide.

Caller believes that the bodies of more than one deceased female can be found in the brush at Gilgo Beach. Caller could not specify number of victims or exact location and could not provide information as to any possible subject. Caller was agitated and emotional and ended the call quickly.

It was a different man who opened the door, and when he saw me, he turned around to look at Charlie, like I was there to pay a friendly visit. Have a chat. Bat my lashes and tap my nails on the desk. Hi, there, just stopping in, what's cooking?

"Hello, Detective," I said and ducked my head a bit. Deference. I had no idea what his name was. "This just came in, and I wanted to walk it over right away." I held the paper up to him and he took it. While he was reading, I looked behind him: Charlie at his desk, suit coat off, sleeves rolled, gold watch, no tattoos—God, Charlie, can we kiss? Can you kiss me? Charlie, at his desk where we had shared breakfast, what I would remember forever as our first date, however informal. It took a second before he finally turned to look. I'd like to think he was busy placing my voice. He raised his eyebrows at me, widened his eyes, like he had just run into a neighbor on a vacation halfway around the world. Like I was an exotic creature out of its habitat. *What?* he mouthed, and gave his head half a shake and got up to come over.

"What the fuck?" the guy holding the paper said. "You've got to be kidding me."

"What's up, Tone?" Charlie leaned over his shoulder when he got close enough. "Tony Russo," he said to me, pointing to him with his chin. An introduction. "My partner." Then I watched him read. He nodded along. He did not do horrified. He did calm. In control. His forehead, unlined. He had some grays, I saw them then when I had the chance to look unwatched. "Probably bullshit," he said to Tony, not me. "Let's just drive over and look. Close it up. Get back here just in time to call it a day and have a drink. This'll just be a quick thing." For this he looked at me.

"This will be a pain in the ass, is what this will be," Tony said, his back to us already.

"Tony, this is Virginia, by the way. Where I go with the coffees," Charlie said after him.

My ballgown, ballooning again. Kiss the back of my hand, at least. Let me blush and bow. Let me be a lady. And, please, for the love of God, do not listen to a word I say when I ask you, later tonight, the night of our second date, second quasi-date, after happy hour or during, to do something to me in the front seat of your car or mine, in my house, in your house, in a hotel—you get the picture.

* * *

The phone rang at 4:58. My desk phone. A line I had never before answered.

"This is Virginia," I said. I was all packed up. I had just redone my makeup. I was ready. "Suffolk County Police Department." Winging it. I wasn't sure of protocol.

"Hey," he said. The comfort of *hey*. *Hey*, he would be late for dinner. *Hey*, he would pick up bread. *Hey*, he was dropping the car at the shop and needed a ride home. "Virginia?"

"Hi," I said. But it was not good. I knew it was not good. I heard it in the *ah* at the end of my name.

"Bad news," he said. "Well, in a few ways. The caller was actually right with that tip. A few bodies here. Four. Off the record, of course, between you and me." He was outside, I heard wind, waves. "It's going to take a while. Hours. We'll be here all night, probably. Through tomorrow. No, over there. One sec, one sec," he said to someone else. I saw him waving them away, plugging his other ear for quiet. "I wanted to let you know. That I won't be able to make it out tonight."

Could not be sweeter, just like Evelyn had said.

"Oh no," I said. "That's awful." Pure disappointment then. Just disappointment, nothing else. No sadness for the dead girls, women, children, out there in the cold. Their skin and hair and bones hardened and salted in the ocean air, dead of winter. No wonder at how they got there, what happened to them first, whose hands wound round their necks or pulled triggers or shoved blades, cooking or hunting or otherwise. I didn't care. Did not care. My future, ruined. "Our happy hour," I said then, like a child. I couldn't help it. I hoped I could hide the pout. But I was deflating. It had been so good, so easy, and now.

"I know," he said. "I'll make it up to you. Take you out on a real date. You know, if that works for you."

"Sure," I said. I was watching the sweep of the clock. "Of course it does." There were more people around him; I could hear the hum of truck motors, a man's voice on a speaker, the beep then hiss of a radio. "Well," I said. "Good luck, I guess."

"Thanks," he said. "I'll talk to you soon."

* * *

I went anyway. I surprised myself and went anyway. Evelyn had come in right after I hung up, right up to the edge of my desk, and leaned toward me and said, kinder than anything my own mother ever had, with such tenderness, with such—with such compassion: "Oh honey, it's fine. You'll be fine. This can be a tough place, but you're doing okay." She had been listening, of course. She told me to get my coat. She waited in the doorway. She flicked off the lights and escorted me down the stairs, out to the parking lot, to our cars, which were parked next to each other, some fairy-tale trick, both of their windshields sparkling in the moonlight.

I just followed her. She introduced me to a group of men I might have recognized, maybe could have placed, had they been in their natural environment, the rooms and halls of headquarters. But here, at the bar, with drinks in their hands and their ties loosened and their faces red from the heating and the alcohol, they only tweaked a chord of memory and what could I do but let it ring out. What difference did it make. I knew where Charlie was. He wasn't here. These other men made no difference. They were just men. Evelyn kept moving. I followed her. To a group of women from Central

Records who, it seemed, had put on makeup and removed their glasses and baggy sweaters and had become totally different women. Joyful women, with White Russians in their hands and milk mustaches on their upper lips. Smiling. I followed, past the jukebox I had imagined. Though its lights were out, its cord unplugged from the wall. Followed to a long table at the back of the place. A table of women. I knew Evelyn would have a story about each of them. Same way I knew she would eventually have a story about me.

"This is Virginia," she said, interrupting them, her hand on my right shoulder, "the new girl at the tip line." They all looked up at me, mid-lift of drink, mid-sip. I hoped she'd leave out details, wouldn't mention the call I'd taken. I didn't know how much I could say, what I should keep confidential. I imagined Donovan scolding me for gossiping about details with people uninvolved. I smiled fake and waited.

"Oh, Jesus," one of the women said. "Get the girl a drink after the day she's had."

They all already knew.

Evelyn was my chaperone, and so I let her help me. That's Missy, she married a detective. Left her first husband for him, actually. That's Anne, also married to a cop, met him at work, obviously. That's Renee, that's Amanda, that's Mary. Oh, those two, actually, both Mary, work as analysts, thick as thieves. Be nice to them, okay? Be very nice to them.

In a lull, the woman on my left asked me about myself. Asked me if I was married, is the way she put it.

"Nothing yet," I said and shrugged. I felt the drinks Evelyn had given me. Red wine from a bar, a bad idea generally. Sour at the first few sips, but now it was warming and thick and smooth as any wine I had ever had. Doing the job. "I mean, I'm single. I live alone."

"Well, that's perfect," the woman said. Her eyes widening, her face bright. Her name was Joan. "This is a good place for you, then. Most of us have gotten wrapped up in something here. One way or another." She laughed and rolled her eyes toward the woman on her other side, who had leaned forward to listen to us. "High school with guns, we call it," she said. "Right?" The other woman nodded.

"Big time," she said.

I felt an urge in me, at first just a little pang. To tell them about Charlie. *Yes,* I wanted to say, to gush, that was the word, that's what I wanted to do. *Charlie Ford. Know him? I'm sure you do. We're going to go out, we were supposed to go out tonight, but then all of, you know . . .* Trail off there. Let them connect the dots. Show them that I, too, was going to get wrapped up in something. Was well on my way to it. I wanted to see what they would say, what advice they would give me. *Tell me what to wear,* I wanted to say. *Tell me what to do, how you all did it.*

But I didn't. I just listened. To all of them. I smiled when I should have. I drank my wine and listened. They were kind. They seemed decent and kind. They talked about the things that I knew I would one day talk about.

I can rattle off their names, all of those women, still.

*   *   *

It was on the eleven o'clock news. Press had gotten there quickly but were kept at a distance, just close enough to get the backs of the cops, their jackets marked "POLICE" in reflective letters as they bent and scraped and dusted and bagged, flashlights bobbing in arcs. I looked for Charlie's coat and thought I saw, when a camera panned the scene, the fur of his hood, the line of his back as he stood talking to another man, both of them hands on hips. Charlie.

I watched when I got home that night, from my bed, under the covers, another glass of wine on my bedside table. This one untouched. I ignored the calls from my mother and then the texts which started out with *Did you see what's happening? Did you hear about this at work?* and crescendoed into panic. *Are you okay?! please call home asap there is a crazy person loose in case you didn't know!!!*

And then I fell asleep. But not before thinking of him, of Charlie, with me, in my bed, full of wine, both of us, touching each other all over for the very first time.

CHAPTER NINE

Place was a mess on Monday. Busier than I'd ever seen it. Something setting people moving, a new purpose. It was not a small county, Suffolk, and it had one of the largest departments in the country. But it was not accustomed to big-city crimes, crimes that would spawn encyclopedia entries and reenactments on TV shows: several bodies at once, no immediate solution. A mystery.

Even in the people uninvolved. The girls at the front desk when I walked in: somber, sober, silent when they looked up from their computers, almost in unison, to wave hello. They were waiting. Ready for anything. Different girls from the ones I had chatted with on Friday night at the happy hour. Now they were cooled off, pulled back. No more pink cheeks, beer spilling, dripping to wrists, showing me pictures of their kittens and/or their boyfriends, husbands, men they had met in this very building. And the women on my walk to the office, all the women. The secretaries behind their opened tinseled doors, hushed on the phones, ears pricked for the next thing, listening for the calls of their bosses. Yes, Sergeant; yes, Lieutenant; yes, Chief. Yes. Just say yes.

"Good morning," Evelyn said when I neared her desk. She stood up like she had been waiting for me. Like she was going to take my coat and hat and hand me a stack of papers to sign. She followed me into my office.

"It's going to be a *day*," she said. She had a pencil tucked over her ear. "I don't want to scare you off, so that's all I'm going to say. But I'm right outside, don't forget." She sighed in the way of people on stage. "Well, happy Monday, honey," she said. "Hold on tight."

I skirted the phone as I walked to my desk to sit, almost afraid of it. Had forgotten to take my coat off, stood back up, took my coat off. Stared at a blank, dark computer screen. Had forgotten to turn my computer on, turned my computer on.

I sat and watched and waited for the phone to ring. Anticipated its bell, its slight shake from the mechanism going wild inside it. The department had released little information. Just the bodies of four women found on Gilgo Beach, ages and identities TBD, no cause of death, no identifying features, nothing. *If you have any information whatsoever—* every notification blazed in red print at its bottom, on the department's website, on the news—*please call our tip line. Completely anonymous, any information can help.* The tip line. That was me. Hi.

Charlie came in around ten, with a coffee for me, but also with Tony and also their boss.

"You already know Tony," he said, setting down a coffee. "And this is our boss, Sergeant Bill McHale."

"Good to meet you," McHale said and leaned over to shake my hand. "Nice to see where our Charlie disappears to every morning." Our Charlie. You bet. He thumbed at him.

"This guy hand delivers you coffee every day and we can't even get him to throw his garbage in the trash can. Unreal." He shook his head.

"I just spoke to Donovan. He should be up any second," Charlie said.

"This caller," McHale said to me, "she's going to call back. She wants to give us that information, get rid of it so it's not just on her anymore. It's weighing her down. They always call back. We just have to have a plan in place for when she does."

"And we need to have you ready for that." Charlie nodded, all business. "We need to have you transfer the call right to us, if you can."

"Okay," I said. "Of course. I can do that." And then, movie timing, the phone rang.

"That's another thing," McHale said. Second ring. "Everyone else is going to have an idea now. It's going to get busy. Real busy." We all looked at the phone. *Go ahead,* it said. *Get me.*

Third ring.

"Good morning, Suffolk County Crime Line. Virginia speaking." I made it nice, whipped cream and cherry nice, because they were watching. I let the nice gild my voice, and I tilted my head toward them. Advertisement: girl on a phone. Nail polish, maybe. Blusher. Hairspray. Trade school. I waited for her to speak. She was going to give me more. Pass the burden and hang up newly lightened. Free.

"Okay," I said and started writing. Weed, between periods, sixteen-year-old from the nice part of town, prior sales, no one cares. "Thanks so much. We will input this information and send it to our investigators right away." I hung up, finished the notes. "Nothing," I said. "Narcotics." I shook my head, disappointed. Like I was one of them.

Then Donovan came in with a flourish of his overcoat, his cheeks red with cold. He went straight for the chocolates, found only two left, and took them both. One after the other.

"Gentlemen," he said and sat. "Busy, busy, busy day." He was still a ship captain. On the deck. Weary. Older. Just finished writing a note home on scrimshaw. He sighed. "What's the plan?"

"Ford tells me we can't get records on callers so we're going to have to wait until she calls back. Or someone else calls back," McHale said. "It can't just be one person who knows about this."

"I think we may be able to get the number," Donovan said. He was rubbing his chin. "If we transfer the call over to you, the number may come through. I think. I mean, it's worth a try. Or if you have other ideas, you just tell Virginia here your plan. We can get someone else up to help her if you think we'll need it," Donovan said.

"I think it should be fine, as is," McHale said. "Let's try and get the caller transferred to us, then. Anyone who calls about this, if it seems like a legit call, try and get it down to us." I looked away from them and to Charlie, who was standing, leaning against the front wall just by the door. He squinted at me, and I wanted him to wink or smile, but it looked like he was thinking.

"Sounds good to me," Donovan said and huffed his way to standing. "Just let me know what you need and when and I'm happy to help. Right, Virginia?" This for politeness, his including me.

I only nodded.

They all shuffled toward the door.

"Wait a minute," McHale said. "Ford, stay back and tell Virginia what we're looking for. What kinds of things we need asked, just in case she can't get the caller to agree to talk to us." And then to me: "You're doing a great job. I only want Charlie to give you a better understanding of the kinds of things we need to know." He was still grumbling when they left. "It's ridiculous we have to keep this thing anonymous. It's a good way to make our lives difficult, actually." He closed the door behind them. Then it was just the hum of the heating and the whir of the computer and the bell in the phone, waiting to go, and Charlie and me.

He was on the far side of my desk. His tie knot looked loose, like he had gotten frustrated and pulled at his neck. I pictured him, digging through brush while the cold wind blew his hair. His gloved hands on the skin of the women. Or not, I don't know. Maybe he wasn't supposed to touch them. Maybe that was someone else's job. Maybe I should suggest the breakfast truck.

"You look scared," he said.

"I'm not scared," I said. "It's just a very surreal thing. It's very weird."

"That's certainly a word for it," he said. "*Weird.*" He pointed at the empty dish. "Donovan ate all your chocolates. I was eyeing them."

"I have more if you want," I said. "They're in the closet—hang on." I came around my desk and went toward the cabinet by the door. "I have a whole bag left," I said and made a hand movement by my head, making my fingers say *lots*. Evelyn would be proud of me. I was expecting the phone to ring, knew it would happen any second, felt the sound of it in the back of my teeth. *Hello, Suffolk County Crime Line, Virginia speaking*—it rattled through me, on a scrolling banner, ready to go. "Oh," I said, head in the shelves. "Wait, I don't. What happened? I thought I did, but I don't." I came out and he was right there, right in front of me. Suggest the breakfast truck. Suggest that the two of you walk down those back hallways to the breakfast truck. "I'm all out. I don't know how. I guess the lieutenant was really going at them."

Any other person, any other man, and I would have been furious. How close he was, I would have thought, too close. How assuming. How annoying that I turn around and there he is, under my feet. I almost lost my balance, in fact. He took my elbow, catching me, my back just about against the door. There was a rushing in my ears, a big loud jumble. I knew I was flushed, reddening deeper by the minute. His hand on me still, just his palm on my elbow, his cupped palm, nothing else touching.

Here it is. One way or the other, here it is.

He vibrated. It came up his arm, through his fingers, right into my body. A spark, a light. I had never felt this before, this connection manifesting into the physical so quickly. He's going to kiss me. Right now. Already. Okay, I thought. Okay. Maybe a little strange, in the office this way. A little risky. Still, this is it. This is something. This is something else.

But his phone. It was just his phone ringing.

"Ignore it," he said without even checking it. "Forget it." He shook his head, came even closer. Put his other hand on my other elbow.

"Okay," I said. Stupid. Reeling. I was effervescing. I think I even nodded at him. "Okay."

He reached up, tugged a strand of my hair, once, twice. Smiled. I think he had just touched my cheek. I think. Maybe we had moved closer. Maybe I had closed my eyes already. Then a click. The door, opening.

It's true what they say, how the air in a place can change.

It fizzed behind me, charged. The metallic thread up my middle tingled, ringing its entire length.

The heat of Charlie's hands was gone. Before I had even realized it, it was gone. And he had moved back feet from me. He must've jumped. He was leaning on the arm of the chair, thumbing through his phone, looking for something to look at. Checking the call he had just missed, maybe.

For an instant, I looked outside, out behind him. Brittle gray, dark for daytime, taut black power lines against the sky. Snow any minute. The color out there was beautiful. All I could think was that I wanted all that cold on my skin. That I needed to be calmed and that it would numb me, quiet every moving part of me. The way my insides rang, I was afraid. It was a collecting, a steady increase. I could not see it to the end. I would have done anything to keep it at bay.

And so I turned around.

"Good morning," the man there said. "Declan Brady, chief of Department." Full uniform, pins and ribbons, collar brass, bright white shirt with stars on the points of his collars, dark tie, crisp, crisp, crisp. He smelled like fresh air, touch of cologne, stacks of paper, and something else, something I had no name for.

He offered me his hand and we shook, and then he was just another man in uniform whose hand I had shaken upon our first meeting. It had happened twenty, thirty times already.

The chair scraped on the floor as Charlie stood up straight. He repocketed his phone. I almost expected him to salute, the way he was standing, rigid and respectful. Reporting for duty. Immediately altered. I was missing something.

"Hello," I said. He looked away from me, cut the air with his eyes.

"Sorry to interrupt," he said. "Detective." Said *detective* with half a smile, all sham, a nod at Charlie. "Are you in the middle of something here? Or may I have a word with Virginia?" But *my* name, my name had the shimmer and lilt of a foreign word coming out of him.

"No, boss, not at all. I was just on my way out," Charlie said. Cowed, ducking, sheepish. He ran his hand over his hair and scratched his neck as he went to the door. He stopped and turned back. I knew he was going to say something to me: *See you later; I'll give you a call; I'll be back for the tips; come down to Homicide when you're done, and we can brief you on what we need; how about we try again for this Friday night?* He opened his mouth to speak. "Chief," he said, his voice different all of a sudden. Subordinate, unsure. "Good to see you, sir."

Oh, Charles Ford, Charlie, the look on his face just before he walked out. Serious, smart, part profile. Like it was struck, etched in the nickel and copper of a coin, shining in the palm of my hand. Something I could put in my pocket.

"Good to finally meet you, Virginia," Chief Brady said when the door closed.

"Yes, sir. You too," I said.

"You have a second?" I nodded. "Very good. Have a seat. Let's talk." I sat. Crossed my legs at the ankle and put my hands in my lap. Everything about me said, *Yes, sir; no, sir;*

of course, sir. His posture, his air, his position just under commissioner, I got it. I understood what was expected of me. I watched him sitting there, and I heard faraway, invisible things: out through the hall, in the other office, Evelyn rat-a-tatted her fingers over her keyboard; on the first floor, a cop rolled his mouse wheel, scrolling through pictures of speedboats; farther away, a maintenance worker climbed a wooden ladder to a blown bulb, stopped at the top rung, scraped a spot of paint off of it with his thumbnail, and watched it float to the floor.

I was still all feral, felt everything at once. Charlie. Those had been his hands on me. I wanted to close my eyes and just think, conjure him. He could become a cloud shape in front of me, a genie in my lap, a picture projected on the wall. Charlie. I didn't want to talk about something else with some other man. I didn't care. I needed to savor what had just happened while I could still remember all of it. Charlie. How close we had been.

"I hear you're doing a great job," the chief said. He pushed himself back into the seat, relaxing. He crossed one leg onto his knee, folded his hands across his abdomen.

"Thank you," I said. "That's so nice to hear."

He tapped his chin with a fingertip. He was thinking. Looking at me. His hair was mostly silver, shot through here and there with gray, and he had it parted and shaped, styled like the fifties and swept to the side.

"I guess I don't have to tell you it's unusual to get such precise information through the tip line. For something so big as this, I mean." He spoke from behind tented fingers, resting them on his lips. I wondered where Donovan was, why he wouldn't be here with me while this conversation

was happening. I missed his mariner's shuffle on the linoleum and his bitten fingernails in my candy dish. I wished
he'd come up. I was useless at this moment, filled up to
bursting and then sucked out. I didn't know what I was even
doing. How I was supposed to speak to this stranger, this
important stranger. "I had to come down and meet you for
myself." He was slow, deliberate. "You know, you must have
had a very cool head to get us this information. A lot of civilians might have clammed up."

"Thank you," I said. "I'm just kind of—I don't know—
winging it, really. Trying to figure it out as I go."

"I'm impressed," he said. He didn't look away much.
Most people, they give you the chance to look around. To
look them up and down, make judgments, spot details, reas-
sure yourself of your surroundings. To make sure that you
haven't been suddenly uprooted and placed somewhere else
entirely. Disappeared somewhere. He didn't look away, so I
didn't have any chance to do this.

"Don't be too impressed," I said. "I'm sure I'll mess
something up sooner or later." But I wasn't thinking right.
It came out flippant. It was too quick. I flinched. I wanted to
shrink in my seat. I looked at my lap and then back at him,
apologetic.

He had his eyes on me. He rolled his tongue on the
inside of his cheek. He nodded. Slowly. I heard the sweep of
the clock, one hundred times. Finally, he laughed.

"I see you've been hanging out with cops," he said and
gestured with his head behind him toward the door. A jab
of dread in me. He had seen what we were doing. He knew
exactly what had been about to happen. And maybe it wasn't
allowed, coworkers dating. There were workplaces like that.

I had broken some cardinal rule, I had done something very bad already. "Looks like the humor is starting to rub off on you."

This man, he was taking up most of the room. Starting to. Everything else was getting smaller and smaller, getting edged out, and soon all I would be able to see was Declan Brady's blue. I answered with the polite smile I used with strangers in grocery store lines, with distant relatives I had seldom met. A little ballerina smile, my mouth closed, crown of my head bowed down.

"Be careful," he said, like an old friend. "We all drive too fast and drink too much." He winked. I didn't like where he was going. I didn't want to hear what would come next. "You should find yourself an accountant or a lawyer. Someone nice and well behaved, with a clean job. You don't want a Homicide guy." Oh no, no, no. I tried to roll my chair back slowly, to pardon myself respectfully, but I banged into the side of my desk and then into the base of a stack of boxes, wobbling the whole thing. I reached out to stop it from falling, then readjusted, rolled back again, and stood, turning to the window so I could just stop looking at him.

The string in me, still going. Stop. I wanted to stop it. I wanted to pull it out. Dry it off and coil it up and put it in a box.

But no, I knew I could do this. I could do this if I had my back to him. I put my hands on my hips, stood straight, lifted my head. Sir, I am an adult. I am capable and grown. And this is not the way we speak to people, to other adults. In the workplace, for goodness sake. That's what I made my body say, posture straight and hard like I had a ruler at my spine. Chief Brady, thank you for your concern, but this kind of talk is unacceptable, and you should be ashamed. Tsk, tsk and a slap on your wrist.

Instead, I just exhaled slowly. It had started to snow. I watched it come down, sticking already. There were Vs of black on the covered asphalt below, where cars had reversed and righted and then left. I saw two women, dispatchers, smoking by the back entrance, hoods up. I wanted him gone. I needed to sit, to close my eyes.

"Finally," I said, just to say something. I chinned toward the window.

"Finally," he said. "It's here." When he spoke, I heard the movement in his eyes as he looked at me. I heard his words hit, slide slowly down my back. I felt them stick to my skin through my clothes. Something completely different altogether. I wanted to hate it. I did want to.

*   *   *

I was still standing, still wondering what had just happened, still with my back to the door.

"Ahh, so I see you met Chief Brady," Evelyn said when she came in a few minutes later. It must have killed her to wait even that long. She shook her head and looked out into the hallway, as though he were not yet far enough away. "Is that the first time?"

I nodded.

"Wonderful man," she said and watched me. She was looking to see what I would do, I could tell.

"Yeah?"

"Very smart. I mean scary smart. You know those kind?" She was pretending to pick pills off the sleeve of her sweater. But it was a show. There was nothing there. She opened her mouth, like she wanted to say something. She lowered her voice when she finally spoke again. "I've heard he can be"—she stopped, thought—"a bit of a hothead, though. A little tough. His way or no way. Or so I've been told." She looked behind her again. "But he's never been anything other than nice to me. A real gentleman."

"Sure," I said. "He seems fine."

"Fine? Of course he is! He's absolutely lovely, like I said. I'm just giving you some background. I always wish some-one had given me all the details when I first started," she said. "I think it's a good thing to know about the people you spend so much time with, right? We're with these people more than we're with our own families. Think of that. Or don't—I don't know. Ignore me." She sighed and looked out the window. "Ahh. More snow. This is all we need." I turned to look too. As though it needed confirmation. We both watched for a few seconds. When she left, she waved with her fingers as she backed out the door.

*   *   *

Hothead. Tough. I looked him up. On my phone, of course. I'm no fool. Googled Declan Brady, chief of Department, Suffolk County Police. Decorated officer, member of the force for more than twenty years. Active in his civic associa-tion, annual cancer walk, here he is with a Boy Scout troop, smearing sandwiches with peanut butter for the homeless; Chief Brady on Veterans Day, giving a speech. Hometown hero kind of feel. This from the local papers. "New Top Cop," another one said. "No nonsense in Suffolk: Veteran cop takes the helm of one of the largest departments in the country." A photo of him at his desk, American flag behind him, pointing at something in a stack of papers. His shirt was short sleeved. It must have been summer. I kept digging. Pictures from earlier in his career: dark hair, old-style patrol car, Brady leaning on its open driver door, sunglasses, smiling. Face still the same. Him at a podium, mid-sentence, group of uniforms behind him. "Private Life of Public Servant," one said. I clicked. Which high school, which position on its football team, academy at twenty-one, single, never married, now forty-five, vacation place in Florida, his favorite restaurant: Italian and affordable, his favorite book: "I read everything I can get my hands on." Another quote, this one in bold, boxed, in the middle of the text: "I was born to serve and protect the people of Suffolk County." I read it through, then scrolled to the comments below the story. *Brady's the change this county needs, a real cop, FINALLY,* one said. *Almost twenty-five years' experience, I'll take it, better than we've had in the past,* another one said. *He will clean this place up. All this man is a hero, how did we get so lucky? Everyone loves Chief Brady.* How nice. I kept going. *Let's not forget that Deck Brady's personal life includes fucking a hooker in his patrol car and letting her steal his gun.* Oh. Farther down, in response: *What about the prostitute he shacked up with who also stole his gun?* And in response to that: *And his blow—he loves his blow.* I kept going. *Womanizer; Stand-up guy; A cop's cop; The hero we need; Strategic and smart as hell; Sex-obsessed cheating scum; Who cares what he does when he's not working as long as it's not illegal? Even if it is illegal,* someone had written in response, *who really even cares?*

Hothead, Evelyn had said. *Gentleman.*

I closed the tabs quickly when the tip line rang. Slid my cell into my coat pocket like it was contraband and someone was watching me from somewhere. I got the phone on its third ring.

I had a small hope it was the woman again. Hoped for her half-crying, washed-out voice with any new information that I could print out and bring down to Charlie. An excuse to go over there. To pick up right where we left off.

"All right, listen to this," the guy said. Pompous. He thought he was doing me a favor. I'd put him in his forties, no Long Island accent, every word measured. "No one's saying how these girls went, but I'm pretty sure it's something gruesome. I'm going to guess blunt trauma to the head, something that would wreck their faces. Or they were strangled. The guys who do this want to punish them, right? Abuse them. I've done a lot of research," he said. I didn't like the pleasure in his voice, the satisfaction. He seemed too excited. "A ton."

"Okay," I said. "And?"

"I went down there. I've been a few times, actually. I've stopped to look at the brush, walk the causeway, just get a feel for the place. I couldn't do it through pictures alone. I wanted to actually be there, to get a sense of the vibe, I guess, is what I mean. The energy. I wanted to have the ocean there behind me, the night time. You know? My car running next to me with the lights off. I was really trying to get it into my system what this guy must have been feeling." It sounded like he was smiling at me. His voice through the phone, greasy and smiling. He didn't wait for me to say anything. He didn't care. "And I think it's important, critical, to consider that this is someone who is probably really familiar with the area. You're not going to have someone out from the city who just stumbles onto this as a dump site. Who's

74

going to make the drive with a girl in his car and then brave that brush, the sticker bushes and everything? Not likely. We're looking for a local."

We.

"You're walking around down there, doing this all, after the bodies have been found?"

"I was testing my hypothesis," he said, and I pictured him doing it. Out in the cold, dark clothes, his sedan idling next to the road. His face a blank spot. Masked with fog, with night. "My other thought is that he didn't use a car at all. That he came up from a boat on the bay side. Much less of a chance of being detected. No headlights to worry about, no one patrolling the waterways in the middle of the night, in winter. So maybe your guy is a fisherman. Or a pleasure boater. Something like this. I'll look into that next."

"Okay, thanks," I said. I couldn't get rid of him quick enough. "I will send this info along right away. Bye."

Male caller believes the victims were strangled and/or beaten or otherwise disfigured in their faces. Says the subject is a local who may have arrived to the site via boat from the bay side of the causeway. Caller claims to have been at the scene since the discovery of the bodies in order to test his "hypothesis."

This was just the beginning. Donovan, McHale: they were right. It got busy. Everyone had an *idea*. They all pronounced the word in italics. *Now hear me out,* so many of them started. *I have an* idea. *Just think of this.* I wrote whatever they said, printed it out. By two PM, I had a batch of them on my desk, waiting to be walked down the hall.

My mother called during this. The height of it, around three. She had a knack for things like that. I took her call in the corner. Standing up, finally. I had skipped lunch, bathroom, looked awful I'm sure. I went to the windowsill, my back to the room, and listened to her chide and then sigh.

"I guess they don't tell you anything, right? About what they find?" she asked. She didn't wait. "Something like this happened when I was younger too. He went around after young women, and all the girls he took looked the same. Similar, I mean." It was like she wanted it to be sensational. A danger to everyone. No one to be safe. She was drinking something—I heard a hard swallow. She was seated too. Softness in her posture. A resignation. "They all had the same hair."

"I can't believe all this snow. I had shoes reheeled and I wanted to pick them up after work, but I am not driving around in this," I said. "I might have to put you on hold. If the phone rings. It's been so busy." We were having two different conversations; we just happened to be on the phone with each other. I thought to tell her more about Charlie. How this was his case. You remember Charlie, the Homicide detective I mentioned? The one who brings me coffee every morning and is going to take me out properly sometime in the vague near future? The one who just hours ago tried to kiss me, held my elbows and stroked my cheek and almost, almost.

I'd never.

"Fine, hon, of course." My mother, sighing again, a long one. A Mom special. "Well, your father's out running. In the snow, this idiot. Did I tell you that? That he's running now? I'm waiting for the phone call when he's found face-first in a ditch. He's too old to run. He's going to kill himself. I'd say a midlife crisis, but he's too old. I told you he sleeps in the spare room now? Moved his computer in there, a bunch of books. Calls it his study. Who knows with him."

"Oh, wow. Ridiculous," I said. Hardly listening. Looking at the snow. Thinking of Charlie.

"I mean, I'm happy to have the bed to myself—don't get me wrong. Maybe it is a midlife crisis. Can you imagine? Next is the sports car and the secretary. I'm more than willing to organize and pack his things." She laughed, shifted in her chair. I could hear her stretching her legs out under the kitchen table, wincing at the pinch in her lower back. "We can give him a going-away party. A little bon voyage."

"Wait—you know what? I have to go," I said. "I have a meeting."

"A meeting," she said, and I heard the impressed in her voice.

"Well, yes. Kind of. I'll talk to you later."

"Be careful driving, V. Call me when you're safe at home, okay?" she said.

"You got it," I said and hung up, rushing.

Maybe the girls, my girls, out in California, three hours behind us so this part of my life hadn't even happened yet. They would want to listen. They would understand. Advise. Their husbands were proof they would know what to do. I could tell them. Ask them. But I didn't. I put down my phone. Walked out.

I thought I should stop in the bathroom on the way down to him, but I had the stack of tips, and where would I put them in there, and wouldn't it look weird, the new girl coming into a stall with an armful of paperwork, all harried? I went straight to Homicide, knocked on the door, waited. It was a while, minutes. I knocked three times, each time a bit harder. Then stood there, ready to smile. Ready to pick up where we left off. *Look,* it would say, my stance, my face, *here—take my hands, remember what we were just about in the middle of?* It was McHale, finally, who opened the door.

"Hello," he said and worked quickly to place me. "Oh, hello again," he said when it clicked and he remembered. "You have something for us? Or a question? You have her on the phone again?"

"Just some tips," I said. He must have seen some kind of disappointment, a little touch at the corners of my mouth, maybe. He looked over his shoulder, discreet.

"Ford's on the road right now, or I'd have him take these from you," he said, his voice a bit lower. I loved him, McHale. Thank you, Sergeant, I love you, you understand everything, and for that I am eternally grateful. "Newest guy takes the tips, you know. No offense, or anything."

"Not at all," I said.

I had tried.

* * *

Back at my desk, I watched the big lawn across the lot, watched the white pile up. Thought of sledding. I hadn't done it in years. But there was a place by my parents' where I used to go. A hill on a golf course where every nearby kid went when there was even a flake of snow. Now that's a good idea for a date. Creative. Easy. Fun. Him in his coat. Jeans and sneakers, finally out of a suit. Would we ride at the same time? Fly down the hill, spinning, about to tip. Would he hold me from behind, his gloved hands snug in the curve of my abdomen, his mouth near my neck, the scratch of his day-old stubble getting my ear when he leaned close to tell me to hold on. His breath minty, cold, too clean for a human being. Would we crash at the bottom, fall into a pile, stay lying down, breathing heavy, his face feet from mine until he propped himself up on an elbow and shimmied closer and melted the snow on my lips with his? We would. Where would we get a sled? No matter. We would go back to his place and make cocoa, though he'd think to spike it—bourbon, Bailey's, Kahlua—and then we'd get bombed, playing cards at his kitchen table, picking at old sugar cookies and crackers, bachelor food, kiss again; then start, in earnest, to fuck around on his couch. Big grains of sugar on our tongues, dissolving too slowly between our teeth and our cheeks.

The tip line rang.

Hello, Suffolk, etc.

"Don't you guys have profilers for situations like this?" he said.

"Sorry?"

"I'm just saying that you would think, with taxes like ours, that they'd bring in one of those profilers, take a look at everything and then there you go. FBI should be able to send some down, for a case of this size, no? Just like on that show."

Right. Just like that show.

"Thanks so much for the information," I said. "I will send it along right away."

Caller is a waste of time. Disregard.

Outside, the sky had turned white. Wind swirling snow so thick that I couldn't see more than a few feet out of the window in front of me. I saw my own reflection instead.

CHAPTER TEN

I had had too much wine, woke up after the alarm. The snow must have stopped soon after I went to sleep, because the morning was bright and clear, the sun a high white circle. It looked to be about five inches out there, give or take. I had no time to wash my hair, so I coiled it into a bun on the top of my head, wore a button-down with an extra button open instead. I almost left with two different shoes on, forgot my gloves, said *fuck* every chance I got. I had no time to defrost my car, no time to fetch the paper or yesterday's mail for the Big House. It may have been two days' worth of mail. I couldn't remember getting it on Saturday either. When the owner got fed up, he slapped his way to the end of the driveway and got it himself, I guessed. Maybe he let it stay there in the box, icing over, melting again, moldering until the spring. There's no way his wife got it. There's no way she got her hands dirty, the bottom of her shoes dirty with such things. It could wait another day.

I drove to work looking out the bottom middle of the windshield, my head pounding.

The phone was ringing when I walked in.

"One sec, one sec," I said to the room, like a woman talking to a pack of hungry house cats. They'd be weaving, their tail tips brushing my knees.

"I read on a message board that the women were found wrapped in burlap. Now here's the thing with burlap. Could be a landscaper. Very easy access to burlap."

"I'm not sure that investigators have divulged any specific details about the scene, sir," I said. 9:10 AM, no Charlie. I reached for my bag to find an aspirin, and when I leaned down, the cord caught on the side of the computer and the red phone fell off its small table and clanged onto the floor, and the call went dead.

"Fuck," I said. Then I inspected the plastic for cracks. It was fine.

Ten thirty AM, still no Charlie. The latest he'd ever been. A fin of worry swam through me. What did I do? I should have given him my phone number by now. He should have asked, really. It had been a week, a little more than a week. We could have at least been texting by then. He had tried to kiss me, after all. He could have asked for my number. But it was delicate. These things, at the very beginning, were so delicate. They had to be incubated and syringe fed and tended to with fingertips and kid gloves. Soft strokes, light as air. I had blown it. Too much, too soon. Maybe he wasn't trying to kiss me at all yesterday—maybe I was standing too close to *him*. I had weirded him out. He had only asked for more chocolates, and even then, he had only tried to be polite. And all my imagining, all my weird imagining about him. About everything, always. He could feel it. Sense it coming off me. It sent out the wrong energy, kinked the karmic way of things, plucked strings in his subconscious:

Careful with this girl. This is how I wound up wrecking it all, always. Too premature. Still too undeveloped for any of that. Still fetal, caul coated, not even mewling. I blew it. He changed his mind. Had to have. Maybe he saw me too close up, my pores and the scar, and fuck me, I knew it. I should have splurged on better shirts, a better bra. This is where it got me, shopping off the clearance section. Good brands, nice clothes, but still. Clearance.

Worry is a color-changing thing, though, and it turns to anger in the right light. So, then, naturally, the next thing I thought: How dare he! What's he playing at: How many other girls in this place has he brought coffee to, held by the elbows, moved in to kiss? Dangled happy hour like a carrot in front of their faces? He tricked me, that little shit. Fuck him.

Virginia, for God's sake. I stepped in to calm myself. He's waist deep in four dead girls, likely the biggest case he's ever had. He has bosses on his ass, the press—you heard it yourself. You have known him for one week, a little more than one week. Calm down. I tucked my hair behind my ears. I lifted my chin. I calmed myself down.

Eleven thirty—almost lunch time. Still no sign of him. Several new tips, all shit, including:

> *Caller states she is certain the person responsible is her ex-husband, Louis Reardon, dob 9/17/1968, claims he participated in "weird sex things," kept rolls of burlap in the garage to wrap fig trees in winter.*

And:

> *Caller states the person responsible has time-traveled from the Revolutionary War, states he is tall, balding*

and that his first and last name begin with the letter M, states that he is "back and forth between time" but can sometimes be found at a home on Cooper Avenue in Amityville, describes house as a high ranch with artificial flowers in a downstairs windowbox.

And:

Caller states that he is a fisherman and frequents the area where the bodies were found. Caller states that he has on many occasions seen cars pull off to the side of the causeway, their drivers removing things from the trunk and disposing of them in the brush. Caller suggests investigators patrol the area, look for said cars.

I printed them all.

I kept looking at the fallen snow. I couldn't get enough of it. But especially when the wind blew, sending flakes down from branches and telephone lines and the roof of the building so they swirled and caught the sun and glimmered and shone all the way to the ground. I wouldn't go sledding with Charlie; the snow wouldn't last. I'd have to think of something else. I'd have to come up with a whole new idea.

At twelve thirty, I recoiled my bun, took another aspirin, and pushed my chair back so I could walk to the bathroom. I was going to stop at the vending machine downstairs in the cafeteria too. It was something I had not yet done. But I was hungover and I wanted a soda.

The phone rang just before I crossed the threshold, and I had been playing this game with the threshold: If I had moved one inch beyond it, I'd let the phone ring out. If not,

I'd turn back. That time, I thought, Fair enough. It got me. I let it. I turned back.

"Virginia?" she said before I had the chance to roll out my script. She remembered my name. She sounded better, more sure. Not crying. "Is it you?"

"This is Virginia," I said. Said my own name like the name of a guest, trying it out for the first time. Making an introduction between strangers.

"Is it just you answering the phones there?" she said. It was very quiet where she was. I thought that if I listened hard enough, I could hear the thud of her blood, muffled by her skin and muscles.

"Right now, yes," I said. "Nine to five." At your service. "But if you want, if you'd feel comfortable speaking to a detective directly today, I can transfer you over. I know that they would really like to speak to you."

"Oh no. No way. I have to hang up now." The end of her sentence got quieter. It was because she was moving the phone from her face. I was going to lose her.

"Okay, that's fine, that's okay. Don't worry about it. Stay with me, then. We can talk." I pulled my legs up onto my desk chair so my voice got all cozy and close up. We are sharing a tent in the woods on a scouting trip, you know. We are best friends. I braid your hair during earth science class. I hold your hair when you're vomiting at a friend's wedding, too much cabernet. I tuck your hair behind your ear on the day you file for divorce, your lousy husband shoving his clothes into his car's trunk. "We can talk just you and me. Though I will say, one of the detectives is very, very nice. I know him personally. If you change your mind, you let me know, and I'll patch you through. Or I can have him come down here and talk to you—whatever you want."

This seemed to soften her. She cleared her throat. Then I heard her TV come on.

"I called again because of the snow," she said. "There may be more of them out there, and all this snow. On top of them. It's too much."

"More of them?" I said, but I made it slide out easy. Just conversation. I was asking about specials at a bakery, a shake of my head as I point at the case. That's how I made it sound. But the snake in me again. It had slithered to the tips of my fingers. They were cold. *More of them.* "How many more?"

"Who knows," she said. She almost laughed at me for asking. "Who knows what he's been doing. They're all escorts, though. You guys know that yet or no? I knew them from around. They just kept disappearing."

I tried to look at the clock, but it made me dizzy, made my head hurt more. I wanted to dim the lights, pull down blinds that didn't exist. I only wanted to hear.

"Okay. Okay, what else can you tell me?" I said.

"No, that's it for now," she said. "Actually, I have to go."

And then, I thought, I'm dreaming. I thought, Wait, am I dreaming?

"Wait," I said. I am spinning in my bed, five hundred yards from the Big House, ten o'clock news on mute, ten-dollar pinot pumping through me. I am dreaming this voice and the sparkling snow and these girls, and this job even. I've made all of it up. No Charlie, no husband, no future life in a three-bed, two-bath. Four-bed? No? Nothing. Good-night, good morning. "Wait a minute."

But I was not dreaming.

"I can't. I really can't. I hope this helps them," she said.

"Can you do me a favor? Can you call me back?" I said. "If you think of anything or if you want to talk, can you call me back and we can talk again? I'm not a cop, you know. I'm just a regular person. What they call me is a civilian. I'm thirty. Nice to meet you." I was nauseous, disintegrating. Could see my skin thinning, beginning to disappear. Speaking nonsense. Yes, definitely asleep. Or the hangover was peaking. Peaking. The anxiety gritty and sharp all over the place. Pain glittered through me. My head. More girls.

"I don't know," she said. "I'll try." And that was it.

I held the phone until I heard the dial tone, and then I put it in its cradle. I reached back to touch it, and it was still warm, its own life inside of it. Its own guts and blood.

I typed it up the best I could. Chose nice, official words that made it sound like a newscast as it went aloud through my head. I heard the anchors reading it, their voices rising and falling:

> *Repeat Caller* Caller states that the slain girls were working as escorts, as she was, and that a further search of the area may reveal additional victims. She is unable to provide any identifying information about a possible subject and is unwilling to speak to detectives directly at this time. Note: This is the same caller who provided the original information regarding bodies.

On the walk over I had a purpose. I had information and a purpose, and he was going to answer the door for me, and we could take it from there. Resume where we left off. Halfway down the hall, I realized I had forgotten the rest of the tips in my rush out and had only brought the one from the girl. I could turn back, start again. Or get them later and have another reason to walk down. That was best. That made sense. I shook my head.

Knock knock. Charlie would open it, stand in the doorway. *Long time, no see,* I'd say. *Where have you been all my life.* I'd lean on the jamb. No, my God, no. *The guy who usually brings me coffee skipped out this morning, and I'm dying without it, and I'm wondering if you can help me.* Severe eyebrows, a smile. *Can you spare a cup?* How about we just keep it simple: *Guess what I have for you,* and here I'd wave the paper in front of him. I'd lean forward a bit. I was wearing my nicest bra. It couldn't hurt to try. *I have so much for you.* I was almost there. I was so close.

"There she is," he said from behind me. And honestly? I wanted to fall. I wanted to crumple on that floor. I wanted him to catch me, to pick me up, his hands under my arms, and say something in a whispered rush. Something, anything. *There you are. I've been looking all over for you. Want to grab lunch? You look so nice today.* I was just this side of stable. I was floating, all over the place. I needed him to help me. *I've been thinking about you, about yesterday and—*

But it wasn't Charlie.

Brady walked fast. Long strides. He caught up quickly.

"So you do leave that room of yours after all," he said, abreast, gun side to me. I felt the electricity of the thing. Thought of a woman stealing it, lifting it right out of its holster. What woman would do that? What kind of girlfriend? My fingers itched at the idea.

"Yes, sir. I got a tip," I said. "I think it could be important. I mean, not that I really know or can judge what's valuable.

You know. But it's the same girl who first gave the information." I stopped myself, lowered my voice. "About the bodies. She called back." I thought he would be impressed again. I looked up at him, but his face didn't change. It stayed straight, looking forward. "I'm supposed to walk them down." I nodded toward the long hallway in front of us. He kept me talking, could have kept me going and going just by being quiet. "That's what they like."

"I bet they like a lot of things," he finally said and stopped walking, made it so I knew I had to stop walking too. He looked at the floor for a second and then rubbed his hand over his mouth. "Actually, I was just on my way down to Donovan," he said. He hadn't been walking toward Donovan. "I have a different assignment for you today."

"An assignment. Okay, sure," I said. "Would you like me to come pick it up?" I imagined a *special project*: data entry, reams of paper, numbers running together, all blurring into one until the minute I went home. Hours of typing. Heavy phones, heavy typing, related administrative tasks. As assigned by supervisor(s).

"Different kind of assignment. We need you on the road today. News conference at two at the scene. We've been having staffing issues in the press office, so I'm going to need you to help me out down there."

"But," I said. Panic. I pictured myself fumbling, dropping something, apologizing in front of rolling cameras and microphones while my words came out in puffs of steam against the cold. "I don't know anything about any of that."

He shook his head. He looked at me like he was going to put a hand on my shoulder and tell me some big secret. The phone, back down the hall on its table. Ringing ceaselessly already, I knew it, the girl with something she needed to say, to add, something she would say only to me. A warning. A secret. Something pivotal and case breaking. The phone would wear out from its ringing. Its little bell dying or catching fire. I had to get back there.

"You really don't have to do anything. You just stand there in your nice coat and your nice shoes and you say, 'No more questions' when we tell you to. That's it."

"But what about the phone?"

A secretary passed behind him, smiled big as she approached, but cut it just as fast when he didn't turn around. He widened his stance, put his hands on his hips. That same thinking face from yesterday. A commotion down the hall. We both turned to look—a group of men, uniformed, laughing loud—and he turned back to me first.

"The phone can go to the front desk. Same as nights and weekends," he said. "I'm reassigning you."

In my office, the phone stopped ringing. Cooled off, the spotlight on it dimming.

"Two, okay," I said. "But it's almost 1:30."

"That's why we have to move," he said. "Let's get your things."

"Shouldn't I drop this off first?" I said about the tip after we had about-faced, started back.

"Bring it," he said. That long, brisk stride. His gun side. Everything about him urgent. He made me nervous.

* * *

He had a parking spot right out front, his name on a sign behind it. A big truck, black, tinted windows, hidden lights. He opened the door for me and went to slam it shut after I got in, but stopped. And how strange. Because then, gently, as gentle as a mother, he tucked the front flap of my coat under the back of my calf, so that it wouldn't get caught in the door. He didn't let a fingertip touch.

Outside: the memory of high school hooky. The sensation of being out of the proper place in the middle of the day. A sizzle of worry at getting caught. But who could catch me? No one could catch me.

Snow glinted everywhere, blown across the big field in front of headquarters, shaped into dunes and dips by the wind. The sky was blue, cloudless, too cold. I folded my hands in my lap, trying to hide my nails. I had a chip in the paint on my thumb, the smallest place where the red was gone, and it made me feel self-conscious. He was the type who would notice. A patrol car flashed its lights in recognition as we passed, its driver nodding. The scratch of the police radio beneath everything. I caught scraps of it but couldn't get my head around all the lingo.

He swung the truck onto the road, and it was then, when we were onto the pavement, that he spoke.

"You cold? You can turn the heat up if you want." He took his hands off the wheel and rubbed them together.

"No, sir. I'm fine, thank you." Prim and fussy. A real lady.

"You can drop the *sir*," he said.

"Right, okay." I moved my hands, shoved them under me. I didn't want to fidget.

"You out with the Homicide kid last night?"

"What?" I asked. It took a lot to make my voice even. He kept his face straight ahead, swerved coolly around a car making a left-hand turn. He lowered the volume of the radio, and the scratching disappeared.

"You smell like booze," he said. He still didn't look.

"I had some wine. When I got home." I said. Slowly, like I was retracing my steps, trying to remember where I had mislaid something. Starting the script of an alibi. "A glass? Two glasses, it was, actually." Actually, it had been three. "Before bed. While I watch TV, I drink wine sometimes. Or while I read." But I could tell he'd see through it. He'd see I didn't read much anymore. He could already tell what I did home alone at night. How I walked the mail up the drive. What and whom I thought of when I got under the covers and switched off the light and closed my eyes. He knew I was lying, he knew everything, my alibi was nothing.

I was waiting for him to say I shouldn't be doing that at all. That I was a nice girl, a nice young girl, attractive, too pretty, even, to be home alone drinking wine, and I should be out on dates, enjoying my life. I was waiting for him to start in about the accountant again. About someone clean and nice, just like myself. Just like who he thought I was.

"Shit," he said, then hit a switch on the dash. "We don't want to be late." The car in front of us pulled over, and we blew by. I saw its driver looking up at me as we passed, relief all over his face.

* * *

I hadn't been there in ages. A thin strip running parallel to the mainland, jutting into the sea. A barrier island. In summer, its causeway seethed with traffic. Beachgoers. We used to go when I was much younger. My parents and their friends and the children of their friends. We used to stay there for hours, till sunset, in the thrall of the Atlantic. Sandcastles, warm sandwiches, the constant dark threat of the undertow.

In the winter it was a different world. Everything gray, white, brown. Thin and brittle, ready to break, to splinter from the cold. The wind down there was relentless, no tall trees to block its way. It had removed most of the snow from near the road except for a thin edge hemming it. Deeper in the bushes it looked untouched. I watched for deer, birds, something alive. Brady sped up, siren silent but lights still going, even though there was no one near us. I saw a blockade up ahead, three police cars across, bumper to bumper. Brady pulled to the middle of the road, slowed only enough to give one of them time to move, and then rolled through.

"My old precinct," he said to me when one of them waved. "Home sweet home."

Fifteen cameras. Local, regional, some national affiliates. Reporters, their backs to the gusts off the water, huddled together against the cold. They were all in a clearing along the causeway, yellow crime scene tape flapping, stuck into the thorny brush, draped like crepe paper at a party. Picture perfect. Brady pulled up and stopped, the closest car to all of it. No tire screech, no gravel flying. All calm. He put the truck in park and opened the door.

"Stand behind all of them," he said. He was getting into a thick blue coat, "POLICE" in yellow letters across the back. "When it's time, you call it. Tell them it's over. Tell them to follow up with the press office if they have any more questions. Okay? That's it. Very easy. You'll do fine."

"But how do I know when?" I said. I was afraid to get out of the car. I picked at the spot on my thumb with my other hand. "Who says when it's over? Who will tell me?"

"I do," he said. "When I look at you, you tell them it's over."

He closed the door, and I saw him walk to the group of cops, all dark coats, hands on hips. He slapped McHale on the back, slid his hand up so his fingers rested on the man's neck. And there was Charlie. This is where he had been all morning, of course. He had come straight to the scene without stopping at the office, or he had been here all night, searching, still working as the dawn broke over the east end of Long Island and slowly moved west, bringing with it the dim daylight of winter. There was Charlie, pacing, face toward the ground like he was still looking for clues.

I stayed at the back, like Chief Brady said. I tried to get as close as I could to the rest of them, for warmth but also to disappear, though no one was noticing me anyway. I kept my eyes up front, where the men were standing. They were lining up, shoulder to shoulder. In the middle, the commissioner, a white-haired man who looked tired, ready to leave already. McHale, some other men I didn't know. Charlie and his partner, Tony, leaning toward each other to talk. Brady stood at the edge, out of the frame. His coat whipping in the wind. I watched as he lifted his head when the commissioner said, *Everybody ready?*

It was really the most I had heard about the case too. Four women, likely between the ages of twenty-eight and thirty-two, all found in this general area—the commissioner half turned, motioned his hand behind him, keeping it a flat plane, parallel to the ground—undressed, in various stages of decomposition. The medical examiners put all of the deaths within the past year. Identifications unknown still.

"It is not unreasonable to say that we have a serial killer on our hands," the commissioner said. A flutter of camera clicks. "Four bodies, all the same manner of death, same place. It's not unreasonable to go ahead and say that."

Serial killer. I said it in my head. Tried to see if the words would do something to me.

Behind him, the wind was still working. It went through the bushes, pushing them side to side. In the spaces it made—in between the gray-brown wood, the thorns, the wrappers, cups, garbage—I pictured the women. The grass and branches tamped down around them. Their fingers, especially, I pictured their fingers. Loosely curled, palm up, index out a little straighter, like tempting you to come close, closer. Or balled, tightly balled, fingernails into flesh of palm, diverting attention from the pain elsewhere. Their nails. Broken or still neatly manicured. I didn't want to picture either. As the wind switched, started in from the bay side, I thought I saw a flash of color in there. A fan of auburn hair lifting, waving, then lying flat. It was a girl on her side, a blanket of snow pulled up to her chin. Then five of them, ten. A slumber party. Where were they? I thought of the piece of paper in the car, the tip I had taken, folded on the dash. Magnetized, its own force field around it. I thought of the caller, the phone ringing on its table at that very minute: more girls, their names, who's doing it. Every answer, there, on the other end of the phone.

And I was going to miss her. Again.

"This is all we have for you right now. I can take a few questions," the commissioner said and stepped back. They pounced. *Commissioner, is it true, Commissioner, people have said, Commissioner, what does this mean for—*

Charlie did a good version of involved. Nodding along, tired looking, somber and professional. He looked over the group a few times, brown eyes roving. But it was so cold, and there were so many of us, and so his eyes passed right over me. I was having a hard time imagining him then. Couldn't think of his hands. The look of him in my office chair. He was wearing the wrong coat, not the parka but a "POLICE" one, like the rest of them. Even his hair seemed different. I wondered when he had had time for a cut. Pictured him at the barber. Then pictured him in front of a bathroom mirror. He would make a good husband. Patient. Gentle. Our first would be a boy. Charlie too. We'd keep his hair long. Dark brown, a halo of curls—

They were all trying to talk at once, the commissioner was holding up a hand to quiet them. And then Brady, staring at me. Worse than withering. It was a hard stare, nothing behind it. Blank and stern and cold.

"That'll be all," I said, his eyes still holding mine. It shook me. But I spoke, got it out. Loud enough, teacher inflection. Dismissal, goodbye, see you tomorrow. The reporters directly in front of me turned to look. All the others wondered what they had heard, where it had come from. But it did the job. It got them to stop. "That's all for today, everyone. Any additional questions, please call the press office." I finally looked away from him.

I walked over to his truck and watched while the group dispersed, packed up their equipment and filed off. Brady was with the commissioner, two other white-shirted, white-haired bosses. I stood, moving from foot to foot. My heels deep in gravel, my hands in my pockets, my breath white against the cold. The one thing I was supposed to do. He would tell Donovan that I couldn't keep track of the simplest job. He would suggest they start the search for someone to take my place. He would order it, that urgency in his face displacing anything else. People listened to everything he said.

But Charlie, then, walking toward me. The wind in his hair, pulling his coat open. It is an awkward thing when two people are coming toward each other and are still too far away to speak, but they have already made eye contact. The difficult part is figuring out what you do in that time.

"Hey, you," he said when he got close. His look was real surprise. "They have you doing press now too?" He was near enough to block the wind, to warm me up. I shook my head and made eyes like *You would not believe.* Out of the office lights, he looked younger, the brown of his eyes almost golden. "You look nice with your hair up," he said. I touched my hair, a reflex. I felt my cheeks going hot. I wanted to tell him no, it was just dirty, I was just in a rush, I was hungover, but I stopped myself.

"Thanks," I said instead.

"I guess you did okay without a coffee this morning," he said and winked.

I was going to lift off, float. Hello! Hi! You're back! Thank goodness.

"I didn't know you had to be down here for this. I could have stopped at headquarters on my way and picked you up. We could have ridden together."

We could have. And wouldn't that have been nice. "I didn't know either," I said. "Chief Brady told me only a few minutes before we left."

"Oh yeah, right," Charlie said. When I didn't say anything, his smile fell. "Wait, really?"

"Yeah," I said. "Is—why?"

"Really?" He stopped. Ran his hands through his hair. "No, that's—Okay, that's—Okay," he said finally.

"So," I said. And he just looked at me. What someone would call mystified.

I was going to tell him about the tip. I had just opened my mouth, just breathed in lungfuls of that cold air to tell him about the tip. The air made me clearer, and I was going to tell him how it was the same girl again, how I had been on my way to walk it down to him, and that's when I saw Brady, who asked me to come along to this, but maybe I'll walk it down when I get back? Will you be back in a few, Charlie? Or later? And you can bring me that coffee, after all? But then there was Brady.

"Ready?" he said to me. Sighed, like we were leaving a friend's house after a too-long dinner party. Like he wanted me to drive so he could fall asleep on the ride home.

"Chief," Charlie said and nodded downward once. Thank God he didn't reach his hand out to shake because Brady didn't hear or he pretended not to hear. Instead, he held out his arm, indicating behind me, toward his car. *After you*, the gesture said.

"Well, bye," I said to Charlie. And it came out weak and stupid, a schoolgirl. End of recess. Stupid.

To his credit, he didn't hesitate. "See ya, Virginia," he said to my back.

The wind was in my coat and my ears rang from the cold, and when we got to the passenger side of the car, Brady opened the door for me. As I was climbing in, I saw Charlie watching, his car parked facing us, just a ways down the road. He had his arm around the back of the passenger seat like he had been about to back up. Still watching. Still watching when Brady went to shut my door, stopped, opened it, and fixed my coat same as he had just an hour before, and then shut it, slapping the window before he walked around to his side. I was staring at Charlie, waiting for recognition, a smile, a wink, a wave, anything. Maybe he couldn't see me through the fifteen windy feet, two windshields and the glare of the sun and the shine off the snow. Or maybe he could see. Maybe he could see when Chief Brady—seated, seat belted—reached to my side of the dash, took the tip and slid it into his inside pocket. Made a joke about how I almost missed my cue back there, not angry at all, laughing, even. Good natured, affable. Maybe Charlie saw me smile at that. Ballerina smile, but still. Maybe he saw Brady reach again to fix my heat vent, over and across, couldn't see where he was reaching for, though, his hands hidden from that vantage point. Maybe he saw what he thought was a rapport. An ease. Familiarity. Involvement. Something. Maybe he put two and two together, misconstruing, and made up his mind at that very moment: That's it, off limits.

That ends that, I thought. Because I knew how it went with men. Not everything, not a lot, even. Not by a long shot. But I knew enough to know that.

CHAPTER ELEVEN

Sure enough, next day it was McHale who came down to pick up the tips. He was waiting by my door when I walked in.

"Hi, Sergeant," I said.

"Good morning." He pressed himself back against the wall to let me pass. He would have disappeared into that wall if he could have. "I don't have a coffee for you," he said and showed me both empty hands. "That's, you know, that's not my thing." He wouldn't even say his name. Then he laughed. Right, of course. And let me guess, he's out on the road. "And he's out on the road again. Out at the scene, so, here I am." Covering like a fraternity brother. What else could I have expected. He stayed by the door while I switched on my computer, rolled back my chair.

"Lots and lots," I said and tapped the stack of them, I smiled because I was trying to sound polite as I spoke. But I was furious. "Though I can't promise they're any good."

"I'll have someone sort them." He stood there look-ing, thumbing through, shaking his head as he read. "Oh, and . . ." he said, like he was just remembering. But I knew exactly what was coming. "We're putting up a bin. One of those wall file things, on our office door. That way you can just drop them off without waiting there for us. Saves us time, saves you time. The office has been empty a lot, with all that's going on—half the time we're not even there. So." So. There it was. That was it. I had been right. Though it had been much more abrupt than I thought it would have been. So much more obvious.

I pictured a whisper network, a flurry of text messages, sotto voce asides in the halls and a game of grown-up "telephone" starting the second we drove away from the beach. Vulgar things between men: *You'll never believe what Brady's getting into now.* Even more explicit. *Chief's screwing the new girl. Stole her right out from under Ford's nose.* Regardless of how they heard it, they had all been given the same message: keep your distance. High school with guns.

Chief Brady had pissed all over the ground at my feet and for what. How dare he. I raged. I hated him.

Sergeant McHale said goodbye over his shoulder as he left. Afraid to spend even another unattended minute with me.

I had to fix this. I had to do something. But I didn't know what. I would have to wait for it to come to me. I would have to wait for the hiss and flare of a match that would illuminate my solution. So I stood up, straightened my shirt, brushed my hair back. I did some deep breathing I had done in yoga once. Let my diaphragm rise and fall, visualizing the whole time. I imagined the clearing away of the anger, a little mop, scrubbing at the really tough stuff, soap bubbles and dirty water and then finally the smell of cleanliness. Every interior surface spotless though dull from use. Empty. Clean.

I would just tell him. *Nothing is happening,* I would say. *Charlie, I don't know what this is all about, the way this place*

works, I don't understand it at all, but nothing has happened.
How about we plan for Friday night, you and me?

I walked out of the office, two-finger wave to Evelyn, then into the hallway. I thought that I would feel a sense of preparation about it. I wanted to. I wanted a sudden shift, metamorphosis, tectonics. I wanted to be an intrepid explorer with a pack on my back, at the ready. But nothing. I didn't feel any of it. It was partly sunny outside, expected high of twenty-seven degrees. Seasonably freezing. The snow was pushed into huge banks around the parking lot. It was December 15.

I stopped at the bathroom. A female officer stood at the mirror, redoing a French braid. I watched in awe.

"I've never been able to do that," I told her. I made special note of my voice. I was much friendlier than usual, more forward, but my voice itself sounded the same. Its timbre, its pitch. I was leaning on the sink. I was wasting time. I could have stayed there all day.

"Once you get the hang of it," she said through bobby pins and the elastic in her lips, "it's like second nature." She finished and twisted off the end, let it fall down her back, and left. I wasn't done talking. I had thought of a few more things to ask.

Pick a stall, sit, stay. I washed my hands three times, using a different scented soap each time. I dried them carefully, each finger. I looked at my face for what seemed like ages. All the same. I touched a small pink spot where my jaw met my neck. A minor irritation. From my pen, maybe. I sometimes rested the tip of my pen in that crook while thinking. Or from the collar of my coat or the cold. Other than that, nothing. I thought I could hear the lights humming, some hidden message in there. The settle of the walls. The flush of a toilet in the men's room down the hall. But nothing in me, latent or bubbling up or otherwise. Quiet. A smooth sea.

The hall was empty. Not unusual. I heard my heels clicking as I went toward Homicide. They were the heels I didn't prefer, the better pair still at the shoemaker's. I turned the corner and got closer, saw the bin McHale had mentioned: a hair crooked and screwed to the door, "Gilgo Beach" handwritten in black marker on a white label.

I will press my ear against this door. I will then tap the wood in code so he'll know it's me. *I need to speak to you, Charlie. This is ridiculous, stupid, let's meet up and I will explain everything because, you know what? You know what's so funny? The funniest thing, there is nothing to explain, actually, isn't that wild! Ha ha. This is a big miscommunication. I had no idea things were like this here.* You *are the man I was supposed to meet. That's why I wound up here. It's you.*

But it was no use. And I knew it. All the way through me, I knew it. I was ruined for him. People were saying Chief Brady had taken a shine to the new girl, and everyone knew what that meant. Charlie was elsewhere, on the road, gone for good. From inside the Homicide office: only typing, chair wheels, the soft fall of paper onto paper. Down the hall, an old-fashioned water fountain in the beige cinder-block wall. White porcelain, the kind that gurgles up from a metal spout. I thought I heard it dripping. Next to it, a ladder, a maintenance man installing a long fluorescent. He hadn't seen me. I waited for him to screw it in. A good sign, always, the flood of light. I knew before I saw it what was going to happen. It was in his body language, the most minute tip backward and then the overcorrection as he leaned forward again. We both watched—him from the top rung—as the bulb hit the floor and exploded, white powder puffing up.

Magic. Match hiss. There you have it. Going, going.

I pivoted, quick left, my body on a track. There's the explorer; there's the pack. I was propelled by something else. I can't really say. It just happened. It was all the things I knew making me do it. The second before I entered, I took a flyer from the wall just next to my head. "Donate Unused Sick Time," it said. I folded it into thirds. It just happened.

"Good morning," I said to the secretary closest to me. "I have something for Chief Brady? From Lieutenant Donovan?" My voice curled up at the end. A bud in the sun. Southern sweet.

"Well, hiya, hon. I can take that for you." She looked down at the paper. She had bright orange hair and glasses so shiny, so reflective, I almost couldn't make out her eyes.

I raised my arm, pressed the paper against my chest using both hands.

"I shouldn't," I said. "He said confidential, hand deliver, blah, blah." *Men*, my face said. *Am I right?* I was cool. Normal human body temperature is ninety-eight-point-six degrees. I was at ninety-seven, tops. I felt my heart through that flyer. I felt it calm and well behaved, beating away. Not a flutter, not a misstep.

"Gotcha," she said. "Remind me of your name again, honey, and I'll tell him you're coming in. He doesn't like to be surprised."

"No one does," I said. "It's Virginia." She turned from me to dial him. On her desk a framed picture: three fat orange cats.

"All set. Go on down," she said when she hung up.

I knew what I would say. This is inexcusable. There seems to be some sort of problem. I'm afraid that this is not what we had in mind. Unfortunately, with all due respect. We'll need to remedy this, ASAP. Let's circle back. Let's touch base. Let's clear this up. How dare you. *Sir.*

It was a long, narrow hallway. No windows, dark carpet, doors the length of it on either side. A tunnel, a burrow. At its end I'd pop up in a dirt-floored den and find a family of bears tearing apart its lunch: a smashed beehive, all paws honey drenched, bees still buzzing; or a baby deer—Mama and Daddy deer on deck—shreds of pelt and innards, everything streaked with red. I had never been there, but I knew to walk to the last room on the right. It was the only open door, a square of light on the floor in front of it. A sign.

"Good morning, sir," I said when I got there so everyone, everywhere in the world could hear me. "I have this for you, from Lieutenant Donovan." He was sitting, leaning back, a folder open across his lap. He put down whatever he was reading. He did not look surprised to see me. On his desk: paperweights, an ornate lamp, a framed black-and-white of two patrol officers in front of their old cruiser, all wings and tail fins. He waved me to him with one small motion of his hand.

This is when I say it. I was going to say it. I cleared my throat as I went to say it. Felt the first bit of sound coming from deep in me. *Why?* I think it was going to say. But then I stopped. I stopped because I knew Detective Charles Ford was already long gone. It was over. He was. He was of no use to me any longer.

So.

So, I walked to Chief Brady, to his desk, right up to it until my front pressed on its edge. And I waited for a second without saying anything. I let him look me in the eye. And then I handed him the paper. He unfolded it, read, and looked back at me. The history of the world on that paper. Solutions, numbered into the hundreds of thousands. Infinite. Maps and keys and secrets and everything. All of it. I felt my skin change, raised bumps pressed the inside of my shirt, rubbed uncomfortably in the thighs of my pants.

This is the something, I thought. And it took forever. It took a second. I had changed my mind. Because I knew.

I swear I saw something in his face, his eyes. A shift. A light.

"Shut the door," he said then.

He did not ask me why I was there under a flimsy pretense, standing in front of him with my arms at my sides like a good and respectful subject. He wouldn't have understood it if I'd explained. After I closed the door, he pointed to a chair. He didn't have to say, *Sit*.

"I'm glad you stopped in with this," he said and waved the folded paper. Like the room was miked. Or a two-way mirror somewhere. "It looks perfect. I was just on my way to see Donovan, to tell him I needed some help down at the beach again. You have the flyers all copied, ready to go?"

"The flyers are ready to go," I said. There were no flyers. "They're on my desk." There were no flyers.

"No need to take two cars. I'll drive. Meet you downstairs in ten minutes. The side entrance. I'll call Donovan and let him know."

And there you have it: neat as the folds of an origami swan.

Behind him, the sun came in rushing and frenzied. What a sight.

"Ten minutes," I said. "Got it."

On my way out, the secretary I had spoken to was eating yogurt, a big spoonful fresh into her mouth. When I said, *Thank you*, all she could do was raise her eyebrows in reply.

*　*　*

He was waiting, his truck running, exhaust clouding out behind it. I walked to him with a slow and measured gait. Down an aisle, toward a podium, through a courtroom. I held a stack of blank copy paper, a prop, tight to my chest.

"Ready?" he said when I climbed in and shut the door behind me. After that there was nothing else but the sound of the radio as we drove.

The beach seemed different. Wider, a huge expanse, cold blue water stretched tight on both sides. I searched the bushes, moving my eyes through the blur, for the flash of hair, the *come here* of the waiting women. If I could see them, I could help. Nothing.

The causeway snaked on in front of us, gray and long and flat, until it vanished quietly into the sky at the end. I could see, up ahead, the roadblock, the flashing lights, the choreography of bodies at work. Charlie down there. Far, far away. Another world.

Before we got to them, to where they were, Brady turned off abruptly into a driveway on the bay side and stopped the car in a spot at the end of the lot. He turned the radio down and looked straight ahead, out the windshield. Winterized boats bobbed at the docks, bubblers at their hulls.

"You needed to see me privately?" he said. The light coming in was grayish through a passing cloud. I could feel the ocean behind me, pulling. The bay in front, pulling. I saw myself from the sky, my coordinates superimposed on a photo: 40.6197507, –73.3933600. We were at the very edge of the water. We could not get any closer without going in. It must be so cold, I thought. And I had to think of that cold. My skin was burning. Everywhere, all of me burning.

He looked at me. He was going to make me do it.

"I did," I said. Definitive. Lit match flickering. I could have been watching the two of these people, there in that car. A man and a woman. Watching and waiting. Strangers. She's so certain, I'd think, zooming in. Look how her face is set. She has made a decision. From my vantage, I could not see red in her face or the heat she was feeling. And him, is that a bit of a smile? A little bit? What are they even doing? What are they waiting for? I'd zoom back out, bigger picture, get distracted by a patrol boat docking at the other end.

I didn't move.

A quick checklist in my head, a rundown: underwear, nice but not the best, not the high-waisted pair I had eyed for weeks and then finally splurged on. But clean-shaven everything. I hated waxing. Perfume dabbed at ears, at elbows, nape of neck, back of knee, cleavage.

And all the other things I was thinking.

Recline my seat, back, back, he could reach over. Sit straight, turn to him. Tiny whitecaps. That high sun. A car pulled into the lot behind us, bass from its stereo loud. It circled slowly, tires crunching gravel, and then exited. Wait for him, wait for his hand on my face. Do Snow White, the surprised look, mouth opened. A rosebud. Pink stained, everything ready. Nearly ten AM. Lean, lean up, out of my seat, across, no gearshift in the way, okay, slip my fingers under the collar of his shirt, thumb under his tie. Eye him from there, up through lashes. Let him get used to the look of it. Let him think this was all his idea.

He leaned to me, exactly as or just a split second after I leaned to him. And we kissed. It was like any other first kiss. Fizzy and warming, a chemical change. He tasted like mint. It was chaste, because of the space between us. Though he did put his hands in my hair, his fingers firm against the back of my head, pressing me to him. He did do that. But that was the extent.

When he pulled away, he bit his lip like he was trying to stop a smile. He looked at me from his side of the car and shook his head.

At my desk, thirty-eight minutes away, the phone rang and rang and rang.

That's it. Just kissed.

He did not hold my hand as we drove back. He did not tell me about his history; his career; his nuclear family; his missing gun; his love of street drugs; his women past, present, and future.

"We'll keep this between us for now," is what he said.

For now is what I heard. The promise of it nestled in there at the end, the potential, snug as a sleeping baby. I was looking for anything. I would have held on to anything at that point.

"Are you free to have dinner with me tonight?" He looked at me for this. Tonight. This is the difference, I thought. This is a person who knows what he wants.

Tonight? Tell him no, I heard my mother saying, saw her pulling her hands as she begged me. *Make him wait, make him ask again, make him wait for Christ's sake. I made your father wait two weeks for a date. Not tonight!*

"Yes," I said. "I'm free."

"I'll get you at seven."

"Seven is good," I said. "I'm guessing I don't even need to tell you where I live, do I?"

He smiled, rakish or a schoolboy. "You can but you don't have to."

He was handsomer than I had thought. Suddenly his profile alarmed me in its handsomeness. Panicked me. His jaw, his broad shoulders, his hand on the wheel, smallest tap of two fingers. He had changed. All of it had. He was a bright spot, the sun come from behind clouds over a newly mown field, hay strewn and fragrant, the moon out too, though strange during daylight. Unexpected. Regardless, he was both, already. He was a comet tail lighting the way through space. He took the place of someone else who hadn't even existed, really. Someone who I might have imagined anyway. Completely conjured.

You want to know why, I know. A change of heart like this. So sudden, so jarring. So, this is why: My opportunity had changed, and I had to change with it. That is adaptation. That is maturity. That is the way we make it to our goals.

For now.

I saw my mother wave her hand at me and walk away, disappointed but not surprised.

CHAPTER TWELVE

Something that you must, must, must keep in mind: I only took the job to find a husband. Another thing, one I always forget: Whatever you're trying to find is never in the first place you look. And one that I don't think has been mentioned yet: the dead girls, a serial killer, none of it frightened me in the slightest. At the end of the day, it really had nothing to do with me at all.

CHAPTER THIRTEEN

Declan Brady. Deck for short. *Deck Brady*. I wanted to run my tongue on that name. I wanted to swallow it whole. Deck Brady was going to fuck like it was his first time or like he did it for hours every night. All animal. Spit and instinct and just this side of vicious, I'd bet. He was that kind of man.

He ordered red wine, which surprised me. I had thought scotch, something else brown and strong. A Manhattan, maybe. He wore a sports coat and pants I didn't take note of and a baby blue shirt as crisp and fresh as the white ones he wore with his uniform. He ordered a rib eye, rare, which is exactly what I'd figured him for. It was a steak place famous for its thick-sliced bacon, so I ordered the thick-sliced bacon. I didn't touch much of it.

You can see us from far away, talking and gesturing, taking a break for a minute to sip our drinks, but that's it, only a minute. You will see it with music over it, so you won't hear what we're saying, only see that we're smiling, that that swagger of his that you've read about has fallen away, and when my hands are palm up on the table after I've asked him a question, he takes his index finger and taps the exact center of my left one, making a point. A tap for each syllable of his answer.

He told me about his career history and about his mother, how much he loved her. His father, a cop too. God rest his soul. He had two glasses, as did I. After they cleared our plates, I declined dessert, though a nice-looking slice of key lime pie delivered to a different table was momentarily tempting. He had coffee, a double espresso that he ordered *corretto*, which impressed me. I did not have anything. When we were ready to leave, he came over to my chair, held my elbow as I stood, and walked me out the door that way. We waited for the valet to bring the car around. It had gotten colder, so he took his coat off and put it over my shoulders, on top of my own. I smiled up at him and he brought his hand toward my face, like he was going to cup my chin, maybe, or put my hair behind my ear, but the car arrived at that very minute. His work truck, familiar to me already. He pulled his hand away.

"Let's get you out of the cold," he said when he opened my door.

Of course I had worn the better underwear. The very best underwear I had. A set. Black. The bra, a balconette. I had oiled myself in the shower, took minutes to massage it in everywhere. I wanted him to be taken aback by my softness, to wonder why no woman he had ever touched before me had had skin like this. I wanted him to think hard about it. To think of how long he had been missing out on it. *Ethereal* was the word I wanted to come to his mind. And if not that, *exquisite*.

"That was very nice," he said as we pulled past the Big House, up to my driveway. Me, I was dying. *Nice.* I was just this side of manic. If he didn't touch me I was going to do something stupid. I was going to ask him in. I was going to beg him to come in. He didn't move to put the car in park. "Well," he said. We just idled.

"Well," I said too. Thank you for dinner, I had such a lovely time. We should do this again. That was very nice. Nice.

"Would you like me to come in?" he said.

I must have nodded. Or the buzz inside of me made my head shake *yes*. At least I wasn't the one who suggested it. At least I only had to say yes. So, yes. The billow of the ballgown was back for our walk to the house. A princess this time. A princess leaving a cotillion, her suitor's coat still on her shoulders. And, oh, because this is important: I was really wearing black cigarette pants, a beige scoop-neck sweater. The wool of it so soft it spoke to you. *Touch me,* it said.

I was wrong. About this too: neither. He was slow with me. He was thorough and by the book and slow. He took my clothes off piece by piece. Shirt first. I saw him notice its softness when the wool whispered to him, got his attention. He ran his hands down my shoulders, both at the same time, an old-fashioned move, one I had seen a lot in romantic films. He knew what he was doing. He knew that I had never had this. And I couldn't believe I had ever imagined anyone else. That I had risked my destiny. That I had come so close to ruining it all. How foolish of me, how shortsighted.

The second, the very second of it starting, my mind flashed colors. Bright heat. I broke into molecules, reassembled around him. Above me, like that, he was someone I had known forever. A whole history between us.

"Jesus," he said, his mouth against my neck. "Virginia."

"Yes," I said. It was throaty and certain and very much unlike me. Yes.

And it was right then that I knew I loved him already. Don't ask. But I absolutely did. And I knew that he would be the one.

CHAPTER FOURTEEN

"Virginia," she said. She was outside, a main street. Exhaust, car horn, squeak of a coffee shop door in need of grease, an ATM spitting out twenty-dollar bills. *Chick chick chick beep.*

"Hi," I said. "It's me. How are you? I'm so glad you called me back." Friends, far away friends. Long time, no speak. I felt around on my desk for my notepad.

"They haven't gotten anything yet, have they," she said, not asking. She had started walking. Her voice bumped and changed with each footfall. "I feel like they won't. That they never will."

"You know what?" I said and tried to make it sound like I couldn't believe it. "They don't say much to me." That part was true at least. Not anymore, they wouldn't. "They're basically like, 'Talk to the callers, take the notes, and we'll keep you in the dark about all of it.'" I was feeling chatty. I wanted her to like me. To feel more comfortable. "I could hook you up with a detective. You might be able to get something out of one of them." They wouldn't tell her a thing.

"No," she said. "I don't want to. I really do not want to. Can you just let me talk to you? Please?" If I pushed, she would hang up.

"Okay, of course. I'm listening. I'm here." I drifted. Deck. In my bed. Afterward. A shiver in my core just thinking about it. He picked up my hair and let it fall, let it drape over his face until he exhaled in a puff and blew it away. The light in the hall was on and lit only the outline of his profile. I couldn't see the face he was making.

"I think it's a client, the guy who's doing this," she said. Another car horn behind her, its driver lying on it, giving it a real good one. She waited for it to stop. "The guy who I think is doing this," she corrected herself. "This is what I'm thinking."

"Okay, that makes sense," I said. Just before he left, he leaned over me, brought the blanket up to cover my chest. He kissed my forehead and said, *I'll see you tomorrow. Client,* I wrote. "Any idea of who this guy is yet? Anything you could tell me? Has anyone ever told you who he might be?"

"If you asked every girl I know, all of them would tell you it's a client of hers. Every single one."

"Well, do you think it's a client of yours?"

"Yeah, I do. Sure," she said. "It could be any of them."

"I'm guessing it won't help for you to give me a list of their names, then."

"Their names," she said. "I don't have them." A door shutting too quickly. I slid my foot in.

"Well, what about the girls. These friends of yours," I paused. I wanted the word to hit her. *Friends.* "What were *their* names?" As far as I knew, they didn't have IDs yet, or they hadn't been made public, anyway. *Virginia,* he said. He must have said it ten times, twenty. His voice going up and down like it was a song. As he moved. *You know what I thought the first time I saw you, Virginia?* he asked. His face touching mine. *Tell me,* I said. I had my hands in his hair. I couldn't get him close enough. I wanted to eat him, to have all of him inside of me at once. He told me.

"I'm going to tell you. Are you ready? To write this down?" she said.

"I'm ready whenever you are."

She had left the street. Ducked into a storefront or library. It was quieter. When she whispered their names, I almost felt the heat of her breath on my ear. Recited slow and evenly—in candlelight, in incense smoke, the perfume and pollen of a million lilies—with the reverence of a litany.

While I waited for the printer to warm up, this: shit. I *should* have made him wait. My mother was right. What kind of woman, the first date, the first fucking date. And what kind of date? The only reason any of it had happened was because I walked myself into his office. Propositioned him, basically. I leaned on the wall by the door, felt like sliding down it until I was sitting on the floor. I would put my head in my hands, rest it on my knees. A kid in a TV show about high school. What a mistake. I kept making mistakes.

I hadn't walked the building in—it had been a lifetime. But I got there, got to the bin, didn't think to listen to what was happening inside. And just, just as I reached my arm out—the paper, the bin—the door opened and there was Deck, back in uniform, Chief Brady all over again.

"Ms. Carey, what a surprise," he said. "Roaming the halls." He let the door close behind him and stood in front of it. "What are you doing all the way over here?" A touch of an edge in his face, his mouth.

His mouth. His lips. "A tip," I said. I waved it. "From that same girl. I was just dropping it off."

"Let's have a look," he said. "Walk with me."

A foot at least between our elbows.

Last night he had gone home, drove the whole way thinking of me. He had slept alone and woken alone, and he had showered and shaved this morning, dressed himself, buttoned his shirt up while looking in the mirror, his skin still tingling in all the places my hands had been. I smelled his cologne.

"What does our favorite tipster have for us this time?" he said as we walked through the outer office toward mine. Evelyn looked up at me, raised her eyebrows twice, and then quickly looked back at whatever she was doing.

"Morning, Chief," the cop there said. Deck only lifted a hand in reply. Half a wave, not even.

"Their names," I said. I thought to whisper it, that that's the respect it deserved.

"Names. Interesting." He sat on the edge of my desk and read. "That meeting I was just coming out of. With Homicide." He nodded behind him, down the hall. He would see if I reacted. I made sure my face did nothing. "We have a new procedure, going forward. You'll drop a copy of the tips to my office. Everything you give them, I want to see too. With something like this, we need everyone on the same page at exactly the same time. You understand."

The door was still open. I heard the phone ring in the other office, the cop pick it up, the rough chop of his *hello*. I felt like Evelyn was watching, looking in at us. I knew she could hear. But it was all appropriate. As much as I wanted to touch him, I was standing where I should have been, just behind my desk. Still, I could pass him another sheet of paper, let my hand graze his. I could inch my fingers nearer, palm flat, so just my nail touched his thigh. Remind him. *Remember? Everything?*

"Of course," I said instead. "So what's happening with it? I mean, has anything that's come through here been useful?" I nodded toward the phone, hoping. "Do you have any ideas? Have there been developments?" I stopped when I saw he wasn't going to say anything. He was just watching me. Then I realized. "Oh, you can't tell me. That's right. Of course, you can't tell me."

He folded the paper I had given him in half, really worked the crease. If he kept going, the paper would fall apart. Just break into two pieces, no effort needed.

"I can tell you whatever I want," he said. His face: head cocked, eyes crinkled. Like he couldn't understand that I couldn't understand.

"Well," I said, standing straight, putting my hands on my hips, "I mean, I *did* have the security clearance. Background check and everything. They came around to my house and asked all my neighbors about me. So, I'm good to go." I was trying to be funny.

"Yes," he said. "I'm aware."

"That sounds like a no," I said.

"This is a good conversation to have, actually," he said. He got up and closed the door, waved outside—at Evelyn, I guessed—before it shut all the way. He came back and stood near me. "I've been thinking about this."

Not good. Door closed and a conversation, this quickly, not good.

"Here's the thing: Do you really want to talk to me about work?" He had his arms folded across his chest.

"I mean," I said. But that's all.

"Do you want this to be about work?" He gave me a second, but he knew I wasn't going to answer. "Because usually I'm thinking about work every minute of every single day. I never stop thinking about it. Ever."

"Okay." Fine. "Okay."

"I don't want this to be about work." He gestured at the space between us. "I don't want us to be coworkers, even though we work together. Does that make sense?"

"I get it," I said. And I did and I let it go, and I swore to myself that I would never ask again. Because what did I care, anyway? Here is a job and here is this man. This man who could turn out to be anything to me. Something. My future. I could weigh them in my hands, but I didn't need to.

When he spoke again, his voice had changed. It had taken on the tone of last night, the wine, the rest of it.

"You. You're like a vacation," he said and shook his head like I had done something wrong. "I can't stop thinking about you." And there it was. Scripted, threadbare from use, a line my father had probably put on my mother thirty-something years ago when he was going through the motions, but, dear God, did it do it for me. "I'm tied up the rest of this week. But are you free on Saturday night?"

I did not pull a thing. I did not look at the wall over his head, pretending to think about whether I was busy or check my phone for imaginary entries. I did not sulk. I did not say that two days of waiting would kill me, please, really, two days?

"I am," I said. Because I was and he would know, regardless.

* . * . *

I didn't figure he would be much for texting. But that evening, he sent me a message. Our first.

Christmas party or dinner on Saturday? You choose and let me know.

I was watching television. Wine, three glasses deep. I would need to be strategic. Go over my response. Really devise something. Dinner was good. Another dinner would be smart. Hours alone, all the talk, he would really have the chance to take me in. It was very intimate. But a Christmas party! I was shocked—a party, already. All I could think of was walking into a party, my arm linked in his, being introduced by my first and last name and no signifier. *This is Virginia Carey,* he would say. And they would nod, all these people, take sips of their drinks as they waited to shake. We'd go in a circle. Maybe the men would approach him later—in the restroom, at the bar—congratulate him on my youth and my looks while I chitchatted with the women, with the wives, about household things. Summer vacations. Landscapers. He would catch my eye during this. From across the room he would nod and smile. Later, he would scoop me up under mistletoe and kiss me on the mouth but without tongue. Cinematic. A leading man. He would lean me back just enough.

A party sounds fun, I wrote back exactly twenty-eight minutes later. I had typed other things. Explicit things, descriptions of what he and I could do in the car on the way and in the host's bathroom after that, or in the coatroom if it was a public place, but I deleted them. I was in and out of sleep. I woke at eleven when my phone dinged. He had written back, *Perfect.*

The news, of all things, was how I found out. The eleven o'clock news.

Huge new developments in a case our local police are saying could be the work of a serial killer. Four women, found late last week in the underbrush on Ocean Parkway, have been identified. We are told they are local escorts ranging in age from thirty to thirty-one. Their names are being held pending the notification of next of kin.

I sat up. Heard their names in her voice.

And in a new bombshell theory, sources are saying this could be the work of someone with extensive knowledge of law enforcement procedures, perhaps even an officer himself.

On the screen, B-roll of the scene: dusk, wind in the brush, yellow tape still flapping. I searched that brush as the camera panned.

A source close to the investigation, who has asked to remain anonymous, tells us that familiarity with police investigation techniques may have influenced the placement of the bodies at this specific location. The source also cites other as of yet undisclosed details.

An aerial shot: Uniformed officers at the scene, combing the ground, dozens of them. A dog with each. Police. Police. Police.

They do stress that the case is still in its very early stages, and they are asking anyone with information to contact them. Again, if you have any information, you are urged to call Suffolk's tip line at—

I recited the number—*my* number—along with the anchor. She shook her head when she finished the story, took a minute, a deep breath, disappointed in this world. Then she shifted to a story about potholes.

"The streets are a killer this winter," she said. I laughed at this because it was ridiculous and it was funny and because I was still drunk.

A cop. Doing this, to all these women. Where did this come from? I thought. And then, Isn't that something. And then, A coworker would have told me this. But not Deck.

I don't think I dreamt that night, but if I had, it would've been this: At a party, to a group, "Brady, now. Née Carey." Wiggle the finger with the ring. Five years on, happy happy. Ten years, happy happy. My tongue thick and slow, though, sounding silly as I said it. Then, a bed. Deck next to me. Perfect versions of us—rings on our fingers in a home we owned—asleep in front of the TV, the smooth voice of an anchor in a kind of children's singsong: *Same age as you, same age as you, well-cut hair and same age as you.*

CHAPTER FIFTEEN

They all had long hair. The next morning their photos, blown up to poster size, were lined up on easels in the media room at headquarters, a name underneath each. Three blondes, one brunette. I had gone downstairs for a soda—the hangover, the headache, the bottle I had finished—and then snuck into the side entrance and watched from the back of the crowd. Another press conference. I couldn't make out the print from where I stood, but I knew them. Knew each of them by name, by heart. Their faces made an ache in me. All that smiling, I couldn't understand why. It was obscene to show those poor girls smiling.

From the left, I don't know what order they had them in—age, alphabetically, chronologically as they were found—but I went from the left. The first, a photo from what looked like a wedding, the lime green collar of a bridesmaid's dress high around her neck. She raised an eyebrow at the camera. The next, cropped close, but it looked like the top of a child's head toward the edge of the frame, thrown back in anger, trying to squirm free. Behind them, blurry orange shapes. They were in a field full of pumpkins. She looked as though she had widened her eyes, trying to rush the person taking the picture. The third: A passport photo. The gray background, just head and shoulders. I hoped she had used it. I prayed for a page full of visas. For her feet in the sand, for a dog-eared guidebook and a pocket full of foreign change. Please? The last, the brunette, on Halloween. Her hair held back with a thick black headband. A Peter Pan collar, a blue dress. Alice in Wonderland.

It was McHale up there talking, the commissioner off to his side. No Deck. No Charlie. Anyway, Charlie who?

"I have to stress that this is still a very active investigation," McHale said. "We are still considering everything. And we are asking anyone with any information whatsoever to reach out to us. Either call us directly, or call the eight-hundred number. We want to hear everything." He gestured to his left, a poster advertising the tip line. "I have time for a few questions."

"Sergeant," a reporter at the very front said, "do you think this is a cop from this department?"

"Ma'am, no one, anywhere, at any time, has confirmed definitively that this is a law enforcement official." He wiped his forehead like he was too tired to do it anymore, to stand up there, to look for bad men. "No one has said that. There is talk floating around out there that specific details of the crime scene may indicate that the subject could have known how to avoid detection and leaving behind evidence. But we did not release that information. And, furthermore, this doesn't make the killer a cop. Doesn't make him a cop, doesn't rule out a cop. Like I just said, at this time we are not ruling anyone or anything out."

"What exactly makes you think it *may* have been a cop? What were the details at the scene? Does it have anything to do with the manner of death?" Another reporter, this one closer to me, though I could only see the back of his head and his arm with its tape recorder extended.

"I can't give out any specifics on that right now—sorry," McHale said. "I can take two more questions, and then I will let you lovely people go."

"These women were escorts, right?" a reporter at the front started.

I could swear the phone was ringing upstairs, that I would rush up there, running, spilling soda as I went, and that no one would be on the other end when I finally picked it up. That it was just the phone itself reminding me to come back to where I belonged. Beckoning. Scolding me.

And it was. The first call I got when I got back to my desk was a dead call. Silence and then a dial tone. No breathing, no ambient sounds. Just a glitch, switched signals, a mix-up with wiring somewhere. Then we picked up where we left off, and the phone started ringing in earnest again.

*   *   *

This one, her husband was a cop in our department's second precinct, way out in the county's west end. His name, both names, were miles long. Italian ones with hills and valleys of vowels, lush as the Tuscan countryside.

"Please let me make sure I have this name right, okay?" I said and started again, my pen following along from the first letter. The wine from last night was making me stupid. I tried to finish my soda, get it into me quickly. Michelangelo. Got it. Abatescianni. Yes.

"Right, so, always rough. Used to do the hands-around-my-throat-during sex thing. I thought, *Is this because he's a cop, or is there something wrong here?* No offense, honey, but I figured cop. You know how they are." She laughed, waiting.

"Sure," I said. I did. I do.

"Anyway, he never actually hit me. But still. Rough. And the sex? Hooo boy." She stopped for a minute. Reminiscing, I guess. "Tons of porn, okay? I mean, constant. Couldn't do anything"—she dropped to a whisper—"couldn't get it up without it." She cleared her throat. "So what else, what else can I tell you?" The sound of her thumbing through memories. "Lots of girlfriends before me. Some definitely during, ha ha!" She laughed again. "He's been with prostitutes. Tried to make me get with them too. That was *the* fight. The beginning of the end, actually. That's when I really knew something was wrong. I was like, 'Mike, you're beyond fucked up, wiring problems in your head, goodbye.'"

"I understand," I said. Her own husband.

"Well, I guess that's all I can think of," she said.

"Okay, thank you for calling," I said. "I'll get this information right over to the detectives."

"Were they strangled?"

"Ma'am, I have no idea. I'm not part of the investigation. I'm just a civilian." I let the word absolve me. Showed it like my own little badge. *Civilian.*

"Gotcha," she said. "Well, Mike's . . . Mike is Mike. Decent cop. But a little off. I don't know. Do with it what you will. What they will."

"Thanks again," I said.

I was standing at the printer, waiting, when the phone rang, and the former Mrs. Abatescianni called me back.

"Look," she said, "I was thinking about it, and I shouldn't have said any of that stuff. That's my kid's father. He coaches baseball. He's a cheater, but I don't think that he really did any of this. It was stupid of me. I shouldn't have."

"This is completely anonymous," I told her. "You don't have to worry."

She spoke over me, through her teeth.

"I need you to remove that information from your records. Do not give it to the detectives. Do you hear me? I've made a mistake."

"Of course, ma'am. I understand."

I folded the paper in half, let it float into the garbage can. Deleted the entry from our program. Forgotten. Easy as that. Struck me, how easy it was.

"Sodom and Gomorrah," one man yelled at me. Cut me off in the middle of my greeting.

"Sodom and Gomorrah, Sodom and Gomorrah," he said it over and over, and I let him. I let him peter out. I looked at my chipped nail as he went on. I had to have them done before tomorrow night. I made a mental note to make an appointment. Tomorrow morning? On the way to a blowout? Was a blowout too much? Maybe too much. Red again, though. I would do the red polish again. Sodom and Gomorrah, something about the front steps of the group home in which he lived, a box there, his pen pal, the orderlies, the lyrics of a seventies song, how prophetic he felt that day. "I've seen all of this happen. Many, many times."

"Thank you for calling us," I said, sad for him. "Thank you for telling us your information."

"You're very welcome. I'm glad I could help you," he said, suddenly buttoned up, smoothed out. He sounded like a school principal.

A narcotics call. I wanted to laugh at her. "I think my neighbor has a pot plant in his yard," she said. And I could see her beady eyes, her tiny mouth, lips so tight they might rip at their seams. Her folded arms as she stood at her side window and shook her head. She had a sign in her kitchen that said "With God all things are possible," and she straightened it while she talked to me. *Have you seen the news? Do you know what's happening in this world?* I wanted to ask her. *Go look at the faces of those four girls, and then call me back about your neighbor, you asshole.*

"Thank you," I said. "We really appreciate this information." I smiled big. My cheeks, hard and round as stones, pushed the handset from my face. I wanted her to hear it. I didn't even type her tip up.

Then my girl. Finally. Around two in the afternoon. I had finished my soda. Felt on the mend.

"Hi," I said when I heard it was her. Relief.

"Why aren't they saying how it happened?" she said. Home again. Quiet. The TV. I pictured her with a steaming cup of tea. On top of her made bed—barefoot, with her legs crisscrossed, and wearing a big sweatshirt. Scrubbed clean from a shower, her skin still hot. "Do they not think that would help?"

"I'm not sure," I said. "I mean, I personally have no idea of the details. And I'm not sure what they give out and why. It makes no sense to me, but they must have their reasons."

I think she lit a cigarette.

"They were strangled," she said. "That's what someone told me. I don't know how she knows. I don't know how anyone knows any of this stuff, so don't even ask. I just tell you what I'm hearing, okay? So take that for what it's worth." She exhaled. "Is Virginia your real name, by the way?"

"Yes," I said without thinking.

"Huh," she said. "I figured it was a fake name. You sound young for a name like that."

"It's a family name," I said. "Long story."

"I thought maybe you used it, like, for safety or something. I'm sure you talk to a lot of weirdos."

"I hadn't even thought of that," I said. And I hadn't. "I guess it's too late to change it now."

"It's funny. My fake name is Verona. The name I use."

"Like Romeo and—"

"Juliet," she said, finishing. "Yep, that's the point. I thought it was funny at the time. Like sick funny. Like here I am, fucking you for money, and my name is this, you know, this over-the-top romantic place. The irony." She said *irony* in a long, drawn-out Transatlantic accent she put on. She kept smoking; I heard the lighter when she started another one. "Ah, *she knows about Shakespeare,* you're thinking. But, yeah. I went to college. All of these girls, all of us, we have real lives. College, jobs, families. Like yeah, we fuck for money. But it is good money!" She laughed. "Everyone fucks for something, at the end of the day. You know? There's a way we all wound up here, that's what I'm trying to say."

I wanted to tell her she was right. Say, *Yes, we all do— you're totally right.* But I didn't.

"I have no clue why I'm telling you this," she said. "But I guess they hired you because you're easy to talk to." It was liquor she was drinking, not tea. A hot toddy or a screwdriver. A mimosa, maybe. Maybe she was fresh from a lunch date. Appointment. I wonder what she called them. If she kept a small book with details. What that book looked like. Pink with a red-ribbon page marker, handwriting tight and neat. Control freak, analysts would say. Likes a clean house. Likes the squeak of her finger along her kitchen countertops.

"What did you study? You know, your major, I mean," I said.

"English," she said. "For a bit. I figured there can never be too many English teachers."

"Well, that's practical," I said.

"Oh, sure, of course. But then I got into acting." *Acting* came out harsh. "And that's how things—that's when I changed course."

I should leave her. I shouldn't ask. I should let her tell me what she wants to tell me, and I shouldn't pry.

"It was going okay, actually. Which is amazing, if you think about it. I was going into the city a lot for commercial auditions, that kind of thing. And then, then I got it in my head to go to LA. Because what is an actor—a real actor," she said, voice booming, stage volume, "if you don't move out West and hit it big. Or wallow and fail for a while and then have a really good story for when you make it big a few years later." Exhaled smoke. Laughed. "Never got there. Obviously."

"What happened?" I asked.

"I was working at a club in midtown. I did bottle service. I met so many men that way, I cannot even explain to you. Men just stuffing money in your hands. Just for looking at you. Paying us all this money—shit tons of money—just because we let them look at our bodies. So, next step, I'm a stripper. You can't just ignore that, that amount of money, you know? And then, things just progress. You don't even have to try."

Her voice, more and more untied by the second. Another mimosa, done.

"I get it," I said.

"Then people started telling me I was too old to go out there and start over. Especially in that business. But, one of my best friends, a girl I worked bottle service with, she went out there. Hill. Hillary. I see her in commercials all the time. We talk, still. Pretty frequently, even. We're kind of planning my trip. Spring, maybe, is what we're thinking. She's saying I'll get out West and never want to come back."

"That's great," I said. And I happened to know where Hillary lived. Hillary's bungalow, white stucco, the climbing flowers. The mountains looming against that cool blue, or hidden by the morning fog, or black against the night sky lit with the million little lights of the Hills. And just down the way, just yards from her front walk, on the next street over, three streets and a short drive over, my two best friends. My own two best friends. All of them together there. I heard her sip. Soon Verona would be out there too. If things didn't work out, I could follow suit.

"But it's good. It's all good." That was her closing that door gently, though she did close it. Click of the latch. I heard that. "Anyway, now they're saying it's a cop, huh?"

"That's what I saw on the news," I said. "Does that make sense to you? Like ring true?"

"Absolutely," she said.

"Absolutely? Really?"

"Of course. Look, here's the first thing about cops: we see a ton of them," she said. She laughed again, the start of it girlish, touched with the alcohol and a bit of a giggle. Then it stopped. "We all see a ton of them because they don't have to worry about getting caught, right? And also because—and this is, you know, a stereotype, but true, so—they're, like, hypersexual. The testosterone and all. I read somewhere once that men in positions of power have higher than average levels of testosterone. And if you don't want power, you don't become a cop. So, it makes total sense to me."

"Right," I said. "Gotcha."

"Jesus, the things I could tell you."

Tell me.

"I probably shouldn't."

Just tell me.

"Whatever, who cares."

There you go. A different door opening. No lock, no sticky paint. Greased hinges giving.

"So, there was this guy once. Young guy. Younger than you'd think. Good shape, not ugly at all. But kind of wound up, you know? Rougher than the rest, right off the bat. Talking a lot, very dirty. He had to keep his uniform on. He wouldn't even let me unbutton his shirt, nothing. And then, when we started everything, he would only unzip. We were in the back seat of his car. You know, the police car. On his lunch hour." Cigarette break. Inhale.

"No," I said while waiting. A good and patient listener. Let my mouth hang open, even.

"Oh no. No, no, no. That's not even it. That's not the part." Her voice here high and tight with smoke. Exhale for the finale. "So, next he unloads his gun in front of me. Puts the ammunition on the seat next to us. Tells me to suck it. The gun. Has me suck it while he, you know, while he takes care of himself. He doesn't even touch me. Thinking about it, I don't think his hand even touched me once. So, there you go. That's just one example."

"Jesus," I said. I could think only of the gun, the shine of spit on the tip of it. How deep could you fit that? What was humanly possible? I figured it was the same temperature as skin, having been pressed up against him for so long prior. That if you closed your eyes, and of course you closed your eyes, and if it was warm enough, and if he was making sounds, if he was enjoying it, it would be just like, just like, the wet tip. I thought of the hips of all the men around me, every day, guns clipped in there—quiet and neuter and almost for show—clacking as the men walked. "Jesus, how do you walk away from that?"

"You just walk away," she said. "Same as anything else. Though, listen, most of them are just normal, nice enough guys. Families, normal, all of it."

"Of course," I said. "The majority, I'm sure. The vast majority."

My phone buzzed on the desk. Deck. I didn't touch it, didn't even reach for it. Transfixed.

"I don't know about *vast*." She laughed. "I mean, there are these parties. I've been to them all over the island. Always the same: some rich guy, huge house, has a party, invites all of his friends and has a bunch of us come in. You bet your ass there are always cops there. Half a dozen of them, even. More."

"And one of these parties? This is where your friends met the man? The men? Who did this?" The man who did this. I was thinking of him. His wet gun shining in the light. Young. Muscle bound.

"It's possible," she said. "Who knows for sure?"

"Well, do you know any of their names? The cops or who has these parties, even?" I asked. On ice. Inch by inch. My right foot, the weight of my toes, the invisible nothing of my arch, then my heel. Safe. Left foot. My breathing quickened so I took the phone away from my face. I didn't want her to hear me nervous. I didn't want to frighten her.

"Ahh," she said. "Million-dollar question. No one is really too eager to introduce themselves with a real name, shocking as that is."

Verona, my girl, my dearest friend. Come ruffle my hair when you tease me like that. Come, let's have a drink. Come sit. Come to the mall and help me find an outfit for tomorrow night. Come visit with me at my desk and skim through headshots of all these men and guess, tapping your finger on which one, which one, which one did this. Keep calling me. Keep calling me, please.

"Even that guy in his car. Took his name plate off beforehand. Not stupid."

"No. Right, of course they don't tell you anything," I said. "That would be ridiculous. That would be totally idiotic." But his car number, his shield number, you didn't see these?

"That's okay," she said, almost consoling. "Be glad you don't know."

"What's the second thing?" I asked.

"The second thing?"

"You said—"

"Oh, the second thing. I don't know, I forgot the second thing. I forgot what I was going to say." I kept hearing her sip, swallow. She must have been refilling, silently getting up, uncorking, unscrewing, muting the glug of liquid somehow. Had to have been. She was getting looser, drunker. "Also, you have to think, there's always so much going on. A ton of people. A lot of alcohol. Coke. Ecstasy. Everything you can think of. These people party and they want you to

134

party with them. So it's hard to keep track. Even if I did hear a name once or twice, I hear hundreds of names and meet hundreds of them. They're all the same to me, at this point." She got up, walked, turned on a faucet. I heard the clink of silverware in a metal sink. She was washing dishes. This she allowed me to hear. "Look, the parties," she said and stopped. "The parties are fine. They're not bad. A lot of the time, we don't even do anything. I'll just stand around in a new dress and drink champagne and let men talk to me. I see girls I know, we drink, bullshit, walk around these big houses. Eat a ton. There is always caviar at these things—I don't know why. Like these parties couldn't happen without the caviar. I'm going on and on here. Stop me, Virginia," she said and laughed. How charming she was when she said my name. How affable and confident and charming. That's what she had, that's something that she had that I never would. Openness, warmth. All of these things.

"No, please," I said. "I'm listening."

"Well, look, I'm sure they love you in there, right? The cops? Like they're going crazy over you, I bet. I don't know what you look like, but you sound pretty. You sound young and nice. And, to be honest, even if you're not, it doesn't really matter what you look like with them. No offense."

"I work in a tiny little office all by myself, actually," I said. "I never see anyone. I wish there were cute guys milling around all the time." I knew how it sounded. Too pat. A nineteen-sixties sophomore, pulling her ponytail tight. "Then I could pick one out and get married, have kids, all the rest." There. There's my secret. Now you know.

"Oh, they'll find *you*. Don't worry, they'll sniff you out. It's their job to find things. They'll sniff you out, and then they'll be falling in love with you like that." I thought I heard her snap her fingers, the sound dulled by bubbles. "Drooling like idiots and telling you how much they love you after five minutes. That's their whole thing. Right away: 'I love you' this, 'I love you' that. One good fuck, and then." Poof. She made her hand into the shape of something disappearing and the bubbles dripped down her forearm, got under the bracelet band of her watch.

I wish, I thought.

If things were only a little bit different, I could have told her everything; I could have asked her advice. The chief of police, actually. The chief himself found me. Or I found him. Convinced him. Seduced him, I guess. Long story. Things are fine, but I want more. So tell me—how? How exactly do I make him love me after five minutes? How do you do it? But I should have been thinking of other things. I should have been asking other things: *Where are these parties? Can you describe any of the hosts? Vehicles, identifying features? Scars and/or tattoos? Could you please provide detailed descriptions of all of your clients who are law enforcement? Start with that first one, the one in the car. I have a feeling.* But this was never my concern.

"Oh yeah?" I said. "That's probably some pretty valuable trade secret." Coy, hinting. I couldn't just ask.

"It's just sex. *That's* the trade secret. That's what makes them fall in love with you." She started laughing. "Listen to me: trade secret. I'm shot. Anyway," she said. She was going to go. I felt it.

"Keep calling me," I said. It just came out. Pleading. Weak. Because this whole time it had almost felt like talking to a friend, and I was confused. "I mean, anything you think of, just call and tell me. I know that you've been very helpful to them so far." I didn't know this, but neither did she.

And then, too quick to stop, because I was talking to a girlfriend, chatting, a girlfriend: "It's just that I feel like I have so much to ask you. That I'm forgetting so much right now and I'll remember later." *I have this date, and could you tell me what color, at least, I should wear? Underwear or no? What do you think of pearls, in a semi-ironic way? Who should I be when I'm with him? What do men like? What does he like?*

"Can't I call you? You know, can't I have your number so that when I remember, I can call you?" Too much? She was quiet. Too much. But maybe considering? "What if I have questions about men?" I said and made myself laugh, turning the whole thing into a joke because I had to. I had to cover up the sound my voice had just made, convince her I was kidding and not desperate.

"You don't need me. You'll be fine," she said and drew out the word, her arm around my shoulder, pulling me close. "I have faith in you. I told you the secret." Here, she'd put her forehead to mine and laugh. "Oh!" she said, a pop on the exclamation. "Shit, I have to go. I have an appointment and I'm going to be late, and this guy can be a real dick if everything isn't just so. I'll talk to you soon, though."

Appointment it is.

She hung up without saying goodbye. Merry Christmas, I had wanted to say to her. But she had to go get ready. Makeup, hair. Clothes. She wore conservative things to appointments. Skirt suits, business attire. Light makeup and a grayish-lavender wool skirt suit. Maybe boucle. Knee length. Scoop-neck sweater underneath. She would meet him in a hotel. She would meet him at the hotel bar. He would be a repeat client. Know her drink order, have one waiting. He was always early.

In fifteen minutes, I would be typing up a call, and she would be driving to the hotel. In half an hour, I would be scrolling through shopping sites on my phone, trying to find something for tomorrow night, and she would be stirring her drink, a vodka soda. Her legs held tight together at the knee. She'd slowly bob a foot; it'd hit his ankle. In one hour, I would be watching the clock, the sweep of the second hand or watching out the window or watching the ceiling, waiting for something to happen to me, to my life. And she would be with the man. The client. A cop or maybe not. Making someone else fall in love with her. Watching the ceiling and waiting until he finished.

Deck's message:

I'm not in the office today but I wanted to say hi. I'll get you at eight tomorrow if that works?

I waited to answer him.

Repeat Caller Caller agrees with recent media reports that the person(s) responsible for the slain women could possibly be law enforcement, though she has no specific identifying information.

Also, caller states that she went to college; that she chose the name Verona because of *Romeo and Juliet*; that she thinks I sound young and nice and pretty; and that she could see us being friends, shopping, on the phone, at a bar, at a bachelorette party, wearing sashes and taking shots, etcetera. Caller states there is a simple way to make someone fall in love with you. Very simple, in fact. See note on attached sheet.

A cop. A cop. Not really. A cop. But no. But I began to see him, this cop, his car, the back seat. Shiny black upholstery warm in the spring sun or warm from the heat blowing on high or warm from the press of their two bodies. I began to see his face, it came to me: An amalgam of all of the faces of all of the cops I had met, their eyes one dull brown, their hair one dull brown. That mouth, open in mid-order. Giving direction, always—all of them, *always*—giving a direction. I saw this cop's body, muscled in an average way, thirty-five, average height, average. The image of a man was emerging. Like science. Substances, a solution. I saw a mess of gold, the patches from hundreds of upper arms, bubbling, bubbling up. The blur of blue, sharpening. It was coming. Turn the burner up. Just a bit. Just a touch. There you go. Coming. Condensing, coming, that glass tube, a drop, moving through. One drop. This glass, so thin. Could splinter, explode. All that heat. But then it appeared, slid down the side of the flask at the end. One drop. I saw him as the man, the officer from my first day, the clean-shaven man who saw me hit my head. There he was. Name tag glinting in the morning light: "Abatescianni." I remembered it then. I knew it. That was him.

I did not write it down.

I made two piles: one for Homicide and one for Deck. Then I wrote back to him: *Hello, you. Can't wait. Eight is good.* Added a winking face, deleted the winking face, added the winking face back, sent. And then I left my office, stopping at Homicide's door first. The papers in the bin fanned out at the top, two days' worth. They hadn't been picking them up. I could not hear anything from inside. No paper, no men, no animals, no nothing.

Deck's secretary, like all secretaries, must have known exactly what was happening.

"Hello, Virginia," she said when I walked in. "Tips for the chief?"

"Yep," I said and held them up. Proof.

"Go on in," she said and waved her hand toward the narrow hall. She knew that I knew that he wasn't there. Behind her glasses, I could swear she winked. Her cats were in on it too. One's tail twitched in the foreground of the photo, its eyes slits.

The light was coming in, same as the first time. My feet were silent on the carpet. I smelled him on the air. His desk was clear, aside from the lamp and picture frame. The paperweights. An organized man. I went around its back and put the papers down. I aligned them; he'd like that. Then I looked out from his side of the room. Pretended to be him. How small those guest chairs looked, how silly and small. And anyone who sat in them, how silly and small too. Me.

I leaned down to get closer to the photo. His father, I guessed. Same jawline, same stance. I'd say some time in the sixties. Deck would have been a little boy, playing at home. Making fake guns with his fingers. I swept my hand across the desk. I'd let him do it here. I wanted him to, had thought of it already. On this desk, on his chair. His blue police jacket was on the chair's back. I ran my hand down the sleeve. Stopped when I hit something hard in the pocket. A charge. A jolt. I put my fingers in before I could even think to stop, not that I would have. They just went. It was so easy. A roll of mints, one or two missing, wrapper folded in neatly on itself. I let it drop back in. Who are you? I thought, thought to whisper it. He'd lock the door, walk over to me. *On the desk,* he'd say and gesture with his chin. Right? He'd say that? Or, *Come sit with me,* and pat his lap. And I'd do it. Of course I would do it. He would love me because I would make him love me. He would love me before he even had a chance to think about it, to question whether it was what he wanted.

The hall was quiet. Everything quiet. I reached out and touched the drawer pull. My fingertips. The drawer pull: burnished wood, knob (not handle), warm in my hand. The top drawer. A place made for secrets. Heavy with secrets. Who are you? Who are you? Because what did I know about him, really? An inch. An inch and a half. What are you doing? What am I doing? Don't do this. Easy, so easy, too easy. It opened. Stop, stop. Pens, pencils, paper clips. Two inches. Golf tees. Three cigars rolled with the motion, stopped when they hit a lighter, a big thing, heavy silver. It looked old. A golden mound, a little mound of golden snow, almost. Twinkling like snow. I picked it up. Delicate, fine. The most delicate filigree. Diamond chips in the centers of small golden flowers. Daisies. Too big for a bracelet, too small for a necklace. An anklet, then. A woman's anklet. I held it for a second, with two fingers, let it shimmer in the light.

Okay.

Okay?

Okay.

I put it back. I closed the drawer. I tapped the top of the desk for good measure and then left. I mean I should have put it back and closed the drawer. In another world I would have put it back and closed the drawer. I put it in my pants pocket instead. And it was so light, its weight so negligible, that it was almost like I didn't take it at all. I closed the drawer. I touched the desk again, running my hand on it, then over the back of his chair. He would see my fingerprints, a dropped hair, a fiber. My sweater, my scent, forensics. He would know I had been there.

Heels in the carpet, heels in the hall, past Deck's secretary, and back to my office. And I'll tell you, I kept myself busy. I sorted through stacks of papers that had been on my desk since I got there. I wiped dust from the covers of books and lined them on the shelves. Cleaned some spots of dried coffee that I had missed when they spilled during a long-ago incident that triggered nothing in me anymore. Promise. I was an organized woman. Becoming one. Cleaning my space. Making room for something new.

* * *

I hadn't planned on drinking. I didn't want to be puffy and bloodshot and all the rest. I wanted to look my best for him, for our party. But it was Friday night, dark early, and I was alone, and so it happened. I did. I stopped after three glasses, though, when everything was at its highest hum, up and running, and I thought I made perfect sense.

Hi there. I was going to call him. *Hey, can we talk?* No, please, not that. *Tell me about you, Deck,* I'd slur. *Tell me about your past relationships. Have you ever been in love? Whose anklet? Where do you live? Whose anklet? This is wild, I know, a little late, but hear me out, I haven't properly asked you, but are you dating anyone? And if not, are you pining for a woman whose anklet you keep in your desk drawer?* I had my phone in my hand. The anklet on my nightstand, nuclear, too hot to touch, its gold glittering in the blue light of the television. I had the news on. I always had the news on back then. Waiting for things I may have missed at work. Things kept from me. But nothing, nothing new. I googled it, the girls. The dead women. I clicked on links and tried to read, but the wine. I didn't get far.

So I googled him again too. And I felt a shiver of shame and nerves when I hit "Return," like I was doing something wrong. But then that flush of recognition when the pictures popped up. Those hands? Pointing to that map? I know those hands. That mouth, mid-speech, telling the press about cleaning up drugs, gangs, about the importance of community and communication. That mouth. Mine. So many pictures of him, Top Cop this and that. Even with the wine, I could look at pictures. The wine helped me see the pictures even more clearly. It helped me understand what I was dealing with. Education on a pixel level. Things I'd never even seen.

He was going to love me, this man. Verona'd told me how to do it. Taught me all it took, which was not much, in the scheme of things.

Yeah, but, whose was it though? That anklet? Whose—no, inconsequential. No. Those hands? From the map picture? Totally inconsequential. Something found on the sidewalk, waiting for its owner. An heirloom. His mother's, his mother's mother's. A niece's. The previous chief had left it in the desk. Someone else's personal effect. The secretary's, its clasp was broken, Deck was going to fix it for her. He was handy too, wouldn't you know? A real well-rounded guy. It was mine. It was no one's. It no longer existed. I had made it disappear.

I typed out a text to him, then thought to get up for water, then fell asleep without moving.

CHAPTER SIXTEEN

The birds woke me up. Singing into my windows, the light streaming in behind them. They landed on the sill, a little line of them—two blue and one yellow—and waited until they knew it was safe to come in. They had brought with them a gust of outside's cold. Their wings whispered, feathers on feathers, as they neared my head, as they pulled my blanket down, nipping at its corners. They folded it neatly at my ankles and then started on my clothes.

Up, up, they sang. Trilling, happy, chests puffed with life. *Time to awaken, it is a special day. Today is the day that you—*

When I sat up, I sat up too quickly. I scared the birds and they flapped in panic, crashing into each other, shedding tiny feathers all over my bed. One, the yellow, spiraled toward the floor but caught itself, managed to get aloft again, however askew. Another hit the nightstand, and I heard the soft thud its body made there, the slide of the fragile thing down, down. It wobbled when it stood, but then it took off. They flew toward the window, hit the pane first, all of them, tiny clicks of their beaks on the glass as they tried. Then they managed to get themselves out, finally. Stunned and discombobulated.

It was raining. I had slept the whole night with the TV on. My head. I checked my phone and I felt heat come to my face. I flushed red, a thick and fast red, even with no one seeing. The gods. Thank God. I had typed out a text but it sat there unsent:

i think i love you but why so mysterious with everything

I deleted it and, nauseous, went to the shower.

* * *

My hands. I watched the manicurist working and thought of my hands on Deck later. Palms flat, fingers splayed on his bare chest. Nails digging in the slightest bit. He'd like this. He liked my hands, had said as much. I watched especially when she got to my ring finger. As she filed and shaped it and then later as she polished. How different it would look with a ring. What would the manicurist think when I finally came in with a ring, when she asked me to take it off and put it in her little glass dish so she didn't get lotion in its prongs as she massaged me? *Congratulations,* she would say and point to it as she moved from finger to finger, *finally.* And how much heavier I would feel with the weight of the metal band, the weight of its diamond. It would hold me to the ground. It would keep me stable and steady and prevent me from floating away. Ten grams, tethering me down.

It was coming. It was going to happen. I could feel it.

When my friends had gotten engaged—within three weeks of each other, holiday season two years prior—they'd sent texts with photos of their hands. Laura first. Hers the week after Thanksgiving, when they were skiing in Vermont.

You can see nothing but the hills of her hand, fingers only up to the first knuckle and the gleam and twinkle of that ring. Marquise with a halo, which I don't prefer, but big, fiancé in finance. I could make out the fireplace with its matching gleam and twinkle, the happy couple drinking Broken Ankles. Pink cheeked, smiles, cheers. Rebecca, like I said, three weeks later, on Christmas Eve. They were in Florence, Italy. There for business, his. Her photo was a bit different. Wider shot—he got her whole hand, which she had turned so her palm faced her, shoulder height, and she was smiling. Hers was a round-cut solitaire, my favorite. Over her shoulder, just next to the tip of her manicured thumb—she knew it was coming, by the way—just next to the tip of her manicured thumb, a man playing an accordion. The stars, the Arno. How had he done that? I remember thinking. This man is a magician. She is smiling too, of course. Who wouldn't be.

I did not go shopping after my manicure. I had gotten it into my head to wear a plain sheath, and I already had one: long sleeved, bateau neck, empire waist, stretch wool. Black. Covered up, untouchable. Just you wait. Watch me throughout the evening, over the heads of the other guests, and just you wait. I was not above being a tease.

By five, I was ready. Showered, makeup, hair, though no blowout. I was in underwear and a robe. It was working. Everything was working. I stood in front of the mirror, took off the robe and let it go to the floor. I was taken with myself. I turned to look at my ass, and it was like I saw someone else. Like I had moved quickly enough to see me like someone else would see me. It was going to be good. Everything was going to be perfect. I salivated at the thought of wine.

I rehearsed holding a glass in my left hand, between which fingers I'd put the cocktail napkin so that I could shake with my right when I was introduced. *Look at that, she knows what to do,* they'd think. *Deck, my good man, she's a keeper,* they'd say. Whee.

Tires on the drive. 7:59. Completely dark, thirty-six degrees. No wind, no precipitation. Saturday, December 18. I took my time putting my shoes on. I leaned down in front of the window so he could see me from outside, lit up, a show just for him. I let him see me fix my hair in front of the mirror, but just a second of it, not a fuss. To see that I cared, but not too much. I put on my coat and turned off the light.

He kissed me hello when I got in the car. A peck, a gentleman to a lady. I felt formal and proper and mature. It was a life I was going to live. Slip into easily. The wife of this man.

"My God, am I happy to see you," he said, and I swear to you, I nearly fucking split in two.

* * *

As it turns out, something had happened with the Christmas party. The host's child, home from college, a stomach bug, a fender bender, something.

"But now we have the whole night to ourselves," he said and patted my thigh. We were driving. He left his hand there. Heat and weight. Its own animal.

"Oh," I said. Because this is what happened and I knew it: He had changed his mind, lied to get out of it. He realized he wasn't ready to introduce me. And why should he be? It was too soon. *Hello, here's some girl I picked up at work—no, no, a different one. No, that's Lana you're thinking about, nice girl, but Lana and I are through.* I imagined the wives at the party without me. Lined up on a striped damask sofa, lights low around them, talking among themselves. These were *wives*, a different kind of people altogether. Vetted and credentialed and in. I saw them accepting the passed desserts but abandoning them on the cocktail table in favor of cordials. They all had cordials. I wanted a cordial. The mistletoe.

"Don't pout," he said and leaned forward to see my face. He was smiling at me. He was trying to be cute. To be nice. Trying. "Don't worry, we'll do something good. It was going to be stuffy anyway. You're too much fun for that kind of party. Virginia, come on. Are you really pouting?"

"No," I said. But what did that mean—*too much fun*? It meant I was not wife material, that's what it meant. It meant he had decided already. *Too much fun.* And the anklet. The anklet. And the woman who took his gun, his ex, had he lived with her? Did she still live with him, even? Where was she and who was she? I could see her. Even younger than me, long-legged, a messy blonde who had lived in Paris, gone to art school there. She was wild—*passionate* was the word she used. Took his gun in the heat of something. They made up just fine. She cooed him calm in a perfect accent: *Je suis vraiment désolé, mon cher, oh oui, oh oui.* Or maybe no, maybe older. Wife material. Patrician looks. Well bred. Chignon. Scarf. A wild streak in her, but wife material all the same. The anklet. And what else, what else was in that drawer that I didn't even see? Just another inch and I would have seen so much more. I would have understood everything. I wouldn't be here right now. That anklet. Or I would. That anklet. "I'm not fucking pouting, okay?" I spit it at him. I was an idiot. This was not what Verona had in mind. This was not her secret. I was not fine without her.

I watched him. I could not look away. I watched him as he nodded and rubbed his face with one hand and then slowed the car, pulled to the shoulder. People beeped behind us; we were on a main road. He put the car in park, and then he did not move.

"What is this?" he said and lifted both his hands up, asking, "Why are you doing this?"

I shook my head.

"Do you not want to go out? Do you want me to take you home?"

I didn't speak.

"How old are you?" He knew, of course. But he wanted me to say it. I shook my head.

"Say again?" he said and touched his finger to his ear.

"Thirty," I said. A whisper. It was embarrassing coming out of my mouth.

"You should act like it."

On our right, a strip mall, strings of Christmas lights lining the whole thing. It was just after eight, a Saturday night, the holiday season. A bright yellow coming in from the streetlamp above us. I reminded myself that he had brown eyes. He has brown eyes and he is about five feet eleven and a Libra, I think, and here we are, in his truck, and I did this, thought of all of these things, because I was afraid I was going to cry and I did not want to cry. There was no way I was going to cry in front of him. But also because— and I hated this—he was right. I was pouting and acting like a child, and he was a grown man. A grown man, older than me, who did not need to deal with these antics. I had no excuse. I wasn't even drunk. *Not wife material. Not wife material, at all,* Verona would scold. *This is all wrong.*

"You're right," I said.

A life flashed before my eyes. That old story. I wasn't dying, but still I saw it. A stone colonial, fieldstone, light through oaks and maples dappling the lawn. Sun. Summer. A sprinkler ticking its way around. Children? Yes. One. A boy. Blond and lanky, seven. A pool. Deck skimming the pool. Deck at the grill. I am arranging flowers in the kitchen, and I'm watching Deck at the grill. It is not words going through my head. It is a feeling, a general sense. But if interpreted, if you forced me to come up with something, some of the words would be: *brim, brass, gossamer.* Upstairs in our closet—we share a closet—upstairs in our closet: racks of suits and dresses, shoes and shoes. His uniforms. A little bench in the middle so we can look at it all. Sometimes I try things on for him. He sits on that bench with his leg crossed at the knee and shakes his head yes or no like a gallerist. There are two sinks in the master bath, one holder for our toothbrushes. They rub bristles if we put them in adjacent slots. At night, we sometimes migrate onto the same pillow. Find ourselves in the morning breathing into each other's mouths. Find ourselves naked. Find that we have forgotten the mid-sleep sex, that we thought we were both dreaming it, that we are sticky, sticking together in some spots and tingling with sleep in others. Pins and needles. Find that we have ignored the sounds of our child from downstairs, that he has fixed himself a bowl of cereal, spilling milk on the floor as he goes from fridge to table. He is seven, though basically feral, so he can do it himself. We wake and kiss good morning and let the sun come in, blinding and hot, even at that early hour.

There is a thing we have, all of us. I don't know the science behind it. Whether it is made of meat or bone or if it's in the air inside our bodies. Buried in the mush of our brains, most likely. It compels and catalyzes, this thing. It is part of our decision-making. It kicks off a seconds- or milliseconds-long process, and it makes us act. It makes us choose to act.

And that thing in me took over then. I climbed to him, gracefully, thank you, gracefully. Did not hit anything, did not nick anything with either heel. Though the steering wheel did dig into my lower back the rest went okay, because the mechanics of it, that was all taken care of. That was taken care of for me by the thing we all have, which, by the way, could be something divine, God given. And it was during this time that the town outside disappeared. The lights, the stores, the stars, the night, all of it. There in that car, with Deck Brady, Declan Brady, chief of the Suffolk County Police Department, none of it mattered. I felt sorry for everyone else. I wanted to cry for them. You will never have any of this, and I'm so, so sorry for that.

"How do you do this to me," he said. And then, "God," he said when it happened.

Yes, I thought. God, definitely. But other things too, Deck. Your mouth. That. That too. Your hands, your fingers in the ridges under my jaw, holding my face to yours. You see that? You feel it? You want to get all of me too, don't you?

I've convinced myself that this is the very moment when we felt the world change under us. Both of us. That's what I hoped. That was my excuse.

"I love you," I said. He kept going. He didn't even hesitate for a second. He knew. He had to have known. "I don't know," I said into his chest. I didn't care. Did not care. "I just do."

At dinner I was drugged, rag-doll dumb, smiling from ear to ear, dreamily. He kept his hand in my lap. We sat on the same side of the table. He fed me things, and if I had seen us, I would have rolled my eyes. But there wasn't anyone to see us, that's the thing. There was no one left anymore. I don't know where our food came from, who brought it. A system of pulleys and levers. Mannequins on wheels. A lazy Susan. And the meal itself: soup so thick it lined my mouth in velvet; still-bleeding meat; pasta in cream sauce, and for this I leaned even closer to him. I didn't want it dripping down my dress. I drank a shit ton of liquor. Gimlets, Tito's, not too sweet.

*　　*　　*

I must have told and asked him a great many things that night, because he slept over. I woke up to him still there, his arm around me. He did not stir when I got up to go to the bathroom, vomited three times, brushed and mouthwashed, and came back. A flash of panic when I saw his arm outstretched, fingers near the edge of my nightstand. But he was still asleep. Had only shifted. The anklet, his anklet, my anklet, was curled safely in the drawer there, twitching like a drowsy cat. I snuck back in. Under his arm. I closed my eyes and swore I would keep them closed for as long as I could until he woke up or something else disturbed us. One of our phones—though, no, he had left his in the car. A particularly harsh angle of the sun. Any kind of natural disaster, but most likely in our region, a hurricane or a very mild earthquake. The whole time I would be thinking—before I fell asleep and while I dreamed—this is what it was meant to be.

"Breakfast," he said, "no?"

I had fallen back to sleep. He was standing, buttoning his shirt.

"Definitely." I closed my eyes. "I'm . . ." I said and put the inside of my elbow onto the bridge of my nose, covering my face. The headache forced my eyes closed on their own. "I'm—I don't know." I didn't. I had no idea. I did remember what I had said, though. I heard my voice, a voice just like mine from a different body. *I love you,* it said. Jesus. Holy Christ. This was not the way. This is not what Verona had taught me.

"You'll be just fine." He stopped buttoning, looked at me. "We can straighten you right out."

Brunch. Mimosa, a cup of coffee, a tumbler of water so big I had to lift it with both hands.

"We'll split this," he said to the waiter, pointing to the menu. "And this. Thanks." He closed it and handed it back. "And no rush." We watched him walk away, and then Deck turned to me. I knew he was going to say something. I held up a finger, just about to drink.

"Let me finish this first, okay?" I said, mimosa to my mouth. He laughed, caught off guard, something I had not yet heard from him. When I was done, I licked my lips. "Okay, go."

He leaned forward, watching, and I saw him in an interrogation room, lit from above. Saw the way he would pace the place, arms folded across his chest, waiting it out. He had all day. *Try me, I have all day.* I saw the way he'd sit, how he'd lean back casually, maybe even rock his chair, teetering. His feet on the edge of the table. Good cop, bad cop, both.

I waited for him to say something, pain blooming at my temples. Maybe if I really paid attention to the pain, let myself revel in it, ride its waves, roll in its red. Maybe then? I was afraid my eyes would tear, and he would think I was crying. I blinked.

"I don't think I've ever met anyone like you," he said finally. Another movie line. We were on a set hot with lights, though he didn't break a sweat. A makeup person rushed in for a touch-up; a cloud of powder puffed around his face. He had already tested the line with a bunch of actresses. A string of new ones waited in a line down the side of the studio, smoking. *Cut,* the director yelled each time and huffed back to his chair. *Not what we're looking for. Next.*

This is what it was with him.

I tried to make him out. The place was loud. At the table next to us: four girls, women, in their twenties, cackling at a phone screen, spilling drinks. They fed each other French fries. I was disoriented, too hungover. I looked down and then couldn't look away from one girl's shoes. I prodded myself. Wasn't this what I was waiting for? This is what I was waiting for. This is what I had wished for from all the men I had ever dated. The one with the manual transmission, the artist and his stupid paintings. This is what I had wanted from all of them: certainty and articulation. Forward momentum. When you know, you know. No matter how quick. It was perfect. This is exactly what I wanted.

I could do one of a few things. But I—I choked. I dove.

"Oh, Deck," I said and looked back to him. I heard a foreign sarcasm in my voice. A fake sweetness. "I bet you say that to all of your girls, don't you?" It was sharp. Too sharp. Hard and mean. It was an accident. It wasn't me. One of the actresses had slipped into my chair, skipped her place in line and took mine instead. She had read the wrong thing for me. Wrong script entirely. I had meant to say, *Well, jeez, that's sweet, I'm having a lot of fun with you too.* But she was only trying to protect me. She thought this was the way to do it.

There was the slightest change in his face. A tiny lightbulb popped on behind his eyes. Small nod. It said: *Oh, okay, we're doing it like that then, are we?*

"Usually not to the ones who say, 'I love you' the second time I fuck them," he said. Giving it back, this hot piece of hate. Threw it right back at me.

I went red. I felt it happening. I knew he could see it, spreading, second by second up my neck. I heard the girls stop their chatter, utensils fall to plates, a leaf drop from an unwatered plant in the room's far corner. The busboy, too, wanted to listen. He turned off the sink in the kitchen.

"Why are you trying to be tough?" he said. He looked at me, baffled. Top Cop couldn't crack this one. "I don't think that's you. A mean person." And his voice over the quieted brunch crowd boomed.

I saw several of them nod. *He's right*, their gestures said. *Why do you have to be like that?* They raised their eyebrows at each other. Married couples looked down at their plates, disappointed. *I thought you wanted to have what we have.* They shook their heads. A baby, just about to cry, held its face in a silent grimace.

And then my mother, for the love of God, my mother, there by the door where I hadn't seen her when we came in: *Virginia, you are going to do a number on yourself. Just open up and let him in. It's the only way it will happen for you. Stop with the faraway!* She turned to someone at the table next to her. *That's my daughter,* she said and looked up to the ceiling, putting her palms together in mock prayer. *She just doesn't understand how to do this.* I waited for her to cross herself.

I shrugged. Help me. That's what I was thinking. Help. Someone. My head, fuck.

"I know," I said. "I'm really not." It was still silent when he reached for my hand. The cuff of his coat caught on the edge of the table, pushed his sleeve up just a bit, kept his hand from mine, until he fixed it, and our fingers touched, and the noise around us rose and then swelled, and I looked at my red nails, nestled there in between his fingers. Held. We were holding hands.

It's one of the places where two people can really combine themselves. Physiologically, I mean.

CHAPTER SEVENTEEN

It was going to be fine. We were going to fix it. We drove to a park and sat in its lot for a minute but then left. Even though the park was fine, perfectly okay, we left. We drove to a playground and watched the swings move in the wind, and both of us knew how that type of cold would feel on our skin, and so we left there too, even though it would have been fine. So he drove to the beach and took the spot where we had been that very first day, and he was right—that's what we needed to do to reset it and reboot it, and we tried to fix it there. What I'm saying is, we fixed it all, and in the end it was okay. It was good. It was great.

CHAPTER EIGHTEEN

But no, not really, because the next day he texted me, icy and noncommittal: *Hey I'm out on the road a lot this week, so I won't be in the office much.*

In reply: *Yeah, so, quick question while I have you. I found this thing in your drawer. I apologize for looking, I shouldn't have, but curiosity, bygones. Anyway, this thing—it's so silly— but an anklet? In your drawer? Is it yours? I mean, not yours, but does it belong to someone you know? Is there someone else? I figured it was someone else's. Maybe you found it, picked it up, have it in safekeeping—I don't know. So whose is it? What I mean is, are you seeing anyone else? And also, while I still have you: out on the road. What does this mean, exactly? Are you alone? Is it for work? Where are you? Why can't you stop in? Why can't you come by at night, any night? I'm always home— you know that. Why can't I come to you, see your house? I'm just, it's just that I feel a little in the dark. I don't know where you go. Where you are. Who you are. Do you know what I mean? Where do you go when you disappear?*

I could have. I probably should have.

So anyway, right: Monday. His icy and noncommittal *Hey I'm out on the road a lot this week, so I won't be in the office much*, and I wrote back, *Hi there*, with a smiley face but no exclamation point, and then when he didn't write back, I cursed myself for leaving it out. How stoic I must have seemed, even with the smiley. How cold. How unable to open up. Too stoic. Fuck. All it would have taken was an exclamation point. All it would have taken was for me to use the goddamn exclamation point. I beat myself up about that.

Tuesday afternoon, thawing: *Miss me yet?* I wanted to type back, *Yes*. No, make it all caps. *YES*. Fill a screen with exclamation points. Write it in several languages. *Do you know what you're doing to me?* He knew. But I was being punished. This was part of it. I knew to repent. *I sure do*, I wrote back, sans punctuation, no emoji. Too drained to look for any of it. *Si, Oui, Da, Ja, Yes*.

Wednesday, warmer, warm, I felt his hands, I saw him smiling: *Are you out roaming the halls again?* I wrote back right away, not even trying to hide it: *No, just waiting by your office door, weeping.* A flutter of them back and forth after that. I kept expecting him to walk in, to surprise me. Uniformed and overcoated and fresh from the winter cold. But nothing.

Thursday, finally: *I'll call you tomorrow. Miss you.* Did this convince me of anything, this *Miss you*? Only that I had not completely wrecked things yet. Not completely, not one hundred percent. *Sounds good. You too*, I wrote back. Cool. Adult. If this was a test, I was going to pass. I was going to win.

I didn't wander down to his office with a blank sheet of paper, looking for him. I didn't pop out of my door at the sound of any fast footfall, the walk of someone important. I did not fish for his whereabouts from Evelyn. I typed him messages and then erased them, bashful, nervous. I considered sending a picture of myself while lying in bed, naked, fake sleepy, blanket artfully arranged. But I didn't. I did take these pictures, but I did not send them. I would wait. What is one day, waiting? In the scheme of things, one day is nothing. Two, three, four days—it's nothing. I checked for messages, must have been every two minutes. I hallucinated vibration. I had been taught my lesson.

*   *   *

Friday was Christmas Eve. I had to work. And then I had to be at my parents' at six. They hosted a large party every year. The idea of it, the noise and the shoulders bumping mine and the questions about how I liked my new job and whether I had met anyone special yet because it was time to settle down and soon it would be time for me to be pregnant and what was I doing, squandering my life like this? *You're only young once,* an aunt would say. *Don't waste it.* Ladling something from a pan into her mouth. *You're such a beautiful girl, why are you all alone?*

Easy: because I fuck it all up. Because I say stupid things and I fuck it all up.

I expected nothing. A slow day. A day for me to sit in silence at my desk and wait for my damaged cells to grow back inside. They were singed with embarrassment, still; crusted at the edges with it. I hoped for something vital at their centers. Something I could resuscitate. I would help them along. It was something I would visualize, as it happened. I would allow myself to notice the swell and beat of each new piece, its slide as it found its place and clicked in tight. Coming back, I'm coming back.

The phone didn't ring until noon. I was at my desk, skipping lunch to punish myself. To help with my repair and regrowth. I don't know what I was thinking.

"It's me," she said, cutting me off out of courtesy. She didn't want me to waste my time.

"Verona, hi," I said.

"You can call me V," she said. "Everyone does, basically."

Of course they do. I was just about to say, *Me too.* They call me that too.

"Another girl is gone," she said, rushed it out. "Just gone. Missing. She didn't go home."

"Jesus," I said. "Did someone make a report? Because someone should file a report, like ASAP. I can't do it from here, but I can transfer you right now, and you can sort out how to make it."

"Of course someone did," she said, stopping me again. "It's different, though, with us, you know? We can come and go, and no one notices." She took a sip of something. Home. Quiet. She was looking out the window. Her voice made the sound of a face close to glass. "I mean, it could be nothing. She could have gone away for the holidays or maybe she's taking a break, or who knows. But I wanted to tell you. So it didn't fall through the cracks. So there's a record of it, at least. In addition to the report. I don't know. I just wanted to tell you. It makes me feel better."

"I get it," I said. Flattered in the strangest way. "Good call." And only then did I think to write it down. *Repeat caller,* I wrote. And then she surprised me. She shook me out of finishing.

"Are you doing anything special for Christmas?" she said. Suddenly she was wearing a Santa hat, red pajamas, slippers.

"No," I said. "Nothing special. Just going to my parents' house. I'm dreading all of it, to be honest."

"Seriously. Me too," she said. "Same." I saw her go, open the front door. John and Jane Doe, parents of Verona. Grandparents, cousins, aunts and uncles of Verona. She took her shoes off when she walked in the house. She helped herself to eggnog and wiped its mustache away with her fingertip. She sat back into the leather sofa after dinner and held her stomach. *So full,* she said, moaning. She let her head fall to a throw pillow and listened to the fireplace and the television and the chatter around her, and her family let her fall asleep. They watched her, curled there, hair tucked around her face, asleep in the middle of everything. *Our girl works so hard,* they thought. She was a receptionist at a body shop, they thought.

"What are you drinking?" I said.

"Eggnog," she said. Clairvoyant. "Literally the only good thing about Christmas."

"I'm jealous," I said. "What I'd do for an eggnog right now. Terrible, illegal, filthy things." She giggled and it bubbled in her, up through the phone, until it touched me. It felt good making her laugh. Then a little flash. "Oh, wait. I have to ask you." Like it had just come to me, dropped in, a courier with a wrapped box. An envelope through a mail slot. Of course. "I was thinking—and this is going to sound so weird, but I have to ask. Do you think maybe it was a guy named Mike Abatescianni?" My accent was a wreck. Tripped through the whole thing. "Does that sound familiar? He has a long first name too. Michelangelo." And it was a no-no, giving her this name. When Donovan trained me, he had said, *This is a one-way street,* and pointed to the phone. *Information comes in, but it does not go out.* But I had to ask because I wanted it to be Officer Abatescianni. Because it had to be him. Simple, wrapped up, done. Imagine. Could you imagine something like that? Thanks, Virginia, all solved. We can all go home now. We can all go on with our lives.

"Ahh, who knows," she said. "Because they don't tell me their names, remember?" She was being gentle. She was hand-feeding and then rubbing my gullet to make sure I got it down.

"Yeah, right, right," I said. "I know. Just a long shot. I was just wondering. If that might ring any bells for some reason." I could taste the eggnog. Through the phone. That gamey tang masked with whiskey. Thick and sweet as melted ice cream. My mouth watered for it. That's what I was thinking of.

"Like I said," she sipped, "it could be any one of many. A bunch of us have seen the same dozen or so guys over and over."

"You know, if you ever want, you can come in and talk to the detectives. I'm sure you would be so helpful to them. And they would treat you well. One of the guys is really nice. I think I told you that." It was the first time I had thought of him in so long. He had ceased to exist. *And then you can come and visit me,* I could have told her. *We could meet. We could have lunch, coffee, a drink. Talk.* And why not, there was nothing stopping us from being friends. Who said we couldn't be friends? We basically were. I mean, for all intents and purposes. We talked more frequently than I talked to my real friends. We shared secrets. What did real friends even mean anymore.

"Ooh," she said, like *ooh-la-la*, "so it sounds like there *is* someone there for you after all." She laughed. "Someone you have your eye on? Remember what I told you, right?" She sounded relaxed, calmer. Drunk already? We could get drunk together. We could get drunk and she could tell me more.

"No, oh no," I said. "Not like that. I just meant that there are some approachable guys in Homicide that would really appreciate speaking to you. That's all." That faraway place. With its stacks of paper and quiet men, white shirts, dark ties. That girl, back then. That girl who looked like me, knocking on their door. Watching that stranger in his winter coat, furred hood. Making a future. The coffees. The break- fast truck. All those nice people, gone somewhere. Never to be seen again.

"I'm not coming in there," she said. "No fucking way. I appreciate that, the offer, but not a chance. They make me nervous."

Me too, I wanted to say.

"And listen, you better be careful with him, with which- ever one you have, okay? Promise me. They're charming as hell, but be careful. Not good, some of them. You know. I told you and so now you know." She drank, finished the whole thing, I think, because I heard her put the glass down. "Well, Merry Christmas!" she said, and it was real cheer in her voice. A light. A small ball of light. I was going to keep it for myself. This light, this delicate thing. It was mine now. I was so thankful. I felt better already.

"Thank you," I said. "You too!" I tried to match her. My voice was stringy, thin, put on. Not a match. She just had something that I didn't.

"We'll talk soon," she said, and I heard her lean toward the glass of the window again. She was getting a better look at something. A dog in the yard two stories down. A boat on the harbor—a fishing boat—its clammer protected by a tarp hung up against the wind. The sun bright against the cold winter sky, a mean joke. I heard the ball of her Santa hat fall and brush past the phone and then hit the window. "Bye."

Repeat Caller Caller states that another woman is missing, though she has been reported as such and caller was not unduly worried about her safety. Caller said she is visiting her family tonight for the holiday, though not looking forward to it. Caller also likes eggnog. Caller warned your correspondent to exercise caution in regard to intimate relations with law enforcement officials. Caller was wearing a Santa hat and said *Merry Christmas,* her voice so rich and thick with emotion that the joy she spread through it, the soaring joy—through just these two words—is private, thank you very much. The undersigned had also intended to ask the caller if she was obligated to dress for Christmas, if it was formal, if she wore heels, something seasonal, green velvet, tartan, taffeta, ruffles, rhinestoned buttons, and/or a red satin bow around a low ponytail. Matte red lips. If she ate the seven fishes, if she opened any gifts on the Eve, if she had asked for anything special.

I didn't type it up. There was no reason anyone else needed to know.

*　*　*

All day long and no call from Deck. And then half past six and no call from Deck.

I was trying to stay calm. Even keeled. I opened the front door of my parents' house, and I walked into the kitchen and mixed a drink before saying hello to anyone properly. I kept my shoes on. I had stopped for eggnog because my mother wouldn't have any and because I had been thinking of it all day. I also bought a Santa hat because it was right there, on the counter at the register, in a display of holiday items. A lighter with a picture of a tree. A necklace with little working Christmas lights. A headband with reindeer horns attached. There was only one hat left. Merry Fate! *"Merry Christmas!"* I heard Verona say. I wanted it to cheer me because I was walking a line. I was on the verge of anger. I was trying to stay on the good side. This was a test. I had to stay calm. A test—I could do it.

Once I had the drink half down, felt the sugar on my tongue and teeth, felt the whiskey start its slow roll through me, I put the hat on. I went into the bathroom and fixed my makeup. I breathed deeply while looking at my face. I did a minute of a rejuvenating facial massage I had read about. Thirty seconds of pressure at the temples and then where the jaw connects. Closed my eyes to do it, and when I opened them, I looked more youthful and festive, definitely. My disappointment was concealed.

Almost seven and still no call. Rage: a tremor deep in my plates. But it could wait. I could make it wait. I'd make it go away.

I kissed people on their cheeks and held my non-drink hand flat on their backs. Colognes and cigarettes and cold air coming off them. I waited in the foyer and drank alone. Made my own receiving line. *You look beautiful,* my aunt said when she came in. *I'm so happy to see you,* my parents' friends said. They were a married couple, so they said this in unison. They smiled in unison.

There was a ball of fresh mistletoe on the archway into the living room. I nodded when I saw it, because it switched something in me. It made the whiskey in me turn bubbling and hot. I was no longer on the verge. This fuck. I drank. The rage. Fished my phone out of my pocket: nothing new on it. This fucking fuck. Again, again I had done it. There was something wrong with me, the way I did this. Over and over. I was doing it all wrong. I milled around the living room, stroked the shoulders of people I knew or thought I knew. *Love this pin*, I said to a woman who looked like the neighbor. Lying. *Brooch, I mean.* Ugly brooch. Ugly as sin. I was livid. I refilled my drink. Drank. Checked my phone. Still nothing. I was missing something. What did I not know?

But then I did know! It came to me. I was looking at the fireplace and it popped and spat and that's what made it come to me. It was because I was too subdued. Too demure. I took the back seat too often, and that wasn't going to get me anywhere. I had to drive. This was something Verona would tell me. One of her secrets. *Grab the wheel,* she would say. *Make it happen.* I liked this metaphor. It was primitive and elementary and embarrassing in its simplicity, but it filled me with hope, knowing that I had come up with a solution. An idea. The idea? *I* would message *him.* No. I would *call* him. Why not. This fuck. He didn't get to decide. Where have you been? Where on earth have you been?

I went to the bathroom first. Fixed my lip gloss, mini massage, peed. My hat felt nice. Made me feel better, I mean. Though it felt nice too. The fur of it. Faux but deep. Decent faux for twelve dollars. Festive. Right. I rubbed my lips together. Pursed them, then kissed the air. Smoothed my hair. Took out my phone, scrolled as I walked. This would not be good. I knew that I shouldn't, and yet—his number. Went to press "Send." My fingers would have been shaking, but the drinks made them sure and strong. This would not be good. Regardless—

But then Deck. Deck was there in the foyer when I got back. A mirage, an apparition come to life. Must've looked up my parents' address, found his way here. He was standing alone, one hand in his overcoat pocket, the other holding a wrapped bottle. Shiny silver cellophane. Twinkling. A red ribbon in a bow. His back was to me.

"Hey," I said, and he turned around. "What?" It was confusing to see him there, in such a familiar place. Also, I was drunk.

"Hiya," he said and came toward me. "Cute hat." He put his free arm around my waist and pulled me to him. He was drunk too. I had never seen him so drunk. I smelled it coming off of him. Whiskey this time. Cigars. "Mistletoe," he said, noticing. He kissed me. Liquored tongues, both of us. I didn't bother looking behind him to see who was watching. His coat was cold. His face, so cold. "That's so sweet," he said and licked his lips. "What is that?" I pitched forward into him. The relief, God, the relief, new blood in me. All my new cells, growing, growing.

"Eggnog," I said. "I haven't heard from you. I didn't know what you were doing," I whispered into his collar. "I didn't know where you were. Where have you been?"

He pushed me back, arms' distance, looked. I could see behind him. No one was watching us.

"I know. I'm sorry," he said. His eyes were red. Something was off. Was wrong. He looked different. He was far away. The clam boat in the harbor, the weeping contrails of a jet plane. Far, far away. He had been somewhere and something had happened, and he was trying to make sense of it. He opened his mouth to speak. He was going to tell me something. He said, "Christmas is a lot for me."

"Oh," I said, relieved. "I hate it too." Because I was game. I was a good girl. I went along. "It's a pain in the ass."

"No," he said. "My dad died on Christmas."

But then there he was. Back. Never even gone. Right there just for me. I wanted to cry with him. A heave soared up through my chest. I brought my hand up from my side and slid it into the collar of his coat, put it on the side of his neck.

"Let me get you a drink. You can wait here? Or you want to come with me?"

He followed me into the kitchen and when everyone looked up I said, "This is Declan. We work together." Then I went right ahead and poured his drink. No last names. No eggnog for him. Kept his whiskey neat. They all nodded. It was that easy. *Hi, Declan, Merry Christmas,* someone said. I didn't know who. Declan from work left the bottle he had brought on the counter.

"Show me around," he said when I handed him his drink. "Show me where you grew up."

I expected something when we got to my old room. Some kind of encounter spurred by it. Onto my twin bed, maybe. In one of my old uniforms, fresh from the decade-old dry cleaning plastic in the closet. Him whispering something filthy while he hiked up my hockey skirt. It was quiet, everyone was downstairs, rooms away, ten drinks deep. But no. He stood in the doorway behind me and looked into the room, like we were checking in on our own sleeping child.

We sat in the living room after the tour. On the couch, side by side, our legs stretched out together to the same ottoman. I wanted to throw mine over his, but it was not yet the time. We watched the tree and the fire and everyone left us alone.

"I didn't know anything about your dad," I said. I thought to put my arms around him to help, but the thought came too late. Anyway, I would have spilled my drink, maybe his too. "I'm so sorry. I had no idea. I would have called." This is the point where your voice starts to change. Where you can hear it in your head, like on a screen or recording. That drunk. *I love you I love you I love you*, it was saying under all the things that came out aloud.

"I know that," he said. He touched my chin, just held it for a second and then let go. The decency. *Charming.* I swam. We were in Rio, swimming in a hotel pool. He held his arms out to me, glistening, sunset, the sun setting behind us. He held his arms out to me. You are a vacation.

"I'm really drunk," I said. One sip left, I finished it. "Just so you know." I gestured to him with my empty glass. "Finish," I said. "I'll get us more." He listened.

"I have something for you," he said as I was getting up. "In my car. Bring a bottle out. Tell your parents I said thank you. But I'm in no shape to meet them right now." The first thing I thought of was a small box. Stupid, I know. But it was the first image. A ring. I pushed it away. Maybe it was a locket. I clicked the locket open. A place for a picture of us. Maybe a watch. A bottle of perfume. A dozen, ten dozen roses, filling the backseat of his truck, falling out as I opened the door. A rush of petals and scent. *Merry Christmas!* Or none of this. A longer box, empty inside. *This is for the anklet you've already found.* He knew it was missing—of course he did. But it was for me, the whole time it had been for me. Easy. It was for me, and I could stop thinking about it. I could forget about it altogether. There was no one else. It was only me.

I was proud when I walked into that kitchen. Hello, hello. I nodded at everyone whose eye I caught. *Yes, that was Declan,* my nod said, *the man I work with.* Man. *The man I'm seeing.*

My mother was watching me from a group of women sitting at the table. Their wedding rings, all of them, shining together, synchronized flashes. It was almost all I saw. She pushed her chair back and came to me. I was trying to undo the ribbon on the bottle. I should have just taken it as it was.

"Declan, huh?" she said. I waited for it. *Declan what? He's much too old. Why hasn't he been married? Is he married, Virginia? He's married, isn't he. Why didn't he stay for something to eat? Isn't much of a conversationalist, really.* She raised her eyebrows. "He's very handsome, V. We're all talking about how handsome he is." She pointed over at her friends, and they smiled. All of their rings smiled at me.

"Okay," I said. "I mean thanks. He says thank you. But he had to leave. I'm just"—I reached around her, took the eggnog too—"taking this. I'll be back. In a sec. Okay?"

She didn't care. I could have done anything and she wouldn't have cared because she and her friends had seen me with a handsome man, and that was all that mattered. She went back to the women.

In the hallway mirror, the reflection of a happy person: festive, smiling, drunk, very drunk, steady in high heels, straight posture, Santa hat, pom-pom bobbing, on her way out into the cold, out into the car of a man. *Where do I know you from?* I wanted to stop to ask her. *You look so familiar, and I think we've met before.* But I had to get out there.

Underwear. *Lingerie,* is what he would say. Good stuff. Expensive stuff that was not from a chain, but from a boutique, and what pleased me about this was not the actual gift so much as the thought of his going there, driving there with this task in mind, engaging the help of an employee, with a tape measure around her neck, who admired his no-expense-spared attitude and his classic good looks and thought of the lucky woman on the receiving end of both and brought to him armfuls of sets and placed them on a small satin bench and watched as he judged them, casting aside those that seemed too tawdry or too virtuous, pointing and shaking his head, rubbing the fabric between his thumb and index finger, in a very intimate kind of motion, imagining what it'd feel like later, on me, and then nodding, finally, at the last set, one she had brought from the back, a new set, a set they had just gotten in and had not yet put out, and when she pulled the tissue up, he smiled and thought of my body in there, in the lace panels and straps, the elastic of the openings tight, just right against that softness, that softness of the body that he couldn't stop thinking about. Could not stop. The body. My body.

It was dark. Jewel toned. Ruby or emerald, I couldn't tell. I squinted. Ruby.

"Beautiful," was all I could manage. I looked to him. The streetlamp from up ahead gave us just enough light that I could see facial expressions on a grand scale, but no nuance. He was smiling in some capacity. "But I don't have anything for you." I almost had tears in my eyes.

"It's you," he said. He was unscrewing the bottle again. "You are." I guess I knew he was going to say something like that. Didn't change a thing.

I don't know how long we kissed. "Thank you," I said when we stopped. "Do you want to talk to me about your dad?"

Pneumonia, sepsis, Christmas Eve sixteen years prior. The day ruined for the foreseeable future. Forever. His father had never seen, would never see Sergeant Brady, Lieutenant Brady, Inspector Brady, Chief Brady. He had never seen the meteoric rise. His father, a decorated cop in his own right, a deputy inspector when he retired, would have been beside himself with pride. His son: a chief.

"I think it was really all he ever wanted for me," Deck said. "He didn't care if I had a wife or family or any of it. Just wanted me to succeed on the job." He didn't look to see if it made me wince. It didn't, anyway. My reasoning was going. I was just a bunch of reflexes. "We're going to feel awful tomorrow, by the way."

I leaned back. I'd drink until the sun came up if he wanted to, listening to him. Still swimming. We'd swim until dawn, summer in the Southern Hemisphere, warm already in Brazil. We were having breakfast in Brazil. We were rubbing our feet together under the table. Sandy, salty, *love you* over coffee. Over mimosas or whichever customary breakfast cocktail.

I woke up at two AM at my parents' house. In my old twin bed, alone, fully clothed. He had gone home. I checked my phone. *Yes love of course it's just you, and I am the happiest I've been in a long time,* the message said. I had no recollection, no outgoing texts. All of the things I could have asked him. *Just you,* he wrote. But more importantly *love.* He had chosen the word. His mind had settled on it, and his fingers had typed it out, and he had sent it to me. I didn't respond. I went back to sleep. I wanted to dream of the beach and of him, but I was tossing and restless, and I came up with nothing.

CHAPTER NINETEEN

"I have to go in," I said to my parents on Christmas morning. I didn't. "To work. Sorry." We exchanged presents quickly, when they had just come downstairs, still tightening the belts on their robes and finger-combing their hair. And then I left them in their kitchen, breakfast sizzling in several pans behind them. The Santa hat was on the nightstand upstairs. The small box Deck had given me, tucked under my arm. I looked at the tree before I left. At the ottoman we had shared. I went home and sat on the floor of the shower under the hottest water I could stand.

Merry Christmas, I wrote to him when I got out. *I'm glad you came by last night xx.* The *xx* was a risk. It was attempting something that I didn't really know if he did, or if I did, even, but I was hungover and cloudy. It was hard to think. Then I sent another one before I could change my mind: *I'm home if you want to call. Or come by. For your gift.*

He did. He brought take-out Chinese, and we let it go cold on the table. He ran a finger under each strap, like lifting the flap of an envelope. Like slitting the tape on wrapping paper.

CHAPTER TWENTY

I imagined Verona on vacation that week. I didn't hear from her at all. Verona on Vacation. A children's book. A series. *Verona on Vacation: Los Angeles.* Verona visits her friend Hillary. Then she goes to her aesthetician to get super smooth for her clients! She drinks four raw green juices a day. She hikes in Runyon Canyon while the dust swirls around her ankles, and she looks down at the mirage of a town beneath her. *I'm finally here,* she thinks to herself. *But how did I get here?* Verona loves Los Angeles! Have you ever been to Los Angeles? Write about your visit in the space provided below.

Verona on Vacation: Verona. Verona strolls Via Cappello, window-shopping, and squints to the sky to see Juliet's balcony. Such sun! Spires! See? She gives up, retires to a trattoria with a client, who chews his pasta loudly, smacking his lips. He speaks piss-poor Italian. He does, however, tip big in addition to the *coperto.* His hands are smooth, and his cologne is very expensive. Do you like pasta? What is your favorite shape of pasta?

Verona on Vacation: Rio. No, Rio's me. Rio's all mine.

New Year's party on Friday. What do you think? Deck texted me early that week. Can't remember which day.

There was a blizzard that blurs everything. Lots of people called out sick, stranded home. I had shoveled my driveway and the driveway of the Big House, though, fueled by the endorphins I made in anticipation. The party, finally! I was redeemed. I was fine. I had passed some test. I wrote back to him: *With you? Anything.* And I was not kidding.

*   *   *

Friday morning, New Year's Eve, warmer than it had been in a while. The air was wet with melting snow. I took my time walking in. I liked the wind whipping my hair, making a mess of me.

I knew, of course, that it was going to happen eventually. Just numbers, odds, a matter of time. He came up behind me. I heard his feet on the pavement and then the beep of his ID card as he unlocked the door and reached around to hold it open for me. A force field between us, a good yard. There was a place in me that should have been affected. I knew exactly where it was and what it would have felt like if I'd been functioning properly. On the left side. By the spleen? I want to say spleen, between the spleen and the stomach, a soft little box. Red and reserved for this type of thing, this kind of emotion. I should have felt a jump there, a cold shiver, an *ooh* said in a whisper, but it was just lukewarm air. Not even rushing. Unmoving, lukewarm air.

"Hi," I said. "Thanks."

"No problem," Charlie Ford said. Charlie Ford should have said. "You sure got yourself set up quickly," is what he really said.

I was inside and he was just out. The threshold between us. I could have turned my back and walked away. Left him there, holding the door and watching my damp hair swing at my back as I got smaller and smaller down the hall.

"Sorry?" I said.

"I said, you sure got yourself set up quickly." He was different than I remembered. Everything about him almost unrecognizable. Who was this strange man.

"I don't know what you're talking about," I said. "I don't know what you mean." I shook my head *no* for good measure.

"Right. Well, good luck with that," he said. "Good luck with him. You'll see. Happy New Year."

I walked away and felt him watching me until I heard the door whisper over the terrazzo and then click shut. He knew enough to take a different set of stairs up. He knew enough to wait in the stairway until he heard my footsteps stop at my door, heard me unlock it and then go all the way into my office. Smart man, at the end of the day. But regardless, even if he hadn't been, I would have no part of his interference.

CHAPTER TWENTY-ONE

It was a huge thing. Right on the beach. Modern lines, wood panels, and concrete. Lots of windows, lit from inside, filled with people. Cars parked up and down the street. This street not far from where we'd been parked the very first day, the very first kiss, the sea all around us. The causeway, again. Oak Beach.

"Wow," I said when he slowed in front of it. "This? I think I might be underdressed." I tightened my coat around me.

"You look beautiful," he said and shook his head at me like he didn't understand. "I already know you'll be the most beautiful girl in there."

Oh, Deck, you win. You win everything.

"Do you mind if I smoke cigars?" he asked. He was leaning across, hand in his glovebox. In its light I saw his gun, several cigars, his shield.

"Of course not," I said. He took out the cigars and snapped the glovebox shut.

"A lot of women can't stand them."

"Good thing I'm not a lot of women," I said.

He held my hand on the walk up, took my elbow when it got rocky, guided me by the small of the back when we were on the stairs up to the front door. We had shared a bottle of champagne on the drive over, plus the ice, my heels.

"Whose party is this? Did you tell me and I forgot?" I said after he rang the bell.

"My father knew this guy's father," he said. "There'll be a bunch of other guys from work here." Then This Guy opened the door. Short and dark haired, shiny. Rings and a silk shirt, dark suit.

"Look who it is," he said to Deck, and the two of them hugged, slapping each other's backs. "Come in."

I'd say a hundred people, that I could see. Cocktail dresses. Lots of flounce and shimmer. Lots of pops of color. All at or above the knee. I regretted my tea-length dress immediately. Hated my tendency toward classic silhouettes. Thanked God for the exposed shoulders and the slit at the side, which I tugged open in the millisecond I had before the man turned to me.

"You have Audrey Hepburn with you tonight, you lucky fuck," he said and took my hand. I look nothing like Audrey Hepburn. Then or now.

"Language, Pete, come on," Deck said. "This is Virginia Carey." My heart. The jump it had at the start of a waltz. A hundred harps rose together in the other room. Say it again, Deck.

"Thank you for having me," I said. "Happy New Year." I almost bowed, I think. I almost placed my hands in prayer position and bowed.

"It's my pleasure," Pete said. His voice was hot. He was just looking. Just standing there looking at me. "Well, you sure did okay for yourself this time, Brady. Very nice." He started at my feet and went up, up. Stopped at the top. My shoulders, anyway. "You know your way around, pal. Go help yourself. I have to let these people in." He spit when he spoke. I couldn't take looking at him. I begged Deck with my eyes for our next drinks.

A group of people behind us, more couples pushing us farther into the house. With them, a rush of cold air. Pete took our coats, shooed the two of us into the bigger room. Deck walked me to the bar, still holding my hand.

"Chief," someone yelled from over by the sliding door. Half nod, quick uptick of the chin, and that's it. Instead, he turned to me.

"Preference? He has everything."

"Whatever you're having," I said. "Just less of it." He got us two glasses of something brown, mine with ice. We clinked and sipped.

"Well," he said, "where do you want to start?"

*　*　*

I was right. Always Virginia Carey, never a signifier. And I liked it. I liked watching them nod slowly as we shook, tilting their heads to the side, trying to figure it out. I hoped it was because he didn't bring many women around. Or if he did, they weren't as young. Or if he did and they were, maybe these people were always so curious and confused. Maybe they walked in awe of Deck Brady and his very many or very few dates. Right away, I recognized two other cops from work. Older detectives, always in suits, from a command at the far corner of headquarters, whose purpose was not completely clear to me.

He led me around and I thought I would never tire of holding his hand. That I was meant to do this. Born to do this. Hold this man's hand at cocktail parties and events while he introduced me and I smiled up at him. Glowing. Pride beaming from my face. A wife.

I had to go to the bathroom. He walked me there, and I closed the door behind me and reveled in the immediate quiet. I wished we were in my bed. My mascara was rubbing off a bit. I fixed it. I dusted fresh powder. I wanted to tell him that I wished we were in my bed together. I was going to open the door and lean into him, fish for his hand, find it, squeeze it, tell him this: *I want to leave.* I finished my drink, one last look, and then I opened the door. The party resumed, sound exploding, but he was gone. I thought he would be waiting. There were so many people. Too many people, and I would never see him again. This has been the story of how I lost my first and only One True Love. Gone like that. Finger snap. I hope you liked it.

But there, there was Pete, his hand on my bare arm. He could have seen me naked and I would have felt less unclean.

"Audrey," he said and pushed his big wet lips into a cartoon frown. "You're lost."

"I don't know," I said. "Deck? Have you seen him?"

"He let you out of his sight? I'm shocked," he said and shook his head, though his hand stayed put. "I'll help you. I bet I know." He plunged forward into the thickest group, all blowouts and smooth shoulders and perfume, hems of skirts. Steering me with his hand still there, his arm looped loosely around my neck. He stopped every other second to speak to someone, and I waited while Deck spun away from me. Farther and farther away.

"There," Pete said. "Out there." He pointed through the thick glass of the sliding door, and I saw Deck's dark shape, the red tip of his cigar when he pulled.

"Oh, thank God," I said. I actually said that.

"Wait," Pete said. Took my glass, refilled it, gave it back, and opened the door. A good host, a perfect host. When he closed the door behind me, the party disappeared again.

I walked over to Deck. The crash of the Atlantic was loud and he was at the railing. He didn't hear my heels on the wood. I put my arm around his waist, and I felt him go rigid, turn quickly to me, as if in defense. Ready to fight.

"It's me," I said.

"Ah," he said, softening. "Here she is."

"Here I am."

"Look at that," he said and pointed at the water with his cigar hand. "Something amazing there. I know everyone says it, but it's true." It was true. The expanse of it. Different in the night. A flat continent, another world. "You can't get tired of it." I could see that. It was soothing, in a way. All that space, made of something changing. Something you could disappear into. Disappear. And then—I don't know, it just hit me—then I really wanted to go home. Him and me. I just wanted it to be him and me. The rest of the world was too big. The ocean, the girls so close by. *More of them,* she had said. More of them right near us, right across the causeway where the others had been found.

"Let's go home?" I said and pressed my face against his chest, just like I had wanted to.

"We just got here," he said. "It's not even midnight yet. You don't want to wait?"

Through the glass, I saw people dancing. Men with women, men with several women. Behind them all, a huge TV screen: broadcasters in Times Square. I did love New Year's Eve. I always had. Down on the beach the sand looked white. We could walk the beach, I thought. Under this sliver of a moon. I could hold my shoes and we could walk the beach. The length of this island, onto the mainland, walk the whole coast, state by state. At least we would be by ourselves.

"I don't know," I said and drank a long sip. It made me shiver, the taste.

"You're freezing," he said. He had a hand on the place where my neck met my shoulder. Smoke rolled out of him, up and away, into the dark. "Come on. Let's go in." He put his cigar on the railing and rubbed my arms, trying to warm me.

He slid the door open, starting everything over, and I finished my drink like a shot, closing my lips and my eyes to keep it all in. Then I exhaled, slow and even. It took one more of those drinks, and then I was fine. I followed Deck around, crossing and uncrossing my ankles as I stood next to him, nodding along. Kitchen island, foyer, office, den, library, couch. On the couch, I sat, finally, and let my thigh touch his and folded my hands in my lap. It was someone from work. I think he was talking to someone from work. A stern-looking man with a mustache and cop posture. His voice was low. It was ten forty-five. A weak wind nudged the scarves of the broadcasters, nudged and then gave up. Their noses were red. I felt unwell. I hadn't eaten. He must have seen. He must have read my mind. He motioned over a waiter with a tray of little squares, red and green pieces, something shiny. *These look like toys,* I wanted to say to the waiter. But he would have thought me strange. I took one and ate it instead.

"This is Paul," Deck said, turning to me. "You've seen Paul around, right?" I was still chewing; I could only nod.

Paul had with him three women. They were all tall and thin, blonde. Tan. *Are you models?* I wanted to say. But it was so stupid. I just kept chewing. My head bubbled, but I was getting better. The little toy I had eaten was helping. I imagined it chugging through me, a tiny train on a mission, refreshing everything.

"Hello, girlfriend." One of Paul's women was leaning down to me. She had an accent. "You interested?"

"What?" I said and then, for some reason, "Hello."

"Hi," she said again and smiled. She was very beautiful. She was the most beautiful woman in the room. Deck had been wrong. Well intentioned but wrong. "Are you interested?"

"Interested?" I looked at Deck. He had his head turned to Paul, listening, but he was looking at me. We were looking at each other. "I don't know? What do you mean?" I asked. I was drunk. That's when I really felt it.

She took her hand to her face. I thought she was going to push aside her hair, this blonde hair she had, my God, but she put the tip of her index finger on her nostril. Just touched. So soft. Her nail was long and red and pointy. Similar shade to mine. I made a story for her in my head. Ana from Brazil. Here for work. Flying home on the third. Liked Paul's attitude, his can-do attitude. What he came up with in the bedroom. Liked his confidence. *Charming.*

Oh. Oh, I know now.

"Oh," I said to her. I looked back to Deck. Still watching. He had not taken his eyes from me. He raised his eyebrows. His look said, *Go ahead.* It said, *Why not?* It said, *Sure.*

"One minute, one minute," he said to Paul when he saw the look on me. One of the things about this man, about

Deck, I'll tell you: the most intuitive, perceptive person. Saw it all. Did not miss a thing. He came closer to me. "You okay?"

"I'm fine. Look, these girls, this girl here"—I looked to Ana, still leaning toward me, patient and generous Ana—"she's asking if I want some. Can you tell her, *No thank you*? I don't want to be rude. I mean, I don't want her to feel bad—that you, that you're who you are. I don't want her to be nervous. That she will get into trouble or something. Do you know? That's all." I tipped my empty glass back and wished. Pete. Where was Pete when I needed him? Pete. I was swirling, regardless. I was really out there.

"Yeah, it's fine," he said. I think he almost laughed. He leaned forward and kissed the top of my head. "Don't worry about anything. You can do it if you want to. You can, but I can't. I shouldn't."

Ana smiled at him and something pinged at me. That she could see something in him. Something that I couldn't see.

"Oh," I said.

Now, I had done coke before. Not a ton. More than five times, fewer than ten. With exes. With college friends. I had done it. I could have just said no. I could have easily done that.

But I let her set me up, Ana. Ana and her two friends whose names I didn't get, but who were just as beautiful as she was. They had stories of their own, but I forget them. Ana set me up and I leaned forward to the cocktail table, and it was exactly what I remembered it to be. I felt Deck's hand on the small of my back as I sat up. I felt it move, felt just the tips of his fingers curl around my side. I wiped my face like a lady. Used just my index finger above my top lip.

Pete was back—of course he was—two drinks in each hand. They were spilling all over him. Streaks down his silk.

"Bad girl, Audrey," he said and went to *tsk* with his index fingers but only spilled more liquor. "I saw that." He handed me one. It was brown but it tasted like water. I was thirsty. I had become thirsty. I finished it. Wanted the rest of them.

"Leave her," Deck said to him. Paul was still in his ear. Ana, though, Ana had moved to the back of the couch so that her ass was just about touching the back of Deck's head. It terrified me. It enraged me. Her dress was of a fabric I had never seen before and would never see again. Thick and soft and tight. Deepest blue. Made of evening sky. I could see the molecules of her perfume. Transferring from her to Deck. An invisible reaction. Science. Chemistry.

"Deck," I said. My voice sounded good. Nice and strong. A ringing bell. "Excuse me." I almost thought to call him sir, but stopped. I breathed out one half syllable of a laugh.

"You okay?" he said.

"Can you help me? With something?" I stood up. Newly electric. A monument. A suspension bridge. All taut. Wires and cables. Everything working, no excess. I brushed off the front of my dress. I took him toward the bathroom. Tried the knob. Someone in there. I bit down. My teeth were sound. I felt that.

"Come," he said, and then he led me. Stairs, hallways, the dark and then bright of another bathroom, this one bigger. Yards of white marble. "Are you all right?" he said after he shut the door behind us. "Do you want some water?"

"No," I said. My teeth. I needed.

I kissed him. Quiet and gentle, lips just touching his. Just touching. Like a sheet of paper could have fit between us. Then something else. It rose and rose. It backed him onto the vanity. It unbuckled him. It was dark and deft and moving. He did nothing. Hardly touched me.

"Love you," I said. I had to be careful how hard I bit his lip. I could almost feel it give.

"You know, I was wondering," he said when my mouth wasn't on his, was elsewhere. "You say you love me once, then nothing. I was thinking you went and changed your mind."

"Dirty trick," was all I could manage to say. Then he pulled me to him. Pulled my dress up. There was a towel rod I could hold onto. In the mirror behind his head I watched myself. My face changing. I wanted more. More pressure. Something. "More," I said and heard it before I saw my mouth go. His hands moved up, thumbs at the front of my neck, fingers cradling the back of my head. Pressure. A little bit more. A little bit more. "More," I said again. Fingers all the way around now, touching in the back. Tight. "More." It was a whisper.

"Jesus," he said. "Fuck." Fuck, fuck, fuck, Jesus. He pet my hair. He kissed my cheek, my mouth. "God, I love you too. I do," he said. "I love you."

The harps. The waltz. The crash of waves. I had done a number on his neck. I had known him nineteen days.

After that, after that I was a new country. I walked out of the bathroom behind him and felt routes expanding out inside me. Charting. Stretching toward borders, unclaimed lands. Rivers rippling with trout, the view from a mountain. A pioneer. A tent, a lantern, and a fire. A leather-bound book to track my journey. I squeezed his hand.

Trade secret.

All these years had passed, and it was only eleven thirty. Everyone was where we had left them. The broadcasters seemed warmer, their scarves unmoving.

Ana was looking at us. She could see the change. Pete too—he could see the change. He rushed over with more drinks.

"Chief," someone called again. Again and again, everywhere, people called the word *chief* as though trying to explain to me who I was with.

I still heard the music, though. So I didn't care about anything else.

"Here he is," one of the men said when we got there. I don't know. Forgot his name. His face was familiar. All their faces were familiar. Six or seven of them. Ten. Could have been Donovan or the commissioner or anyone I had seen in the halls at HQ. Could have been Charlie Ford. Was that Charlie Ford over there? Back against the wall, arm around a redhead? Wanting to tell me again that I'd fucked up? To wish me good luck? To warn me, to threaten me, to hurt me, to say, *Just you wait*? I didn't care. All I wanted to do was leave. All I wanted to do was go home and think about my new life.

"—Chief Brady, and this is Audrey," Pete was saying and pointing to me. "Smile, Audrey, you have such a beautiful smile." He had forgotten my name. He couldn't find *Virginia* anywhere in his head. Fine, that's fine. Introductions. I shook hands and shook hands. Hello. Pleasure is mine. So good to finally meet you. So good to see you again. Layers of names. I saw them flutter by on index cards, pile on the floor by my feet. Sergeant Tommy Barnes, Lieutenant Bill O'Hare, Chief of Support Services Denny Casey, Lieutenant John Mancini,

Lieutenant John Shore. I looked down. My favorite shoes. I loved them. I wasn't wearing the underwear he had bought me, but I wasn't wearing any underwear at all, so it was okay. It was better. I crossed my legs at the ankles and looked up at him. His profile. The edge of his smile. The harps.

That voice.

"I'm V," she said reaching her hand to me. "Audrey, was it?"

No, *I'm* V. It was Juliet. No, it wasn't Juliet. It was. It was. It was what.

Deck was next to me but talking to someone else. Then he turned his head, I saw it coming, saw his mouth move, he was going to say: *It's almost midnight.* But wait. Wait a second. Back up.

"Yes," I said to both of them. She was my height, same build, blonde hair, full lips, blue eyes, eyebrows on the thicker side, pearl earrings. Red dress, classic cut. Tasteful.

The dress. That's what I saw first. On a cobblestone street. This is how it came to me. Pieces of her. The dress. Then legs. Thin tanned legs coming out, heels on those cobblestone streets. Clicking, getting stuck in the cracks. Big sunglasses. The stucco of one building, then another and another. The sun coming through between them, a beacon. She had sweat on her upper lip, just a bit. She left it. She brushed her hair back, thought to tie it up into a bun. *Ciao,* she said to me.

Then that Italian sun finally got to us, and the lights in the party went up and the harps expanded to deafening—all those notes at once, all those beautiful notes—and someone in a robe, robes, gilt and brocade, came down just to show me. With a golden hand, a golden finger, haloed and brilliant. Came just for me, just to tell me this.

This:

You know her.

Verona.

Verona on Vacation: Oak Beach.

God, I wanted to say. *Hi. It's me.*

"V," I said and shook with her finally. She nodded. *No, not just you,* I wanted to say, *I am too. Remember me? V? Virginia?* But it would make no sense. She didn't know who I was, and how could I tell her?

I thought to try something else. I hope you enjoyed your Christmas. You look so pretty. How was your day? I'm so drunk. Oh, and listen, this is the man, right here, this one, the one I was telling you about, what do you think? I did what you said, and I think it's working because he just said—

The party. This party.

The house. The men. The girls. This party. Wait. Her hand, I moved my fingers along hers, a friendly gesture. *This is one of the parties, isn't it?* I wanted to whisper, I meant to say. Show her I understood, like I had understood for ages, since I had pulled up at the place. *Is he here?* I thought to look around for the man I had made in my head all that time ago. *My God, is he here right now?* The man she and I had made together. The man made from the drop, distilled down. That dull brown hair. Thick hands. Average. The killer. But I couldn't get my head to turn. I couldn't stop looking at her.

She squeezed my hand back.

"Are you okay? You having fun?" she said. "No offense, but you look a little—" She made a face. No smile, wide eyes, a scared child. "You want to come with us a sec?" she said and nodded behind her. To the two other girls standing there, to the whole big house unfolding out behind her. All there, all right there. "Come."

"Okay," I said. There was no thought in it whatsoever.

Deck didn't try to keep me there. He just let me walk away.

She took me up the stairs, still holding my hand. Through the same halls, back to the same bathroom I had just been in. *Look,* I could say, a docent, a guide, a yellow flag bouncing in my waist pack, *look, here is where he said,* I love you, *here's where he sat and where I sat and this is how I made him say,* I love you. *It worked, it all worked, just like you said.*

I said nothing. One of her friends shut the door behind us, locked it, then pulled her dress up as she walked to the toilet.

"Does he care if we smoke in here?" she said, sitting. "I forgot this one's rules."

"I don't think he'll have any idea," Verona said. She was at the mirror, her shoulder touching the towel rod. Just touching. It could still be warm from me. "I think he's concerned with a lot of other things right now and you can go ahead and smoke." She had licked the tip of her finger, was re-fanning her eyelashes. When she stopped, she just stood there looking at herself. Then she caught my eye in the mirror. Raised her eyebrows. I thought she might wink. Now is the time I say it: *You know me. We talk. All the time. Please, tell me, is the man here? Did you see him downstairs?* You know me, I said. But my mouth didn't move. I was watching. I was watching myself the whole time.

And then the first friend finished, flushed the toilet. And then the second friend, wrist deep in her bag, rustling, came toward us.

"It can wait a second," Verona said to her. "Put that down"—she gestured to the counter—"and come, Ceece, Jesus." Then to me. "CeCe doesn't listen. Refuses to wear waterproof." She licked her finger again and rubbed it gently, so gently under CeCe's eye. One and then the other.

Second bell, school bathroom, late to class. Laura handing me a ball of toilet paper, saying, *Wipe your face. Do not let him see you with your face red. Because you do not care. I know you care, but he cannot know that. Do you understand? Promise me.*

"Audrey?" Verona said. "Right?" I smiled, half nodded. "This is Audrey," she said to her friends. "Audrey," she whispered to herself, as though committing to memory, still fixing the smears.

"It's fine," CeCe said. "It's fine. You can leave it." But she made no move to pull away.

"It's not fine, though. You want big smears on your face? It's not a good look. Not fine." Verona leaned back, looked at her work. "Why you refuse is beyond me. But it's better. Good enough. Now we can." CeCe opened the small bag, started making lines on the white counter. "You feeling okay now?" Verona said to me. "You just needed a breather. Happens all the time." She, quickly, so quickly, moved her hand to my chin. Raised it, came closer. The way the man takes the woman's face in old movies, the way he steers her into kissing him. "Not bad," she said. "Can you show Ceece how you do this?" Verona said. "Maybe she'll listen to you." This close. This close I felt her breath on me, yes. Her fingers. Her skin, no wrinkles. Not one. No grays, no small hairs above her lip, no imperfections whatsoever. This close. "You want?" she said and then finally took her hand from me, gestured loosely at CeCe, the lines on the counter. "Can't hurt."

I didn't know if that was true. But I nodded. I did it anyway. I had not said a word.

I was a ball. I was a weight I was a mote I was a ring.

I held her hand on the way downstairs. We went back to where we had been. The men opened up for us, a circle loosening, admitting. We could have been anyone. But they were men and we were women, and so they let us in.

"There you are," Deck said. He slid his arm around me. The feel of it forced my eyes closed, for a moment, for a second, even though all I wanted to see was what he looked like when he found me again. I did not let go of Verona. "The ball," he said. He looked toward the television. A huge group, a mass of all those dresses. Ana the Terrible and Her Magic Dress. I saw the top of her head, bobbing, coked and happy. I could have been coked and happy. I will be coked and happy too. I am coked and happy. I am.

But her hand, the girl.

"Wait a minute," I said to Verona. "One minute. One more thing." It had been minutes already. It had been many minutes that I was holding onto her. "Listen," I said to her. She had her other arm bent onto the shoulder of one of the men, leaning into him. It was Denny Casey or Johnny Casey. Mancini, maybe. Her fingers curved and loose and just hanging over it. No, no. Those fingers. I saw her nails lined with dirt. The fan of that blonde hair on the ground, the wet dark. Marks on her neck. I couldn't help it. I couldn't shut my eyes against it because I would see it there too, on the backs of my closed eyelids. My imagination just went sometimes. It went and it went. It was a problem. It was a serious problem.

Listen, please, do you see him? The man from the car? His wet gun, all the rest, remember? Remember what you told me? I moved my mouth to do it. Nothing came out. I tried again.

Which one is it? Where is he? We were just looking at each other. *Who is the one who did it? We are friends, right? We are friends now and I'm just asking for your help. Help me.*

Help me.

She looked down at our hands, then back up at me. I saw her eyes move to Deck, his hand on my waist, his face near my neck. He was talking over my shoulder to someone else. His head turned toward whomever. And the way her eyes moved. It was furtive and it was a warning.

A reel. That's how. She and I, we were watching the same one. A movie reel, frame by frame. I saw the same things that she did and assimilated them as she did, and then she widened her eyes at me, like she did in the mirror upstairs, and bit her bottom lip the slightest, the slightest bit. I did, too, because I was doing what she did, like there was still the mirror between us. We were just a children's book. The worried heroine, only this time, two of them. Capes caught up in the sticks in the woods. A pink one, a red one. Over-turned baskets. A shadow approaching, a figure with its arms raised. The dark. I saw it happening. It was coming for me.

No is not the word. Not the word for it. I cannot think of an apt comparison. Stone. Ice. Something dead. The snake inside shedding its skin. The snake inside eating another snake, starting with the head. The snake inside eating a goat, or no, eating a man, the outlines of his body, still kicking, stretching the snake's skin from the inside. Making its scales shift. I had to ask. I did not want to ask, I don't think, but I had to. The drugs and the liquor and him right there and the harp music, still, though faint—I had to. I had no choice. "Look at him. At him, I mean." I moved my head toward Deck. He was still talking to someone else and had not moved his arm from me. "Do you know him?"

"What?" she said. She tilted her head at me. "Him?" Her eyes went to Deck again. She took in his face and then looked as far down as to his knees, and then she looked back at me. I was watching her the whole time. If I hadn't been, I would have missed it. It was an instant, a second. A big ship's sail blocked out the sun, moving slowly. A jet plane's shadow darkened the ground as it went overhead. Then her face brightened again, though she did not smile. "Of course," she said. She stood up straighter, and I looked at the hollows of her clavicles. "Everyone knows him."

"But," I said and stopped. "But, like." I looked at her hand in mine. Her bones under her skin. So fragile. I could crush them all. My hand a snake's mouth starting with her fingers, moving up her arm, taking the rest of her piece by piece. "But, like, he is not a bad guy." Told not asked. I did not ask.

She leaned toward me. I was biting the tip of my tongue, starting in on myself. I thought that in order to stop it I would have to reach my hand up and move my teeth, remove from my teeth the tip of my tongue. Physically. I was my own snake, my own meat in my mouth.

"Oh, these guys? They're all just charmers," she said. "A bunch of sweethearts." She winked at me. It wasn't a whisper; she was performing. She tapped the nose of the man she was with and left it there for a second like he was a puppy. "Isn't that right?" she said to him, and her voice turned syrup. Oh, my dear friend. You are here, right here in front of me, and we need to talk. We need to hash this out. Let's go back upstairs, to one of the dozen bedrooms this time, take our shoes off and get under the covers and talk. Leave the nightstand lamp on so I can see your face. And you can tell me everything. Everything you know, you can tell me privately. But please tell me it is not him. It is not mine.

The man she was with had gotten closer and closer to her. His nose was touching her neck. *You look so good tonight,* I thought of him saying. *Happy New Year. I'm going to fuck you hard. Are you ready for me?* He had his mouth open against her, the fronts of his teeth pressing on her skin, ready to feast. I hated him. I needed her more than he did.

"You know what I mean, don't you?" I said. Her eyes flicked to me and then away.

"No," she said to me. He was still at her neck, kissing it.

"Can we talk for a second? Can I borrow you for just one second?" I said.

"Okay," she said. Same as how she always said it on the phone. No hesitation. "One sec," she said to the man. She pinched his chin, let her thumb rest on his bottom lip. Almost the same way she had held mine. Her nail was almost touching his teeth; I saw it. A rope of spit. "Okay?"

We moved to the hallway, where I could still see Deck's back, his silver hair, talking to someone else with silver hair and someone else with silver hair. I blinked. Shook my head.

"I—" I said. I had her there. All I had to do was ask. There she was. "Thank you. For, you know, for upstairs."

"No problem," she said and smiled. She didn't go to move, but I felt it in her, the potential energy there.

"But, also, I just—I'm just wondering something." Enough. Just say it. Move your mouth, loose the tongue. "That man I'm with, what do you know about him? Do you understand what I'm asking you?"

The waiter, his tray of fake food, passed behind her, and she pressed in closer to me. Roses, heavily roses. Her hair touched my shoulder, rested on my shoulder. White near her nostrils. Not as neat as I was. I could reach out to fix it. I should have. She was my friend so I should have.

"Nothing," she said and stepped back when the waiter had gone by. "I have to get back over to that guy."

I brought my hands to her shoulders then, one on each, and squeezed. I didn't mean to, I didn't mean to squeeze, I just needed to keep her, I just needed her to help me. Her skin was so warm.

"Is he bad? Has he done bad things?" Don't you understand? Can't you hear me? Why don't you know my voice? Why couldn't she tell the feeling of my skin on hers? She should have known. She should have felt it and known right away. We were the same temperature, two bodies, and we knew, we knew each other. Upstairs, so close to my face that we were breathing in each other's air. She saw it all. The pores, the hairs, the errors. She knew me. She knew this was all I cared about, all I wanted. She had told me how to get to this very place.

"He's fine," she said and closed her eyes, an extended blink. On TV, they were gearing up. A tight shot of the crystal ball; I could almost make out its slow start down. I exhaled.

"Okay," I said and let go. Opened my hands. It was all I needed.

"It was so good to meet you," she said, super sweet, fake, but sweet, but hardly looking at me anymore, already turning away. Her veins had become racetracks, same as mine. All the engines still firing. Loops and ess curves. She was worse than me, maybe. But no one cared about anything. She was going back to her man, and I was going back to mine. I let it finish. The end. *Ciao*.

If it were possible, when I got back to Deck, I would have begged him to put his hand inside my back at that exact moment, move me like a puppet, ape my voice and say all the right words, then steer me to the television so we could laugh and cheer and toast and kiss like everyone else. Kiss. Our first New Year's kiss. We would remember it forever. December 31, 2010. Minutes after we had said, *I love you*.

We could have been home, in bed, the two of us. With no strange ghosts to tell us bad stories. With another bottle of cold champagne in an ice bucket and the ball going down while we weren't even watching. We should have left when I said to have left.

"Come," he said when I got to him, just like I had hoped.

"Ten," everyone said. "Nine." He was cast for this, he was born for this part. He wrapped his arms around me, pulled me closer. Swayed me like we were slow dancing. Closer to the television. "Two. One." Behind him, I saw it come down, glittering, hitting the bottom. And then 2011 lit up. Shining right in front of us. Nothing but promise.

He did lean me back. Had my neck in the crook of his elbow like that old photo of the people in the street, V-J Day. He was squeezing. *My head is a hive,* I wanted to tell him. *I shouldn't have said those things.* Also, *I know that girl, and I think we should leave.* He was squeezing and I wanted him to squeeze harder, needed him to so he would stop me from thinking, feeling. Wring it from me. My hands still hot from her. I needed him back in that bathroom again or in his car or on the deck, even: freezing, windblown, body temperature finally edging down, his hands back and forth on my pricked flesh, no mind to warm this time, just pressure and movement and no room for anything else. I thought of the words *drowning out*. I wanted him to consume me.

"Happy New Year," he said when he stood me up again, and his lips moving at my ear, this, it finally worked. Brought me back. It tickled all of the smallest things in me. It cleaned out that little box, the little room inside, deep inside. It caused a wild stir in the air there. Finally revived it. Me.

"Happy New Year," I said back, and though I didn't want to—though all I wanted to do was to look at him, at his eyes, the corners of his eyes when he smiled at me; to breathe him in, lick his neck, kiss all over what I had bitten—I looked at the room behind him. She was gone.

That night, he brought me to his house for the first time. I'd like to think he carried me over the threshold, my legs dangling over his arm like a smiling bride in a magazine spread. But I doubt it. I do doubt it.

CHAPTER TWENTY-TWO

New year, new you. Useless. January 1, 2011. High of fifty-two degrees, unusually mild. Sunny. I stayed in his bed. Let him do whatever. Asked him to close the blinds and got up only to wash him off me, get cleaned up for him again. He tore one of the straps of my bra, the Christmas gift. Swore it was an accident. *I'll fix it,* he said. *Replace it, I mean.*

At dusk he left to get us dinner, and I thought to look through his things to see if he was dangerous. If I could find anything that told me he was the one. The one doing it. I fell asleep instead. That was my decision, right there.

CHAPTER TWENTY-THREE

Had they been touching? Had I seen her touching him at all? Did she smile when he spoke? Was she jovial? Did she seem jovial to you? Did she seem frightened? Did she back away? Did the corners of her mouth turn down in disgust? No? In pleasure? I think she had a hand on his shoulder? I think she was saying something to him when I realized who she was, right? I think they were laughing about something, old friends, ha ha? I'm pretty sure? Wouldn't you say it was definitely one of the other men? Didn't you see the cold coming off of her toward that other man, the one she kept her back to? Any of them, actually? I saw. Yes, definitely, the man in question was any of those other men.

CHAPTER TWENTY-FOUR

I would spend almost a week waiting for her. A week jumping when the phone rang, answering breathlessly, whispering my name when I said my greeting: just waiting. Narcotics, narcotics, wrong number, narcotics. She was on vacation again, maybe. Overseas. Delayed. *Stay,* I wanted to tell her. *Everything is fine here anyway. We'll solve it all without you.*

I knew she was going to call. She was going to tell me. She was going to kill me with it. I could almost hear her voice:

I saw him last weekend at a New Year's Eve party, and I heard someone call him chief, so if that helps to narrow it down at all. He was with a girl. Thirty, I'd say, give or take, a girl I don't know from around here, maybe he brought her out from the city? Who knows. Really pretty, classy looking. Oh, thanks, V, I appreciate that. *How was your New Year's? How was your Christmas? I haven't spoken to you in so long. I was on vacation. I was down in South Beach. My God, it was nice to be away. How's it going with that cop friend of yours?* Here she'd needle me. She'd put the sound of a cartoon sexpot into her voice, all lips and waist. She'd toss her hair. Blonde. I really had not figured her for blonde.

I knew it was stupid, but I searched for her, desperate. Just Verona. *Verona is a city in the Veneto region of . . .* Verona plus escort. Escort companies in Verona, land of love. Barbies, one of them was called. Another: Euro Girls. Verona plus escort plus Long Island. An Italian restaurant in a nearby town with a mediocre rating overall but a reputation for great filet of sole. "Best-kept secret," one said. I'll bet. I got foolish, went mad. Made up names that I could pair with hers and searched the walls and pages and profiles of those who came up. Would you believe? Several Verona Careys. I was not creative. Like I said, I was foolish. I looked at their photos, their alma maters, their smiling children. Not her, not her, not her. I had nothing. I wanted to find her, to ask her more, to tell her to keep everything to herself after all, but I had nothing.

Deck that week, he ramped it up. Dinner out. Gentle, gentle Deck. PG-13 Deck wanted to hold my hand. Wanted to kiss the tips of my fingers while we watched television. Mentioned meeting my parents. *Yes, of course,* I said, breathless for this too. Deck attempted something one would call "making love," and it was me who ruined it. Me who made it depraved. We went to the mall. We had coffee together in the mall at around six PM on the Wednesday of that week, and then I watched him try on suits.

"The blue one," I said, sitting on the bench in the dressing room of a high-end department store, mind racing, wondering what we could do in there, that little space. "Definitely blue." We didn't try. Then we had dinner at a large chain restaurant with sticky chairs. We watched a child smear cheesecake on his sibling and Deck smiled at me. Smiled like, *Would you look at that.* I deduced then that Deck wanted children. Perfect. Let's act quickly.

"Let's go away," he said when he was signing the check. The best. The best words. "Want to do Montauk? This weekend?" I loved him.

"One hundred percent yes," I said. I was drinking white wine. White wine made me feel settled, adult. You can't be out of control and drinking white wine. *I told you, anything with you.* Cake slid down the leg of the table next to us. I finished my wine. Verona was somewhere far, far away.

Until Friday. First call of the day, just after eleven. I was watching the snow come down.

"Virginia, hey," she said. Too stern, much too much business in her voice. I sat up straight, waiting for it.

"Hey," I said.

"They found her. They found Gina. I wanted to let you know, so you could, I don't know, tell them or whatever. She's fine."

"Jesus," I said. Jesus. This is why she was calling, to tell me about Gina. Not to kill me. My lungs—with wings. Everything, winged. Sheet music of a church hymn unfolding, taking flight on the wind. I would sing too, sure. "Jesus, that's great. Thank God."

"Seriously," she said. She laughed and coughed, smoking. "I'm pretty fucking relieved, to say the least."

Okay, great, Verona. I'm so glad to hear from you, but I've got to go. Talk to you another time. Another day. Bye.

"Well," I said. "Thanks for letting me know. I'll get this to them."

Goodbye, farewell, fair Verona. Virginia on Vacation: Montauk. The End. Virginia on Vacation: Anywhere but Here. Forever and ever, amen. The End.

There was a lull and we were both quiet. I heard what sounded like lapping waves behind her. I imagined the Atlantic. Calm and smooth. A blue desert. I would sit there forever. Let her forget me. Let her think I hung up or we were disconnected. I should have just hung up.

"And, oh, so, listen. The real reason I called, actually. On New Year's Eve?" she said, asking it. Daring me. It was light snow, the slow kind where you think you can see each piece as it comes down. The big pieces. People always say this means it's going to stop soon. Verona, please stop, I'm begging you. This is not something I want to hear. I could have hung up. But then what. She would just call back. I could leave the phone off the hook. I could cut the cord. "I went to a party. Some big shot, house on the beach. I've been there before. The guy always has a bunch of girls there. He's gross, the guy whose house it is. Awful." That he is. "Anyway, bunch of cops there."

I'm sorry I can't take your call right now, Verona. I'm away, remember? I'm currently out of the office, but if you need immediate assistance, please call someone else. Or don't.

But it was fine. Because it wasn't him. There were so many of them there. I saw them myself. She's just going to let me know that she went to a party with all of these girls and all of these cops, all of these people, together. Just people, together. Just confirm that these parties are still happening, maybe give me an address, the name of the host. Because I didn't know.

She said he was fine. She told me herself. She said: *He's fine.*

"Seven or eight of them, that I knew of. Girls all over the place. Working, I mean. As always." She lit another cigarette. I pictured her, chaining them, blowing smoke to her ceiling. She was painting her toenails too. She was eating popcorn and flipping channels. She was shopping online for a bathing suit, bandeau top, same as the one she had seen poolside at a hotel on Ocean Drive. "One of them," she said, and I imagined her pointing her finger and narrowing her eyes like a detective on the cover of a book. Dark, dark, dark, flashlight with its yellow arc, trench coat, belt knotted at her lower back. "I know him. I've seen him before. I mean, I was beyond fucked up. But I know who he is."

"Oh?" I said. I tapped a pencil on my desk, let her hear the clicks. Virginia is thinking. "It's so hard without names. Without descriptions, you know?" Or wait. Something else. "You ever think maybe it was the guy you told me about? With the gun and the back seat? That whole thing?" I was trying to make her remember because I knew. It was a fact. It was a fact and all we both had to do was acknowledge the fact. I knew it was him.

"No," she said.

That's it? Just no? Okay. Moving on. Someone else, then. Someone else. One of the dozen others there that night.

"He had gray hair. Salt and pepper. Medium height and build, I guess," she said. "Forties maybe? Early forties? Handsome, actually." I tapped that pencil. Don't know, don't know. Do not know anyone who fits that description. But forty-five, to be exact. If we're stating facts.

"So many of them are salt and pepper, though," I said. Which was true. "They kind of all are. All the men here look the same." Which was ridiculous.

"He wasn't a regular cop. He was higher up." In my stomach, in everything of me, a draft. An open door. I tried not to let my voice change. The cold came in. It blew snow down my throat.

"Like a sergeant, or something, you mean." I said, snow melting. I made the word *sergeant* sound like a dawning, like the missing clue. Aha, a sergeant, yes. Well, sergeant rules out Michelangelo. Mrs. Abatescianni was right after all. Verona was right about him too. Rules out several people, many people, most people. It was not the man with the wet gun after all. It was not—

"Sergeant? Yeah, sergeant, maybe. How are you even going to tell them this? That one of them is doing it? Thank God you're not a cop, right? That'd make things bad."

Real bad. Thank God.

"Actually, no, you know what? Not sergeant. Someone called him Chief, now that I'm thinking about it," she said. Just like that. She scratched out her cigarette and stood up. I heard her stretch her arms over her head, saw the hem of her T-shirt rise. Her nice flat stomach, tan even in the dead of winter.

"Oh, is that so?" I said. Probably the room went black, or my chest constricted, or there was a bright flash or a sudden blankness. Suddenly! That's what you would expect, right? What you would expect me to say? Something like that? Couldn't tell you. "Name," I managed. "His name?"

"No," she said. Okay, okay. Breathe. "Chief is all I know. That's what I heard someone say." I could almost hear her nodding. "He's not a client of mine. He's usually alone, actually. But I think he had a girl with him the other night. Though, honestly"—she had sat back down, had lit another cigarette. Breathe, breathe. For some reason I pictured her smoking those long, thin ones—"Maybe she wasn't working. I don't know."

Maybe it was his wife, I could have said. *We talked, you know,* I could have said. *You and I spoke. My hands on your shoulders. The bathroom. The makeup. CeCe.* I could have said so many things. Instead, I straightened, continued with my script.

"Thing is, we really need a name," I said. "That way they can verify what department he's from. It's not necessarily Suffolk, know what I mean? Every county has a police department, right? Then there are the village departments, the state troopers. And so on and so on. So I just want to give them everything we know definitively." Casual, casual, been doing this a million years.

"Jeez, I don't know," she said. "I'm trying to think. I don't know that I've ever heard his full name. The girl he was with was Audrey, though. His girlfriend, whatever she was. That I remember. That should narrow it down for sure."

Audrey. Of course. But there is no Audrey. Audrey does not exist. None of these people have names, and so none of them exist.

"And you're sure it's him?" I asked. Rattling but keeping it out of my voice, keeping it buried. "Did someone point him out and say, 'That's the guy,' or something? There were several other cops there, you said, right? I mean, you said he's not your client?" I was reaching, leading her there and pushing her face down into it. *You told me he wasn't a bad guy, Verona,* I wanted to say to her, scolding. *I asked you at the party and you told me. Why did you lie?*

I heard Evelyn then, out in the other office. Laughing at the cop she sat with. Always laughing. They joked all the time. It made me so tired.

"It's just what someone was saying. One of the girls pulled me aside and said, 'Oh, it's Chief So-and-So doing this. I'm sure it's him, the crazy fuck, but he won't get caught. So just keep your distance.' One of the girls there that night." Quiet. Quiet. An axis, spinning, daylight breaking. Good morning somewhere else. Dawn. New day. I felt it coming out of her. Don't, don't do it, but I knew. I felt it. I almost moved my mouth at the same time as hers. "No, wait. It was Brady! Brady? It was Brady, I think. An Irish name like that. I heard someone say Brady. I can confirm, though, and then get back to you." She exhaled and quieted. Just like that. But oh, my poor heart. The poor, poor thing. It jumped in my chest. Lopsided. Last legs. Death throes. "I can ask around and call you back when I can confirm. So, I don't know—maybe wait to tell them? I'm going away again, so it could be a few days. But I'll try to call you back today."

"Well, thanks so much for calling, Verona." I could have said this and straightened my tie, shot my cuffs, stood up and buttoned my suit coat. Very professional. Name plate on my desk and everything. Don't call us, we'll call you.

"Honestly, Verona?" I said, and my voice had become shaky and weak, but I didn't care. It was the end for me. She had killed me like I knew she would. "I just really think you should be a bit more careful."

"I'm always careful, hon. I'm very careful with clients." Stubbing out another cigarette. Exhaling her smoke. She was looking in the mirror at her eyebrows. Judging the regrowth at her bikini line.

"No, that's not what I mean. Not like that," I said. I still heard Evelyn in the hall. The snow had still not stopped. "I mean careful as in you should really think about what accusations you're making. Because these are very serious accusations." She was quiet. "And it seems sort of unclear what you are even talking about half the time. One day you know the name, one day you don't; one day it could be one of your clients, one day it's not. What if you're wrong with this name and a perfectly innocent person's life is ruined by your accusation?" Two. Two lives. This little voice had risen to a controlled yell. Through gritted teeth. The way my mother used to do, but mean. Real mean.

She was quiet. She might have hung up? I hoped she had just hung up and we both would be spared. We can get past this; we will be fine. Then I heard her, still smoking.

"Well, you sure changed teams, didn't you?" she said. Her voice had gone nasty too. I remembered all the fights I had ever been in with friends. When things got bad and turned to foul after foul. The meaner, the crueler things you could think of, the better. Girls draw blood. Try to. I prayed I'd be able to stop myself. To control myself. Don't draw blood. Don't break skin. You are not the villain. "Do you want the information or don't you? Because I'm trying to give it to you. But if you don't want to take it, I'm guessing there are a lot of other people who will want to."

"Oh, I'll take it," I said. "And I'll give it to them. And then they can figure out how to proceed with one person's account. It's really not my business. It's none of my business or my concern." I started typing words so she would hear the keyboard clicks and think I was doing something.

I'm sorry. I'm so, so sorry, Verona. My eyes were welling up. I'm sorry but this is how it has to be right now. Please understand why. Just hang up. Just get off the phone. You can fix this. There's a solution. But it wasn't going to work. I stopped fake typing. I exhaled. I let the fat tears come. Gave up. I gave up.

"Why are you doing this to me?" I said. It was a whisper.

"To you?" she said.

"I want you to let this go," I said. "Please. Please, you don't understand. I feel like you should understand, but you don't."

"Honey," she said, her voice softening. Honey, yes, please. Call me honey, I am yours. Tell me what to do now. "What the fuck are you talking about?"

"It was me. On New Year's. At the party. I was with him, with Brady."

Silence. Typing from the hallway, Evelyn and the cop, ha ha ha. The snow coming down, fat flakes crashing.

"And I asked you about him," I said. "I was standing there with him, and I asked you if he was bad and you said no. So, please. Why now? Why this now?"

"Audrey," she said without asking. "Huh."

"Audrey," I said. "I didn't even pick it."

"But you're so—I thought you were like us," she said. "One of us."

"I am," I said. "I am one of you." I put the phone in the crook of my neck, put my head in my hands. "Listen, please. Can you just think about this? Before we move forward? Really think. It can't be him. It cannot be him. It is not possible."

Silence.

"Look, I don't know what to tell you," she said suddenly, coolly. Exhaling smoke again, unfazed. I thought I heard her fidgeting with a strap or a lace. Impatient. "These guys. I don't know what to say about them. But I'm helping you, okay? I'm looking out for you. Do you get that?" she said. "I mean, what are you going to make me do, call the news or something?"

Two choices. I could cry or go wild. I had already cried, and it had done nothing. Go wild.

"The news?" I said. "The fucking news? You're out of your fucking mind. You're crazy and wrong and just—just wrong. And I refuse to listen to fucked up, bullshit, back-and-forth from someone who—"

She hung up while I was still going.

I slammed the phone down and listened to the little bell ringing inside from the force of it. I could have smashed the thing.

I saw her on vacation and sunning herself, high-cut bottoms and the green bandeau, flipping on the half hour and running her thumb up the condensation of a Mudslide, eyeing her client so he'd buy her another one.

Repeat caller Caller states that her friend, an escort named "Gina," previously reported missing, has been found safe. Caller states that she thinks the person responsible for the bodies at Gilgo is a gray haired male of medium build, medium height, early to mid-forties, and that he is of a rank higher than sergeant, possibly a chief, within an unspecified law enforcement district, though she is unsure of the individual's name or district. Caller believes he is involved with a woman named Audrey.

Caller may be unstable and/or intoxicated. Caller said the name *Brady*, but caller has given conflicting information in past reports as well as in real life because she looked me in the face and told me it wasn't him, do you understand? She told me he was *fine*, and that's true because it's not him. It is definitely not him.

My finger hovered over the button. I would just click "Delete." I could do that. But the news, she was going to call the news. But this information was useless anyway. Based in fiction, untraceable. Useless. So the good in me muffled the dark in me and moved my hand, cursor hovering over "Print" instead. I clicked. Two copies. I heard the printer whir, warming. Then, immediate regret. Delete—I should have deleted. I would delete, I would destroy. I will destroy them both. I stood up to get them. But then. But then. Evelyn's manicured hand on the jamb.

"Oh, hi," I said. "Hello."

She eyed me over her glasses.

"Personal call?" she said.

"Yes, sorry," I said. "It was only a minute."

"I didn't want to interrupt. I didn't want to hover, but then I didn't want to interrupt." She moved her hands back and forth in front of her as though weighing something.

"Just a girlfriend," I said. I smiled. My lungs, sludgy. I smiled bigger to hide it. Evelyn reached toward the printer.

"You want this?" she said and leaned toward it. Her hand, her hand, her manicured nails.

"We were making plans. To go away," I said. My voice, water, blood rushing out of me. "Those are our things. Our, our itineraries. I printed them out." I saw her hand, closer, closer. But I moved. I got there in time, I don't know how. I flew, leapt, landed, just in time to get there first. My hand on the hot printer, on the hot pages. Our fingertips touched. But I got to them first. Took them to my chest like a baby. "Very exciting," I said. "We can't wait to get out of here for a little while."

She had heard it all, the whole thing, and I saw her calculating, trying to make her mind get somewhere. Pushing, digging. So I couldn't let my face move. Did not even move my eyeballs. I hardly breathed. I stared at her. I think she saw a glimmer. Digging, digging, looking for ore. I think she may have been close. Just about to strike. And I might have said something if she got there. I might have just told her the truth. Admitted it, start to finish, and then asked her for advice on how to proceed. But then she gave up, just like that. I saw her weak smile, hot in the sun, tired of digging. I saw her lean her shovel against the shed's front and wipe her brow. Done for the day.

"I was coming in here for something, but now I forget what it was," she said.

"Gosh, isn't that the worst?" I said. Gosh. "But come back when you remember!" Cheer, all cheer. I smiled at her back even as she walked out. Because someone could see me. I felt like someone somewhere could see me. Could see everything I had done.

When she was gone, I folded both sheets into sixths and put them into my bag. Then I unfolded them. I put them in my inbox under a pile of papers and a copy of the Rules and Procedures from 1999. Then I took them out and refolded them and slipped them into my overcoat's pocket. I erased the record from the system. Delete, destroy. I sat down, hands folded, calculating. Delete, destroy, delete.

Here is where I change again.

CHAPTER TWENTY-FIVE

But look, Deck did not need me to protect him because he did not do these things. Did not. I was making something from nothing, mountain, molehill, letting my imagination run wild to an unhealthy extent. It was not unheard of. This is how I lived my life.

We can't go busting down someone's door on just one person's word, Donovan had said. Donovan: A smart man. A good man. I trusted him and his tested wisdom. He had steered a ship through a huge storm. A tempest, really. The whole boat tossed up in a water spout, and who righted the thing? Lieutenant Donovan did. He made candle fuel from whale blubber and those hard crackers that kept his men alive. He knew what he was doing. He was a good man. Hard tack, that's what it's called. Also, he made salt pork.

Verona was going to call someone else. She was going to call the anchor from the local news and tell her everything, and there would be a report at five, citing new developments, an unnamed source, another bombshell, breaking news, a crack in the case. She was probably on with her right now, blowing smoke out in a French exhale and weeping. *It pains me to say this about a public servant and all, tasked with our safety, but I didn't know who else to tell. I had no one else to tell.*

* * *

Deck came in that afternoon around one. He caught me with my back to the door, watching what I was sure would be the last of the snow. I didn't jump at the sound of him because he didn't scare me. I only spun my chair around. And there he was.

"You all set?" he said. He stood, looking pleased, hands on his hips, like he had just come up with a solution. Like he had just solved a whole big thing. But he had no idea. He knew nothing.

"Well, hello," I said. He sat down in the chair in front of my desk. He stretched his leg, nudged out the doorstop. It creaked slowly closed on its own. We waited. "I'm all ready to go," I said when it had shut.

"Great. Meet me downstairs at three. The side entrance."

"Three? Really?" I said. "My hours are nine to five."

"Don't worry—I'll talk to your boss about it," he said.

"All right," I said. "If you say so." He looked at me, his arms crossed in front of his chest. He chewed at the inside of his cheek. Did he look more serious? Older? Angry? I saw a different edge in his eyes. Something sharp or, if not sharp, something unpolished. Raw. He was tired. He was probably just tired. He smiled then, the way he did. Subtle, only the edges of his mouth.

"I say so," he said. "Just send the phones to the front early." That edge. Was it an edge? Was it him? Was this the face of a man I loved? *The* man I loved. He bit his cheek, curbed his smile, like he didn't want me to know what he was thinking, that he was amused. "So tell me what else is new and exciting in your life," he said, sitting there in that chair, same as the very first time I had met him. He still took up the room. More of it. Everything. I looked at the brass on his collar.

I shrugged. "Just you, really," I said.

It was him. He was the one. He was my one. Was she right? She was right. He was the one. He was either the bad guy or he wasn't, and maybe he was going to kill me, but I was not scared or worried at all because it was going to end soon, one way or the other.

*　*　*

At three the snow had ended, and I climbed into his truck, looking over my shoulder to see if anyone was watching, if anyone would see me go. Not a soul. No one was watching anymore. He pinched my cheek gently when I was buckling my seatbelt.

"You're all mine," he said. "Finally."

But I always am, I thought. Thought, did not say. "Finally," is what I said.

Over the hum of the tires on the road, I heard the phone in my office. Ceaseless. Haunting me. I hoped Evelyn would get tired of its ring and unplug it, sneak right in there and crouch down and do it. She would never think to pick it up. Or I hoped that a mouse, disturbed, desperate, would emerge from its hole and gnaw straight through the cord, turn its back on the sparks and smoke and resettle itself into its home. But as we kept driving, putting distance between us and the building, the phone became quieter, quieter, silent. I could forget about it. And since Montauk was more than an hour's drive, by the time we got there, I was far enough away that all I could hear was the ocean.

An old mansion on a hilltop turned into a hotel. Some people said it was haunted. We managed to get there in time for the sunset. It was cold, below freezing, but we stood outside and watched. The sun streaked everything orange. Softened his face into a painting. I put my hands into the sleeves of his coat.

"I'm glad we got away," he said, his mouth pressed into the top of my head. He pulled me in, his arms stiff around me. A cage. Tight. He was stronger than I thought. "I need to be with you without anything else around."

"Mm-hmm," I said. Breathing him in. How tender, how sweet. He was mine. He was good. A decent man.

There was a player piano in the lobby, and I watched its keys go. I would have stood there watching for hours, but he pulled me to the elevator with the lightest tug on my sleeve.

Something changed when we entered our room. He seemed strange. Maybe it had happened on the way up and I had missed it, the exact second. He was cagey. That edge again. Up and down, could not stay still. Switched all the lamps on, then some of them off. Lowered the blinds, adjusted the tilt of them so only a sliver of outside showed through. Then the TV. Busied himself with the channels, stopped on the news. Oh no. Oh, dear God, no. Not the news, I beg you. But he changed it and put on a cooking show, volume muted.

"Want a drink?" he said, rattling around by the refrigerator. He had cracked enough ice out for two glasses before I even answered. I heard the hiss of the liquor when it hit, melting them. "Here," he said and handed one to me. A full glass. "Cheers, baby." *Baby?* This is not a word he used, not toward me. Baby. Strange.

It was good whiskey, I knew that. And that's what I chose to focus on. The good whiskey he had brought with him for us to share on this, the occasion of our first getaway.

"Very nice," I said. He was already at the closet by then, where he had put our bags. I could only see his back. Zip. I wanted him to sit with me. Zip. I finished my drink in a sip. "Come sit," I said and patted the couch. I was warmed immediately. Felt it going through. Zip, zip, zip.

He came back with his bag, still digging, zipping and unzipping pockets. A bit frantic. And then, couldn't help myself, I pictured it. All of it. All of the worst things. In there, in that bag.

"What are you looking for?" I said. "Come sit." If my body had cared at all, it would have been racing. I would have sweat everywhere and shortness of breath and the thwacking pulse of something very tiny. But I was under control.

"I am," he said. Disturbed. Not smooth. Unusual. His hair had fallen in front of his face. Even in the wildest middle of anything we had ever done, I had never seen his hair fall. He was nervous. Deck Brady was nervous. It was unprecedented. It should have been worrying. But still: nothing in me. Nothing had changed.

"I'm getting another drink," I said and went to get up.

"Don't move," he said and brought his hand to my chest, stopped just short of putting me back down onto the couch with force. "Have mine." He hadn't touched his after the first sip. Again, unusual.

"Hey," I said. I reached forward and put my hand to his cheek, and he looked at me, finally. He was bent in half over his open duffel, everything inside it messed, his arms elbow deep. "What on earth are you doing?"

And then he stopped moving. Closed his eyes as if in relief. He had found what he was looking for. He started to bring his hand out of his bag.

His gun? He would not use his gun. Too loud. Anyway, his gun was in his glovebox. His gun was on his belt. His gun was on his belt in a locker at work because he had finally learned his lesson about letting it out of his sight. He would do it during sex, I figured. Sex being so inextricably linked to everything else between us. The seed of us. The reason. Rope? No, no rope. He would use his bare hands with his nice nails and his nice watch, throttling, my hair against this upholstery, falling over the side of the couch, knotting beneath his knees as we both shook. His mouth still on mine, where it belonged.

His hand, toward me. His fingers, opening.

It was a small red box.

He looked at me and held it out, and there he was. Everything glossy and polished again. Even his hair was back in place. The golden twinkle of the stars on his collar. He still hadn't changed out of his uniform.

"What?" I said. Racing finally. Everything in me lit on fire. This is the thing that made my pulse go. This. Of all things.

Earrings. Diamond earrings.

"My God," I said. "Why?"

"I never see you with earrings," he said. He had leaned back into the couch, Chief Declan Brady, there sipping his drink like he had been watching television all along. He had been nervous. To give me a gift. How endearing, how sweet. This man, my love. My One True Love.

"Jesus, Deck, thank you." I loosened the back of an earring, went to move my hair out of the way.

"No, let me do it for you," he said, already leaning toward me. "Come here."

* * *

So, what could account for the roughness? Because he was rough. He did not move slowly over my body, reverent and thankful. Did not take the time to make everything sing. Did not. He put his hands on my neck, wrapped them till his fingertips touched, overlapped in the back. He covered my mouth with his hand, and when I bit him, he jerked it back and I closed my eyes, bracing, but then we shifted. We moved and he didn't do the thing that I thought he was going to do.

Afterward, I explained it to myself: He always holds your face like that, his thumbs there under your chin, Virginia. He has done the neck thing too, remember? You do remember glimmers of it. You remember asking him to do it. Then you remember asking him to slap you. Put that away. Put that back. He always has his hands in your hair, wrapped in it, ropelike, a good grip. Always. That first kiss, even. Remember? The very first kiss. He always moves like that, always says those things. Down to the word. He uses the same words every time, and you know that. He does. He does! And you egg him on, you beg him. You beg and beg. But it is not unreasonable that something felt different to you. You are in a different place, after all, a faraway place. And something significant has just occurred—the gift, the trip. And you are still upset about the call too. That's all this is. That's what made things different. This was a significant event between the two of you, and that's what's making you think like this.

He and I had just become closer. Closer still, no inhibitions. Because when we were done, he pulled me down and held me tight against him, so tight I'd smother if he kept me there, I'd die taking my last breaths into his chest, and he said, *I love you. You make me so happy. You know that, right?*

*   *   *

We went to dinner at the only open restaurant in town. We showered first. Then we went. We ordered burgers and more whiskey and watched the band play, set up in the far corner. Eight PM. Aside from us and them, the place was empty. I felt the weight of my earrings every time I moved my head. And even when I didn't, I felt them there. Metal and stone. Something permanent, tangible, driven through the flesh of my body. Stop. We were drunk by then. I was, anyway. I had brought a drink into the shower with us. I drank while I waited for him to get dressed. And so I was a princess there in that booth. Kind of. If I tried hard enough I could feel the scratch of tulle, the whisper of taffeta around me. No opera gloves, though. No suitor's sports coat. But I was doing the best that I could with what I had. Resourceful.

The news was on behind the bar, and I would soon see that she had called. The twenty-four-hour local news channel that looped the same few stories until they updated them at set times. Five, I'd guess. Eleven. A lost dog, reunited with its owners after six months of living in the wild. They showed the dog, skin and bones, its red collar dirty. The family in their front hall, indicating the dog's toys and its bed. I couldn't read the closed captioning to see the dog's name or the family's name or the town where the dog lived and had escaped from. A Dalmatian. Half feral, foraged on its own to stay alive, and then suddenly it's scooped back into the fold, forced to become domestic again. She had called. A story about something at a school, something to do with test scores, a scandal. Could not care less. Another story about potholes. She had called she had called she had called. Then, and I jumped at the very first frame of it—I knew exactly what it was—the brush, in the wind. The gray of the sky down there by the ocean. The same aerial footage of the same police officers and their dogs, combing. Searching. I had seen this footage a hundred times. I tried to read. But I didn't want him to see. But I tried to read. She had called, and it was done. He was asking me what I wanted to drink. Then by the smiley anchor's head, an image: "ONGOING INVESTIGATION" in all caps, with a depiction of a Suffolk County PD shield. If it was anything major, they would have done something different. They would have written *breaking*. They would have interrupted the loop, gone live from the scene. That beach, the ocean. The sight of it a mural already painted on the walls of my skull: the sea, the bushes, the sky rendered in grays and blues, smudges of color, brushstrokes. I went back to him. I felt time moving. It was going too fast. I felt like I had to be quicker, to keep up. I had to figure it out first, before anyone else did. Drunk, in that booth, I knew it was up to me.

"Why didn't you ever get married?" I asked. I'd say it came out of nowhere, but it didn't. It was something I was thinking of, obviously. And normally it would have horrified me. I would have flushed and mumbled something to cover it up. This is how I had gotten myself into trouble in the past. Always rushing, *never happy in the moment*. That's what an ex said. The ex from one of my other lives. But I was all right. All that liquor, him. I didn't care. Because there were things I needed to know. I was running out of time.

He even gave me an out. He touched his ear and leaned closer like he hadn't heard me.

"What?" he said. He squinted, pretending like he was trying to make it out. This actor over here.

"I said, why didn't you get married, ever?" Doubled down. He would have an answer. He had answers for everything. Never caught off guard.

"I just hadn't ever met the right person," he said right away, the slightest shrug moving his shoulders.

Hadn't ever met. I ran that choppy construction around in my head, held a light up to it, looked for breaks and dark places. Does that mean? That means.

"Really? That's all? I'm shocked," I said. "I'm shocked you've gone this long. That someone hasn't snatched you right up." I narrowed my eyes at him. Wanted to wink. Couldn't coordinate it. Drank more. Sometimes a bruise feels good, doesn't it? Like when you press it, the hurt is a little hit of sweetness or a lick of salt. A soft spot that you want to keep at. That you can't resist. I pressed it. "Didn't you date someone seriously, though? Cohabit and all?" I fucked up *cohabit*, added an extra syllable. No matter. "Cohabit, I mean," I said, correcting.

"Is there something you want to talk about?" he said. He sipped and then swirled his drink. That thing in his eyes. It was back. What and where. His sharp edge. A blackness.

"No," I said. The music had stopped suddenly, so my voice was too loud. "Forget it. Never mind." At that moment the band started to play "Southern Cross," which I thought strange, for winter, for an empty place. But I could make it into the sign I was looking for. I could do it with anything. I tried to listen to the lyrics. They would have meaning to me. They would illuminate everything. *Think about, think about.*

He came closer, put his arm around the back of my neck and his face by my ear. "If you have things you want to know, you're going to have to ask," he said.

You're right, I do. I have things to ask you. I want to hear you give me alibis. You were somewhere else, each time. You were working or with your mother or with Pete or at the grocery store—check the video—or with a woman, with Ana, even, Ana and her coke, fucking all night long. I don't care as long as you were somewhere else. You didn't do it. Any of it. Please tell me this.

"No," I said. I shook my head.

"No, there's something," he said. "What are you thinking about? What's going on in here?" He tapped my temple with two fingers and then pulled me closer so he could kiss it.

"Did you do something bad?" I said.

I had known him twenty-eight days. Four weeks. The average cycle of a woman. The length of a regular February. At four weeks, a newborn human will turn toward sound. He will find his own hands and feet, finally realizing that they belong to him. At four weeks, a puppy will wean, leave its mother's milk, try food for the first time, bye. Four weeks is significantly longer than the War of the Stray Dog, 1925, and longer even still than the Anglo-Zanzibar War, 1896, which lasted thirty-eight to forty-six minutes, according to varying accounts. Some people get married the first night they meet. Hours, half hours after they meet. See: Vegas. Some people, like my parents, become engaged very quickly. They were engaged after four weeks. Still married. My whole life up until that point, I'd secretly considered them foolish for doing such a thing, but at that moment I understood. I finally understood.

The band was taking a break. I saw its four members leaning on the bar. The stereo had come on. What is it like to drink so easily, to lean on a bar and sip from a beer and laugh with people you know?

"Ever in my life?" he asked. His mouth. Use that mouth and kiss me instead. Let's leave. Flee. Clear across the country. Anywhere. Don't tell me. Tell me.

"I guess. I don't know. Yes, ever," I said.

"Of course," he said, no hesitation. "Haven't you?" His hand had made its way into my lap. It just sat there. For now.

"Of course," I said. "Of course." I pushed a friend to the ground at a park and she bled, more than you'd have thought. I tricked a girl into sitting on a tack at circle time. I put someone's toothbrush in the toilet at a sleepover. I wrote math answers on my palm, peeked when I could. I cheated on an ex, but I was drunk and he was cheating on me, and I confessed in a flood of genuine tears in the end. Drugs, here and there, but we've covered that.

"Can we have another round of these, please?" he said to the waitress. I hadn't even seen her come over. I think I was up to beer by then. Bottle not tap. I remember scratching at a label.

"But what's the worst thing?" I said. My heart was keeping me alive, but only just. All of the pieces in me, just a body, just flesh arranged in a specific way to keep me alive. It was his left hand that was in my lap, and he was facing me, turned toward me, his right arm stretched out on the booth's top edge behind my head. When the new drinks came, he took his hand from between my legs, where it had only been sitting, unmoving. That's important.

"The worst thing," he said, thinking. He bit his bottom lip, looked up at the ceiling.

The girls. There are ten of them, in all. So far. Some are in a different place. Up on the North Shore, a little bit east. They haven't been found yet. They were all escorts. I pay for sex. It's just easier for me. None of the hard stuff you have with relationships. I mean, look, I'm a passionate person. You, of all people, know this. And so sometimes things get rough. They often do. I am gentle with you, usually, because I love you. I have a life with you.

I love you—you heard that? Well, did you? A life together?

I have no good explanation as to how it got that far with those girls. I don't remember the actual second it happened. The minutes it took. I didn't black out, but I don't know. I just don't know. I used my hands, only my hands. Isn't it amazing that your hands can actually be weapons? It's mind-blowing to me. Part of our body. Perfect weapons. Perfect tools. Something happens when I fuck them. It's something that comes out in me, in the heat of it. I'm just feeling so much at once. Is it an accident? A mistake? Yes, of course it is. But it keeps happening. I keep making the same mistake.

"I've made mistakes. In past relationships," he said. "You know, selfish things. Things I'm not proud of." He looked back at me and shook his head. "I just—it's hard. I work a lot. Relationships have always been hard for me." He stopped, watched my face for a change. Feeling me out. Something else was swimming within him, a river, its dark bottom. Murky, dirt stirred up. Something else. Some other muck.

"I've slept with women," he said and nodded slowly, looking away from me, looking at the far edge of the table. Tonguing for a word, his cheek bulging. "And I've paid them," he said finally. Said *paid* lightly, like draped in silk, discreet, delicate, fine. "It's just easier. Was just easier. I've never been good with a girlfriend. Never *had* been." He very carefully and patently corrected himself. He took the time to cut that *had* out of construction paper and stick it in there, right in between. He wanted me to see the scissors moving, the drips of glue. Put sparkles on too, Deck. Put sparkles. *Never* had *been*. Emphasis on *had*, his.

When I didn't react, he took a sip of his drink and then started talking again. I heard what I wanted to hear. "But the worst thing? I was engaged to a woman once." *Engaged.* "We were young. Really young, and so pretty stupid. I was anyway. It was a mess, and I couldn't figure out how to end things, so I made up a story about why we couldn't do it. Get married, I mean." He shook his head at himself. "I lied and it was terrible of me."

Young Deck, Deck in the late eighties, skipping out on his fiancée, too scared to get married. I was a child when this was happening. Sitting at the kitchen table of my family home, watching our house cat lick itself clean. A juice cup in front of me, a bowl of cereal. And where is she now, Almost Wife of Deck? Dinner party in a town not far from where we sat at that very moment, still at the appetizer course, forks clinking. Girls' night, gossip, lots of pink wine. Watching her college-age children, still home on winter break, play Scrabble with their father. I wanted to find her, ask about him. What he had been like.

A lie was his worst thing. A lie.

"So, you're squeaky clean otherwise is what you're saying?" I said. I was running my finger back and forth along the table's edge. It was wet and my finger slid, no friction. I was watching that. I couldn't look at him.

"More or less," he said. "What are you looking for?"

"No, I'm not. Nothing. I'm just asking."

"Most people you meet are decent human beings." He put his hand on mine to stop it from moving. "I mean, you're decent, right?" He didn't expect an answer; that question was only for show. He was touching my fingers, each one, one at a time. Up its length, back down again. "I'm no different. It really comes down to good decision-making."

"You're a good man, then," I said.

"I am," he said. "I'm one of the good ones."

For the rest of the night, he whispered things to me while we sat there. I wish I had written them down. Because those things, those are the kinds of things you want to remember years later, when you are a different person with a new life and you are trying to think of what used to make you happy. He put his hand back in my lap. We sat there for three hours. We went to sleep at one AM.

Saturday we went down to the dock, looked in the windows of closed shops, promised to come back in the spring and have lobsters with the coldest white wine we could find. We watched the water. Choppy and dark. Scary in its depth and temperature. We went back to the hotel, lay in the bed, clothed, and I stroked his head while he flipped channels: home shopping, an eighties teen movie, news. He stopped at the nature channel, left it, turned to me, and then fell asleep.

I had been holding it in, pent up, ready to burst, so here is when I watched him. Sober, both of us, more or less. Our drinks from lunch already metabolized out of our systems. His head on me, moving as I breathed. Slow up, slow down. He could hear my heart. The sound of my heart would infiltrate whatever he was dreaming. And what did a man like Declan Brady dream of? High school, flying, falling, the same things as the rest of us. But also, what else? Things that only a man like Declan Brady could dream of. Wet and beating things. Shadows. Tight knots and knives and terrible things most people's minds couldn't imagine. Things he had seen, things he had responded to. *I* could imagine them. The darkness in me imagined them then. I traced his eyebrow with the tip of my finger. Smoothed my hand on his forehead. What kind of violation it is to touch someone who is sleeping. I did it. I kept doing it. Ran my palm lightly against his hair. The flat side of my fingernail on his earlobe. This almost woke him. He stirred. A twitch, but he breathed deeply and then resettled on my chest. I moved my hand to his, put my fingertips in his open grip. I looked. Our hands, pressed together on the bed next to us.

I did not love him just because he was there, because he had materialized and in doing so had thwarted something else. Or because I was desperate for someone, anyone. Not anymore. I loved *him*. And I had never been more certain of anything before or since. The string in me sparked up my length. He'd be able to feel its heat through my muscles and skin and clothes. It would wake him and he would know; he would see me glowing with it. I let myself feel it, just let it go, arc and spray sparks wildly. Illuminating nearly everything inside.

On TV, the steppe: a lesser kestrel in flight, heading down for a mouse.

Here is when I thought of other women. Him with other women. He had slept with all of them. Every woman in the world. Hundreds a night, five, ten at a time. Sessions, installments. We are taught to think that no man wouldn't. I thought of what he said to them. I thought of his hands on their skin and how hard he squeezed and how soft it was and whether he wished it was softer. Whether he was longing for someone with softer skin. Waiting for the one with the softest skin of all. An apple, a glass slipper, a ring for the softest skin of all. I thought of what he said when he was done: *Jesus.* That's what he always said with me. What did that mean to him, Jesus? What, specifically, made him think to speak the name of God? And did he do it when he finished fucking all of the other women? This is one thing that I wanted to know.

Here is when I thought of the events, the coincidences, that I had up until then kept under blankets and tape in a trunk with a big brass lock. In an attic. I pulled them out. Why did he come in that day, that very first day? To congratulate me? To thank me? For taking a tip? No. It made no sense. I was no one. A civilian. Why did he bring me to the beach? The day of the press conference. Rewind. Think back. Think hard. He had found me in the hallway, I had been walking to Homicide, with a new tip. *An assignment,* he said then, after I had told him what it was. *After* I had told him. Then he said: *I'm reassigning you.* What did he do with that tip he put in his pocket after the press conference, after he had tucked my coat into the car and Charlie had seen and then had dissolved right in front of me? Why the double copies? The new procedure. He wanted to be in on everything. In control of it all. He had it orchestrated and arranged. And why was he always out on the road, gone for hours, days at a time? Christmas Eve. He was shaken. Why was he so shaken? His father? Really? Just his father? Shaken. And the anklet, for fuck's sake. And whatever else was in his drawers, in his glovebox, items I had not searched for and not found. I turned these things over—these coincidences, these inconsistencies—I brushed the dust off, scratched at the rust spots with my fingernail. I weighed them and appraised them. Really looked for their value. I closed my eyes for a second. And maybe I should have fit them all back into the trunk, nice and neat and closed the lid quietly enough so as not to wake him up. I could have slid the key into my mouth and swallowed. But, but.

A stocky wild horse with a short mane flicked its tail, trotted away as though it had heard a sound. It could have been the marmot, who stepped on a branch, made a crack that echoed and traveled, gathering momentum and volume as it went. That would have scared the horse for sure. Or it could have been the Mongolian wolf, watching. Unmoving. Its breath hot enough—close enough—to stir the hairs on the horse's hide. To make it run for its life. And what an idea: to run for one's life.

There was too much happening. I would have stopped breathing, just given up if I'd thought about it too long. If I second-guessed myself. Again, I know you want to know why and all I can say is: It was time. *Decision-making.* It was time to make a decision.

"Deck," I said, a whisper. He didn't move. My hand still in his. I had looked away from the animals. His breathing was slow, even. I tried to really see him. To look at his skin like I could see the cells—farther than the cells, deeper—the molecules of him moving there. Atoms bouncing around. Like I could see his hair growing and his skin wrinkling as he aged in front of my eyes. My future happening. Us, aging together. We were already aging together, right at that moment, rushing toward death, and we would every minute from then on.

"Deck," I said again. Nothing. A heat rose up in me, soft and barreling, a summer storm. It hitched my inhale. "I love you so much," I said. "And so this is, this is—it's why I didn't tell you this. I couldn't." My eyes filled up. "But the woman from the tip line—the one who started everything—she told me it was you. That you're the one who hurt those girls." I said *hurt* because I couldn't say *killed*.

"We saw her at that party, on New Year's Eve, and she didn't know who I was, but I knew who she was, and she told me you were fine that night. I asked her and she said you were fine." I had started crying. I bit my cheek to try to stop it. "But then she called back. And she said you were the one. And why would she lie to me? About something like that?" My nose was running into my mouth. "But, look, I don't believe her, right? She's wrong, isn't she? She only made a mistake."

That stage in crying, just before full body rattle. But no, no. The end was in sight. It was all over; I only had to keep it together for this moment. Just one more moment. So I breathed. I breathed and I counted in my head, and then I said, calmly, a different person, again a different person altogether, amazing how it happens, I said, "Deck, I don't know what's going on. I don't know what's going on at all, and so I want you to explain to me. I want you to explain to me that she's wrong and that you're good, a good person, and then I want us to get married and I don't ever want to talk about this to anyone, ever again." The front of my shirt was wet. "The tip is in my pocket and that anklet's at my house."

What then. What could one expect then. The things in his bag, the things in his car. Again his bare hands. His hands, he had said, his hands. He was still, stiff, rigid, even. He was a stranger. He was bad or good, depending on how you looked. Depending on the light. Depending.

My words hung. Hours, days. The stocky horse had made it, was grazing lazily at some outcrop, the sun high and relentless. Unscathed.

He tilted his head up toward me, and his eyes were open, irises brown, edged in yellow. A tiny ring of light, a fire around each.

"Anklet?" he said.

"Stop," I said. And it came out as a yell, and my voice was thin, lacy, ready to rip, ready to give. "Deck, please, Jesus Christ. I found it in your desk," I said. "Whose is it? Please." The crying came back. I tasted it. I ate the tears. "Please, just tell me something that makes sense." He closed his eyes; I could see him remembering.

"Yes, God, right. It was—it belonged to an ex. I'd given it to her as a gift, and she showed up at work one day and we had a conversation in the parking lot, and she threw it at me." He shook his head the slightest bit.

"A *conversation*," I said.

"An argument," he said. "It was a scene. People saw. A few of the dispatchers. One of the girls from the front desk. And then there was lots of gossip. I'm surprised you haven't heard that one." The little fires in his eyes seemed to dim.

"So I put it in my drawer, and I honestly haven't thought of it since." The anklet, way back in my drawer in another world, cooled and darkened, newly toothless. "And a tip? What tip?"

"Yes, the tip, the tip, the tip," I said. "The girl from the tip line." I waited for his eyes to rage. I could see nothing else. Just the brown, the yellow. I waited for him to do it, to finish all of it. Me. This is the way it would end. Just like this. And the eyes would change first. That's what would alert me.

"Virginia." And my name, still so soft, so warm in his mouth. The ruffle, the flutter, I loved him, I did. "Jesus, sweetheart, it's not me," he said. He said, "How could you even consider that?"

"I don't know," I said. He didn't move to embrace me, to dry my face, to kiss me, to unknot the drawstring of my sweatpants. He just let me be. He wanted to watch me decide for myself. "She just—she said. I don't know." I didn't know. "She made it sound like—"

"Everyone has a theory," he said. And this, I knew, was true.

"But what if she called back? While we're here?"

"What if she did call back?" he said and waited. Waited for me to say something, I guess. But there was nothing to say. I was nothing left, just the little bits of bone and meat and metal. Just barely those. "Listen, even if she does, it doesn't matter. There's nothing to worry about," he said, his voice that soft growl it got when we were close together. "You know me. You know who I am."

"Do I, though?" I said.

"You do," he said. "And the truth, it always comes out. Eventually. One way or the other. Trust me on that. I've been doing this a long time."

I closed my eyes so I couldn't see his anymore. The dim fire, the rage, whatever it would be. Whatever it would turn into. I didn't want to see. And then, while keeping the rest of his body still, my hand in his, he traced a line around my ring finger, left hand, with the tip of his thumb.

We stayed until Sunday. We were our best selves. No bad habits. Woke up on the right sides of the bed with fresh breath and clear eyes and smooth skin, ready for each other, over and over again. Playing house, sure. I wanted him to see what I would be like as a wife. What it would be like, our entire life stretching out in front of us. Day after day. Our future just beginning. Like I said, we stayed until Sunday. Not a word of it between us. He was unruffled and affectionate, touched me gently any chance he got. *Trust me*, he had said, and so I did. I did what I had to do. I trusted him.

CHAPTER TWENTY-SIX

Donovan was there in my office when I got in on Monday. He had unlocked the door for himself. McHale and Charlie Ford and his partner, Tony. All of them. Evelyn didn't even look up as I came in.

"Good morning, everyone," I said when I saw them. Then I realized what was happening, and I turned and left before crossing the threshold, because the threshold was a boundary, and that's where things would really change.

CHAPTER TWENTY-SEVEN

Donovan was there in my office when I got in on Monday. He had unlocked the door for himself. McHale and Charlie Ford and his partner, Tony. All of them. Evelyn didn't even look up as I came in.

"Good morning, everyone," I said when I saw them. "I'm glad you're all here." I stayed standing, as though I were making a toast or a speech as a maid of honor. A bad dress. Chintz. Pink. Bad. "I have something to tell you." I'd had second thoughts. It was all a mistake. Charlie looked up, his thumbs poised over his phone. I let my eyes tear, didn't even try to stop it. I let a fat one fall onto my cheek, roll down to the corner of my mouth. "I don't know how to say this, really. But Chief Brady." I let my head drop, my chin to my chest. "I think he did it. All these girls." I let it take me, shook with it. Near hysteria. Donovan came over to pat me on the back. I hugged him instead, pressing my face into his shoulder.

"Tell us everything," he said. His hand moved in a slow circle between my shoulder blades. "It's okay, sweetheart, just tell me everything." He smelled like saltwater, of course. It was the closest he had ever been to me, and I realized that he smelled like saltwater and sand. What else could I do but tell them everything.

CHAPTER TWENTY-EIGHT

Donovan was there in my office when I got in on Monday. He had unlocked the door for himself. McHale and Charlie Ford and his partner, Tony. All of them. Evelyn didn't even look up as I came in.

"Good morning, everyone," I said when I saw them.

Donovan was sitting in the chair; Charlie, McHale, and Tony, leaning on the walls. Charlie didn't make eye contact, scrolling his phone, as usual. McHale was reading something. Tony, I don't know. Who cares.

I sat down without taking my coat off. I was too cold. Also, my shirt was wet near the chest placket where I had tried to clean a spot that morning.

"Virginia," Donovan said, "we need to talk about a few things." He rubbed his hand down the front of his face. This captain. Upset with me. Disappointed. The young sailor is written up for violations. Insubordination, wrongful this, failure to. "I hate having to put you on the spot like this," he said. "I apologize in advance for it."

"Yes," I said. "Okay." They could see me shaking. They could see the way my pulse beat in my neck, the lift and fall of the skin there. They were trained at this. They could see the dilation in my pupils, whether my eyes darted or didn't. If I was too agitated or not agitated enough. I didn't know which was appropriate. There was a right way for an interviewee to behave. Was I praying at this point? You could say so. I had my hands in my lap, one on top of the other, and I had the words of the Our Father going, over and over. I hoped my mouth wasn't moving along with it. What if I thought of the terrazzo floors of our local church, of the vinyl on the kneelers, the smell of the pages of the hymnal? I did. What about the priest. When I walked up to the priest, my hands clasped just like now, and when I opened my mouth for him. I thought of that. Had to stop from actually opening my mouth. Imagined instead the dissolve of starch on my tongue, the walk back to the pew, the few minutes when people were quiet and bowed and as holy as they would be for that whole day.

"So, look, Detective Ford spoke to a caller on Friday after you left for the day."

Verona.

Oh.

She'd called back. I had known it was going to happen. I had known it. I had known it and still I had left. Myopic, love drunk. She had confirmed the name, and she was calling to let me know. To kill me with it. The final blow. And since I wasn't there, she would tell anyone who would listen. Enter Charlie. So she'd told him. They'd spoken about it together, these two, both who hated me already. And so now he knew too, and he wouldn't hesitate.

Repeat Caller Caller states that she would much prefer to speak with Virginia and would like this added to the record. Caller states she goes by the name Verona. Caller may *be intoxicated. Caller states that one of her colleagues, an escort using the name Ana, has several times been intimate with Chief of Department Declan Brady in his department-issued SUV after indulging in alcohol, cocaine, and/or other recreational drugs at house parties. Caller states that Ana can confirm that the subject she alleges to be Brady behaved in a manner that was—*

That was—

That was—

—striking in its tenderness and that she was very surprised by that. She hadn't expected it from him, for him to be "a candles and roses kind of a guy." She said he was thoughtful and gentle. Caller states Ana is currently unavailable to speak with detectives as she is en route to Brazil. She is eschewing phones and other technology forever. Send a letter. A telegram. An SOS. Sorry and good luck.

Sorry and good luck, Virginia.

"She hardly spoke to him, I should say."

"Oh?" I said. I looked at the clock. The host had almost dissolved. I tapped my left front tooth with my fingernail. I was waiting for the rest of it too. *Virginia, this is for your own good.* Donovan would say this with a hand on each of my shoulders. He'd be looking down. The sun coming in, Charlie and the others watching. Standing behind him like an ensemble cast. *Declan Brady is a dangerous man. We have good reason to believe that he is involved with the deaths of these women and that there are more women that have yet to be found. He has a checkered past, skeletons in his closet, dark secrets, etcetera.*

"Which caller is this, again?" I said. That, Virginia, that is a very good question. The skeletons, I ignored them. They could stay where they were. They could sit, dusty, rattling against each other, mouths wired shut. I tapped my front tooth, still.

"Virginia, you know which caller this is." This from Charlie Ford, who had finally put his phone down. Who was fed up and ready to let loose. Taking it out on me. Charlie with his *you'll see* finally coming to fruition. It pleased him, I could tell.

"Oh, the girl? That girl who keeps calling?" I said. *That girl.* That girl had told them everything. That girl had ruined my chances. That girl had set the ball in motion, and now they were going to take him from me. In minutes. They were going to surround him and take him away from me, and it would all be over.

"He didn't do it. I know he didn't. I know what it looks like, what she told you, but I know him and he didn't. He couldn't have." I opened my mouth to say all of this, but a rush of cold air from downstairs stopped me. I felt the door open and then creak slowly shut. The skeletons swung on their hangers. His shoes on the linoleum. He climbed the steps slowly, blowing his coffee cool. He patted his coat pocket, realized he had left his phone in his truck, stopped to turn back but didn't. *Fuck it,* he thought, *Get it later.* Kept walking. The hall was a vacuum. I smelled his cologne. Sensed his distance. Could see in the dark and from hundreds of yards away. The vibrations, the electricity of a body, emanating. Messages sent, received. I was an animal then and now and forever because of him.

"Good morning, Chief," Evelyn said from out in the other office.

And then there he was.

I watched them for movement. They were going to approach him slowly, still professional, all of them. Respect undying, even then. They were going to lean closer, lower their voices. *Boss,* one would say, *sorry about this.* Or maybe it would be Charlie's job, his case, after all. He'd skip the polite, knock Deck around, take pleasure in it. No, no. Someone else would have to come in to do it. I had a feeling they had to have an outside agency in, something about jurisdictions. And it would be a stranger who did it, and that stranger would press Deck's arms together behind his back and cuff him, gently, gentlemanly, but cover the cuffs up, decency still, even in this, and then the stranger would walk him out to a waiting car, an unmarked car, an FBI car, probably. I saw his coat blowing open in the wind, his exposed shirt. He would be so cold.

No one moved.

"What's happening, gentlemen?" He looked around the room. "Ms. Carey, good morning."

Something. Something was happening. Was going to happen. Maybe it would take them a minute. They had to read him his rights or wait for the FBI guy to come up and do it himself. The FBI guy was probably downstairs, waylaid, getting a cup of coffee or taking a piss or talking up the day shift at the front desk, three pretty girls. Fidgeting with the clip on his gun and licking his teeth, leaning over to look.

"Morning, boss," Donovan said as he stood up. He was going to. He was going to. He inched closer. He was going to. "You want my seat?"

"I'm fine," Deck said, a little edge there. "What are we all doing down here?"

"Well, see, this is tough," Donovan said, starting. He was going to. "We're, we're just trying to get to the bottom of something."

"Okay, what is it?" Deck said. Impatient now. "How many times are you going to make me ask, boys?" He peeled the cap off his cup. He looked around at them, one by one. Then at me. He stopped on me.

The night before, I had slept at his house, restless the whole time. I kept waking to check if he was there. I couldn't get enough of it, the look of him, the look of him as we started our new life. The first night of the rest of our lives. Him safely next to me. Ten times I woke. More. And always, he was there. Right next to me. Every time. The whole night. Except for once. Only once was he not there, but I heard him in the bathroom. I heard the sigh of the tap, the gurgle of the drain, the shriek of the pipes, hot water faulty. I could swear it. I could swear to it that he was only just down the hall.

The night before, when I actually managed to sleep, I could have dreamt of his being taken from me. I could have prophesied. Deck in an unmarked car, sitting in the back seat, the saddest place I could imagine him. He did not belong in the back seat of a car, ever. And the problem was he couldn't see me through the window, through the glare. In the dream it was summer and sunny, hazy, cicadas, and I was crying so hard that I couldn't wave goodbye. I was sweating and crying, and the sun was turning the top of my hair too hot and the tops of my shoulders red. They were bare. I was wearing a sundress with slight cap sleeves. But I hadn't dreamt at all.

That very morning when I left him, I kissed him goodbye as he was buttoning his shirt, and he took his hands from the buttons and balled my hair in his fist and held me there. For an extra second. Neither of us said *I love you*. I could see that we were on a precipice. I could see a river swirling below. We only kissed.

"A tipster called on Friday," Donovan said. "After Virginia had gone for the day. She spoke to Ford." The end. That's it. And I had been close, so close. I had almost gotten everything I wanted. I had almost made a new life for myself. I swore I saw Ford—Ford to me now, Charlie was gone—narrow his eyes at me.

He kept going. "After a few minutes she got frustrated with him and said she had already provided us with information. Provided *Virginia* with it, actually, and had no interest in talking to us. She only wanted to talk to her." He sighed and looked from Deck to me, then back. "The problem is, Chief, we don't have that information. Sergeant McHale and the Homicide squad do not have any of that information. So we're just trying to find out why it never made its way down there and where it's at now, that's all." To this day, I don't think Donovan knew anything had happened with me and Deck. He only continued to steer his ship, rain falling all around him.

"We go this crazy over anonymous tips now?" Deck said and drank his coffee, winced when it was too hot. Then he smiled that smile.

"Well, it's the same girl who told us about the bodies in the first place, so . . ." McHale said.

That stopped Deck for a second. I saw. But only a second.

"Aha," he said. He said, "Virginia? Do you know what this is about?" Still, my name when he said it. Still, gilded and shining. Its own pulse. Why are we here? Why did we come here today? Why didn't we just stay where we were? Montauk. The lobby. The player piano. The cold ocean on every side. My body ached for that faraway cold. We could have stayed out there. Could have worked on chartered fishing boats, both of us. Could have learned to clean fish, slash and scrape and scoop out guts and bone, let it all fall into a waiting bucket with a wet thunk. We could have waited tables. Made beds and cleaned hotel rooms and cracked cold beers together when our hard days were through.

Let's go. Let's go now. Deck, marry me and let's go now. I looked to him, asking him, telling him, telepathy, with my eyes. This is what it would come down to. This was it.

And then he nodded, solemn. And in that nod a signal, a symbol, a stand-in for a question. The question I'd been waiting for the whole time. My whole life.

In the end he asked me with a nod.

"I do," I said. An awakening. My yes. "Yes, I do remember the call. I'm so sorry. But she said her information was unconfirmed. That she wasn't sure and so she was going to call me back. She was going to double-check a few things and then call me back. That's what it was."

"Oh," Donovan said. "Yes, well, that does happen." He looked to Deck for approval.

"Not a problem," Deck said. "Not a thing to worry about." His eyes soft at me, his eyes different already. Different again.

I heard them going all the way down the hall after they left. The change in their pockets jingling. Their guns on their belts as they walked. Someone silenced a vibrating phone. Someone half laughed and then said, *Ah, fuck.* A door closed behind them and they all sat at a conference table. One of them fidgeted with a pen. Out in out in out in. One of them flicked a paper clip and sent it flying to the floor. Clink. They all listened to the hum of a dial tone as they waited to connect a conference call.

After they left, Evelyn tiptoed in like someone was listening, watching us. She shut the door. She stood there, eyeing me, hand still on the knob behind her. Deciding.

"Come in, come in," I said, hushed like a younger sister up too late, hiding under the covers. "What happened?"

Then she told me what had happened.

The tipster, hereinafter known as "Verona," called on Friday afternoon at 3:18 PM. Just as Deck was chucking my chin or pinching my cheek or whatever he had done, just as we had started our drive. The phones had been sent to the front desk, as ordered by Chief Declan Brady. This was consistent with protocol; the front desk took calls on nights and weekends and any other circumstances when tip line staff was unavailable to perform assigned duties. Verona asked for me by name, hesitated when the front desk attendant said I was unavailable but that she would be happy to handle the call instead. Front desk staff then transferred the call to Homicide, as directed by Detective Sergeant William McHale. The call was subsequently answered by Detective Charles Ford. Verona spoke to Detective Ford, noticeably agitated and uncomfortable with giving him information, and then ended the call abruptly.

"So," Evelyn said when she was finished, "that's where we are." She sat back at this, this nothing information, just about gasping, a depleted medium. I expected her to close her eyes, to ask with shaking hands for a cup of tea and her beloved Pekingese. A throw to cover her lap.

"But what exactly did she say?" I wished for the phone to ring. I saw, on the edge of my desk, Deck's coffee cup. He had left it. It heartened me, just seeing that cup. It meant that he would be back. He would not have left it accidentally. I wanted to think that he was not the kind of person who would leave something behind accidentally. I wanted to think that he did not forget or misplace things. That he was not sloppy.

"She said she had already spoken to you," Evelyn said and looked at me like I was stupid. And she was right: I was stupid.

"That's it?"

"I think that's it."

But I knew that couldn't be it. Verona had wanted to get to me because there was something else, and maybe she had already told Charlie what it was.

It was: She had confirmed. She'd gotten the name from Ana, written it down and everything. I would wait while she fished the scrap from the bottom of her handbag, flattening the creases, clearing her throat to read it like a proclamation. Translating the purple ink and the fat bubbles of her own script and the flourish of the Y, a long tail that wound around and petered out under the B of Brady. You hear that? Brady. I told you so.

It was: She wanted to clear up what had happened between us. And here's where we'd both apologize, talking over each other, promising never to let it happen again, the way all these things between friends are mended. *I'm so sorry*, I'd say. *Please forgive me. You have no idea the stress I'm under.* My mascara would run while I cried to her because I did feel awful about what had happened, I did. *Waterproof*, I'd hear her chide. *Come on, V, you know better.*

It was: She wanted to warn me. First she wanted to compliment my dress from the party, so classic. My hair. Again, the makeup. She wanted to make plans to meet in "real life" soon, maybe next week? But more than that, she wanted to warn me, in no uncertain terms, about this man, this type of man, men in general, every single man.

It was: She had been mistaken after all. She had a different name, a different man altogether. She had been mistaken, God forgive her. Get a pen. Are you ready to write this down?

CHAPTER TWENTY-NINE

The phone.

Silent.

I waited for her. I steadied myself, ready to—ready to what. To beg, I guess. To beg her to return to her life and to leave mine alone. To let our lives diverge from here, never to intersect again. To apologize and plead for forgiveness. I had been cruel. She was just trying to help, and I had been terrible about it and I was so very sorry. Verona, let me make it up to you. Anything you want, but please just let this go.

Deck hadn't come back. It was getting later and later. Too late. I was waiting for both of them. I didn't know which one I wanted more. It was half past eleven. Sunny. High of. Just about. Please with this. No one cares anymore. No one remembers the weather. Something was very wrong.

I could call my mother, while I was waiting. For comfort. For a distraction. I could listen to her move from room to room and look at her life as she did so, making sure all of its pieces were still unharmed, intact. *What a miracle!* she would think upon seeing all of her things, upon running her fingers against the cocktail table's leg and the edge of the kitchen countertop and the knife pleats of my father's shirts,

251

heavy starch. Such triumph that nothing terrible had happened to them in the night. There was a specific spot on a den area rug: It took the vacuum in a way that left profound cleaning marks. She would start there and continue her inventory well into the afternoon, the evening. What pleasure to have this diversion. How I envied her. How I wished to do this in my own home with my own husband's crisp shirts smooth and cool under my hot palms.

The phone.

Vibrating.

A phone somewhere vibrating. But my phone was on my desk right in front of me, silent and dark. Another phone, then. A phantom phone, a phone in my head, a phone in my bones. Verona? But there, there at the very edge of my desk, its buzz slightly fuzzed by the stack of papers it sat on: another phone. I reached for it. Here is an answer, I thought. A prop, dropped in, just like that.

"Back so soon, Ford?" A man's voice from the hall—the same voice that always came from the hall—jokey and with its ever-present smile, and I pulled my hand back just in time before Detective Charles Ford, suit coat on, no parka, purposeful, entered my office. It was strange to see him like that again, the replaying of a far-off and discarded memory. I almost imagined him with two coffees. He stopped feet in front of my desk.

"Forgot my phone," he said and pointed, as though I needed to be shown.

"Oh," I said. I reached for it and picked it up and held it in my hand, though I made no motion to give it back. "Right."

"So? May I have it?" he asked. Slight uptick of his chin, challenging. If you had asked me at that exact moment, I wouldn't have been able to decipher: inflating or deflating. Only that my insides were a rush, a blur, a gasp. So I just asked him.

"What else did that caller say to you?" I said.

This time he did narrow his eyes at me. Tilted his head.

"What makes you think she said something else?"

"No, I just mean . . ." I said. My neck warmed. I felt the wet spot on my shirt. Almost dry. I was waiting. Waiting for my phone to ring, for Deck to come back, for a knock on the door, for someone to save me. Praying. Help. I knew she was going to call.

"Of all possible things, what is it that you think she could have said to me?"

"No, I don't know," I said. "I have no idea." He must have seen me flush. "I was just asking."

"Are you nervous about something, Virginia? Is there something you want to say?"

"What?" I said. "I don't understand." I shook my head, willed my flush to die. I imagined again the ice. "No."

The phone.

Silent.

Verona, please. Please call.

"Right. Of course not. Well, I'm not really at liberty to disclose details of the investigation, as you of course know. So, unfortunately, I can't share anything else she may have mentioned." He made a fake frown face. "But you know what, I think it'll all come to light soon enough anyway," he said. He nodded slowly. "These things seem to just open themselves up sometimes. Lay themselves bare, the answer right in front of you, you know?"

I could only nod.

"The phone?" He looked at my hand.

The phone.

The phone. The tip line, it was ringing. I had forced it to ring. Our telepathy, a miracle still. And here she would be, ready to help me unravel the whole thing.

I held out my arm, reached his phone to him. His fingers touched mine as he took it. Nothing, two hands touching, no life between them.

The tip line rang again.

Charles Ford turned from me and started to walk out. "Good luck," he said without turning all the way around. I heard the *You're going to need it,* regardless of whether it was actually said.

"This is Verona," I said. I skipped the speech. It didn't matter. I had meant to say Virginia, of course. I'd meant to say my own name. And then to start right in on my apology to her. But I got tripped up, fully confused, and what was the difference between us at that point anyway?

"Hello, is this the tip line? To report a crime?" An older man. I saw his hunch. For God's sake not now.

"Yes," I said. "What can I help you with?" Not pleasant, not sparkling. I was just a voice from a body. There was not much left. I had to conserve what I had. Other things were coming. I needed not to disappear.

"My neighbor," he said. "There is definitely something happening at my neighbor's house. In the way of narcotics sales. He has cars coming up morning, noon, and night. The guy leaves his house and walks out, hands something through the car window, and then done. Goes back inside. His name is Samuel Gibson, 147 Myrtle—are you getting this?"

"Okay," I said.

"Okay?"

"Okay, sir," I said. "Got it. Anything else?" I needed to get rid of him. If I had him on the line, I couldn't have her. It was one thing or the other. Always.

"He has these two large dogs that lie in the side yard," he said. Then, cued up, someone called, *Action*, and the dogs— or some other nearby dogs—started barking.

"Mm-hmm," I said. "Right."

I was closing documents on my computer. Trashing files. Rearranging icons. I just had to wait him out. I was scrolling through the email address book, looking at names. It was something I did sometimes, in lulls. I started close, but just above, so I could feel a little bump of surprise when I saw it there, spelled out in print. Barnes, Thomas—Detective Sergeant. Bouchard, Richard—Detective. Boyce, Patricia— Police Officer. Braddock, Emily—Programmer Analyst. Brady, Declan—Chief of Department. His extension. I was just a girl in junior high, writing on the back of a notebook. Curlicues and hearts. Mine and his. Forever and ever.

"This is a bad dude," the old man on the phone said. "My wife has seen him with what she swears is a gun. She's right here. She can tell you herself. Sonia? Come talk to the police. Tell them."

Farther down. Carey, Virginia—Public Relations Spe- cialist. That's the title they had come up with for me. It was a reach. But it made sense, in a way, I guess. After me: Car- mody, Angela—Senior Clerk. Casale, Joanne—Principal Clerk. Joanne of the orange cats and shiny glasses. Casey, Dennis—Chief of Support Services. Cassidy, James—Police Officer. Castro, Maria—Police Officer.

And then: Casey, Dennis. Denny Casey. Chief. Chief Denny Casey. Chief, Chief, Chief.

Of course.

Of fucking course. She's thinking of Denny Casey, not Declan Brady. Denny Casey, chief of Support Services. I clicked his name. In the place where a picture would be was a grayed-out shape of a head, a placeholder. I clicked on my name. Deck's. No one had pictures. I reached for my phone, searched for him: Dennis Casey—Chief of Support Services, Suffolk County Police Department.

A photo from a groundbreaking at a community center, he helped hold a golden shovel. Smiling. He was gray haired, same height as the town supervisor who stood by his side, about the same as the rest of the men in the picture, not unattractive. One of the seven or ten men I remembered from the New Year's Eve party. The one whose shoulder she was on, the one whose teeth were at her neck. The one who, the one who.

The man on the phone was gone. I don't remember hanging up. But the handset was back in its cradle and I had taken the tip, written down an address and a name, and that was good enough. That was just fine.

She had just gotten confused. And why not, why shouldn't she have? The names were so similar. The hair, the height, right? Chief, even. I would have gotten confused if I didn't know Deck like I knew him. It's why she was calling back. She had figured it all out. Of course she had, always a step ahead of me. A smarter version of me. Me but better.

We can clear this up, I thought. We can fix this whole thing. It's so simple. We were all fucked up that night, Verona. Me too. And I know why you thought it was Chief

Declan Brady. It's because you meant Chief Denny Casey, you meant that he is the one, the bad guy. The one doing all of this. You didn't lie to me, you sweet girl, come here, come here, let me see you. Let me see your face. That's a girl. You didn't lie to me at all. You were just confused. I'm confused too. I've been confused this whole time too. But no, you like Deck. You know him from around, and sure you've seen him do coke and maybe he's met a girl at a party, paid for it, a friend of yours, here and there, but he's fine, fine, other than that. He's a gentleman and he's polite. You told me so. It's so simple. Jesus, look what almost happened. Look how far this almost got. Look how many things were almost ruined because we had a little mix-up. That's all this is, a little mix-up. Okay? You're fine, honey. You're just fine. Let's have a drink, a cigarette, something else to calm us down. Let's find something else to calm us down. Let's ask around. We can find someone who can give us something. Come over here. We're all okay now. Jesus Christ.

You were calling me back to tell me that you had figured it out.

That it wasn't him.

Now it was just a matter of time. Until we could sort it out. She would call again. Even if she was on vacation, she would call me back. Even though we had fought and I had yelled and been awful, she would call me back. She needed me, same as I needed her. I had to tell her, to explain. To first apologize and beg forgiveness and then to explain. And we could get the right information to the right places, and sure, it would not be good, it would be very, very bad, actually, that this department's chief—*a* chief, rather, *a* chief from this department—was accused of such awful, hideous things, but we would get the information to where it needed to go, and then it would be out of our hands. The process would have been started.

I just needed to speak to her.

I would summon her, then. I put down my phone and my pen and put my head back against the chair and rolled toward the window and closed my eyes. I envisioned candles and a crystal ball, the smoke from a ceremonial herb, a séance. No, no, a séance was for the dead. We needed ESP. Clairvoyance. I envisioned her. In her red party dress. Cross-legged on her bed. In her green bikini. I sent my thoughts out to her like a group of homing pigeons. The one that took started down the coast. It was shaky and new as it lifted off outside, but it hit its current, flew quickly all the way to Georgia, got snagged in a passing storm, but then picked up speed and went easily all the way down to South Beach, where it found her at the deco-style pool of a hotel on Ocean Drive. She was face down, her bikini top undone. Not the bandeau I had imagined, but a halter-style, blue gingham. She sat up. Realized quickly, cupped her chest and asked the man to retie her.

"What?" he said looking up from a newspaper.

"I asked if you could retie me. I have to make a call," she said. "I'll be right back."

"Not now." He shook his head, didn't lower his sunglasses. He folded his newspaper sloppily. "I have to show you something in the cabana first." He shifted on his chaise and brought his hand to his shorts to readjust himself.

She looked at her legs: tan, skin tight from the hot sun. Out over the pool: a child steadying himself to dive off the board. And then at him: this man she was with. He wasn't bad, all things considered. She was on vacation and he wasn't that bad and her stroke of genius, her realization, her intuition could wait.

"For you," she said and opened her hands like a king showing gold, "*all* of it will wait." She got up and followed him in, the cabana's curtain falling closed behind them.

CHAPTER THIRTY

He had his secretary call me and everything. I figured he had to make it look like I was getting a talking-to.

"This is Virginia," I said when I picked up the internal line.

"Hi, hon. It's Joanne in the chief's office. Are you free to come down and see him? In about"—she looked at her watch or the wall clock—"fifteen minutes?"

"I can come right now," I said and stood up. I would ask Evelyn to watch the phone, to call for me if it rang. Excuse me—Evelyn, Officer Whomever, what even is your name, by the way?—excuse me but it is imperative that you call me if this phone rings. Please pick it up and ask the caller to hold, and then call me to come back here. I'll just be down with Chief Brady for a moment. Or two. Please. *Please.*

"He's in a meeting now, but fifteen will be perfect."

"Of course," I said.

Verona had not called. Deck had not come back to me for his coffee cup or to whisk me away forever. It was almost one in the afternoon.

Joanne had me wait. Sat me down in one of the chairs there. I listened to her talk to the other secretaries. Diets. New Year's diets. Then the sales in the department stores.

Maybe a new mattress? A pair of sandals? A Crock-Pot? Perfect time of year to buy a Crock-Pot. Stews, chowders, bisques—perfect. All of the husbands loved a hearty meal. To me: "You want some coffee, hon?" The cats on her desk snoozed in the sun. Even their tails were still.

He was running late. Twenty-nine minutes late, to be exact. The phone. She was going to call and I was going to miss it. Again.

I heard the door open down the hall. The sound of the men from Homicide: McHale and Ford and Tony and another man who must have been their lieutenant, though I had never met him. Never even seen him, I don't think. McHale gave me a sympathetic half smile. The others looked past me, talked among themselves. The last of them, alone, phone still tight in his hand: Ford. I looked straight at him—defiant, daring him—because now I had an answer. Now I had more than he did. But he wouldn't meet my eyes.

Joanne's desk phone rang and then she turned to me. Smiled. "All good, Virginia. Go ahead."

It was a different hallway. No spot of light on the floor. No bears, unfriendly or otherwise. But I was brimming. It didn't matter.

"So listen," I said as I was walking in. Then remembered. "Hello. Good afternoon." He waved me in and I shut the door. He was sitting at his desk.

"Hey," he said. "Sorry to have her call you down," he said and gestured toward the door. "I'm just neck deep here."

I shook my head. It was nothing. My days were numbered there anyway.

"Listen, listen," I said, starting. "I was thinking of something. Something sort of just came to me."

"Virginia," he said, interrupting, and he had turned, he was in the very process of turning. Hard chin. He wasn't the Deck from my bed. "Just a second. Sit down, okay?"

Bad news. This was bad news. I was a bad news expert, well versed in darkness and filth and sin and the grim, and that's where this was headed. I could smell it. I could taste the bad in the air. In those twenty-nine minutes something very bad had developed, and I was too late. The realization—*our* realization, mine and Verona's—had come too late.

They were there, waiting, just in the other room. And they were going to take him away. There were two of them waiting to take him away, but they were giving him the courtesy to tell me in person. This one last courtesy. I heard them shifting their weight in their feet, both at the same time, their guns on their belts, their nylon coats that said "FBI." I heard the noise that nylon makes when it rubs against itself. I heard them out there. That's why the bears were gone. They had cleared them. Sent them lumbering back to their den. That's what they were doing when I had walked in. Why I hadn't seen them. It was over. It was all over.

"Late last night," Deck said. His voice. Cozy, almost. Like he was starting a fairy tale. Narrating an old film. "No, wait. Disregard." He looked down at the paper in front of him. "About 0200 hours this morning, actually, a call comes in. Female caller, wouldn't provide her name. She could barely even speak. She's screaming, crying, incomprehensible. The dispatcher asks for a location, the caller says, 'In the bushes by Gilgo Beach.'" He stopped to look at me. He saw in my eyes, the smallest nod of my head: *go on*. "That's as precise as she gets. Then she says, 'They're after me.' Dispatcher says, 'Who, who is after you?' The caller says, 'The guy who did this to all of the girls. I know who he is, and he's after me now.'"

I opened my mouth to speak. Closed it. Sat there, twirling my earring. I saw him see me doing it.

"This call goes on for eighteen minutes. Dispatcher says, 'Who is he, what's his name, what's he look like?' All of it. The dispatcher did everything right. The girl was just hysterical, though. I mean, rightfully so. But she can't put a sentence together. Most of the time it's just rustling, her running. The phone rubbing against her face or in her bag or wherever."

Behind him. Out that big window. No clouds. My right ear started to ring. Tinnitus kicking in at that very second. I shook my head. Couldn't make it stop. Figured—silly, silly— it had to do with the earring, the metal in my skin, a foreign body. Darkness seeping. Looked back at him.

"Patrol goes down there, while she's still on the phone with dispatch. Nothing. It's—well, you've seen it—it's not a small area. Not easy to cover quickly. In the dark. The cold. Not ideal." His desk phone rang. He looked at it but didn't move to pick it up.

"Do you have to get that?" I said. It rang again. "Go ahead," I said.

"Yes, Joanne," he said when he picked it up. "No, not right now. It'll have to wait a bit. I'm in the middle of something. Can you push it back?" He looked at his watch. "Three thirty should be fine." He hung up. It was too bright. Getting too bright. I had a headache. Had we drunk too much? What had we had to drink?

We got back from Montauk around three, four maybe. His house. We showered, sat on the couch, dozed. We had happy hour by ourselves while sitting at his kitchen island. He showed me how to make a margarita *properly*. He said: *There is one right way to make a margarita and I only drink them when made* properly. I watched him shake it, concentrating. I told him that no one drinks margaritas in the dead of winter. That this was a strange proclivity. Neared the top of the list of his. We skipped dinner. Later we had prosecco in bed. He had mixed it with peach juice—Bellinis. It's hard to drink while lying in bed, and so it spilled. It went down my chin, down my neck, split into two rivulets, one cresting each shoulder, over onto my back. They died when they hit the sheets. When I was cleaning myself up, I looked in his medicine cabinet. A men's facial wash and moisturizer. A bottle of aspirin. A very thin layer of dust on the bottom shelf, which was empty except for one white button and its attached remnant of thread.

"Canine just found her. The call just came in."

I didn't say anything.

In his fridge: orange juice, the peach juice—nectar, it said—butter, neat rows of light beer and bottled water. A pint of strawberries turning soft, leaking sticky red, a mess on the glass. In his junk drawer, after he asked me to get batteries for the TV remote: a small measuring tape, the batteries I was looking for, playing cards, rubber bands, change, a complete mini-screwdriver set. Not missing a piece. He was like that. That was very him. In his closet: shoes lined up, suits, uniforms. On the very top shelf: hats, a ski helmet, and goggles. I imagined us in Aspen, in Snowmass. No taped boxes, no safes. Nothing. I shut the door.

"First glance, injuries look consistent with those of the other victims. We have to wait for the ME's report, but as

of now. Preliminarily, you know. She was positioned somewhat differently, but the guy knew he had a limited amount
of time. He couldn't do what he normally did. Probably just
did it and then fled."

"God," I said.

"Are you okay hearing this? I thought you'd want to
know," he said.

I didn't want any of this. I wanted him to call me Virginia in that whisper way he had and to touch my chin.
I wanted to get in his truck and drive hours away in any
direction. I wanted Christmas Eve and that day at the
beach and the sweater he touched so tentatively that first
time and anything but this. I wanted to put my face into
his sleeve, his chest, the crook of his arm. I looked at the
crook of his arm. He watched me. I was still at my ear,
worrying it. I felt the back of the earring loosen and then,
finally, I put my hands in my lap to stop them from moving. These hands were their own things. It shocked me
that they were still there, even. That two of my most functional parts had not yet left me. It seemed like everything
else was disappearing.

Down the hall, the phone was gone. The line was chewed
through, just like I had imagined, and the phone had been
removed. The office was cleared out. Walled up. Painted
over. Gone.

"Verona?" he said to me.

"Yes," I said, answering to it.

"That's the name she uses, right?" He had leaned back in
his chair. His arms bent, hands on his head. "It was all over
her phone. Not her real name, obviously. DMV says she's a
Ms.—" He looked back down at his papers, lifted a sheet.

"Please don't," I said. I put my hand up, palm to him. Closed my eyes. This stranger sitting in the same chair that I had been in, speaking for me. "I don't want to know."

My girl.

Cloud cover moved in over Southern Florida. People got up, gathered their things, went toward the hotel's entrance. The pool jets stopped pumping. The bathing suit. The cabana. His newspaper would disintegrate in the rain. Dead.

I had known, deep down. One of the many times I had woken up the night before. It had been a cosmic shift that did it, enough to rouse me even if I didn't know exactly what it was at the time. Our connection. Bone deep, meat and bone. Verona. Half awake, still dreaming, I'd crumpled. I slid down the stuccoed front of one of those buildings on Via Cappello, sun beating, and puddled onto the curb. I wanted to wail her name, to clutch my chest and weep in those cobblestone streets with a horde of other mourning women. We had lost so many women, too many, and one of us would always be next. Our black skirts floated on the wind. Veiled, shawled, we wept and wept.

He had been in the bathroom then. That was when I heard it, the gurgle. Of the pipes. I heard them spit, the sink choking through the walls of his home. He was in the bathroom only down the hall. So close I could still smell his cologne. So close I could feel him through the walls.

"Virginia?"

It took so long. It really took so long for me to see it. To understand what it meant.

And this was one of my problems. I missed the things that were right in front of me, and I saw the things that weren't there at all. Two problems, two opposite problems.

I was still fuzzy, I guess. My headache and the ringing in my ears. The prosecco. The sky opened up, a crack in all that blue. There was a sound when it cracked. Some would say the sound of singing. That that's what you would hear. But I will say it was the sound of tearing paper or the ripping of a seam. The sun was coming down, still streaming—almost painful in its brightness—that's not what had changed. It was in the tops of the pine trees outside, the green of them, the emerald of a flowing robe. A mantle. It was that blue, plush and thick and soft as the most exotic fur. The pelt of an animal found only in heaven. Velvet. I wasn't praying at this point. I was not thinking of the priest or feeling God enter my body through my chewing of the Holy communion. Because I didn't need to.

He had been with me. The night before, he had been with me. His back to my front or his arm across my chest or my head on his shoulder or my mouth on his. Every time I woke up—almost every time, but no, no—every time, say it, repeat it: *Every. Single. Time.* He was there. He couldn't have done any of it. It was impossible. But anything is possible. But it was virtually impossible.

But those choking pipes. Those pipes choked on their own, I knew that. A lifeless gurgle. The empty bathroom. I saw its darkness, the moonlight on the tile, my feet cold on the floor when I'd went to find him. Because there was a time when he hadn't been there. The hall was silent. The house and hall and drive were silent and empty except for me alone, in the hallway and then awake in this man's bed. I remembered that. With certainty at that moment, I remembered.

No cold shiver. No sudden inhale. He got called out all the time. Standard operating procedure. He was outside on his phone, didn't want to wake me. He was in his truck, speeding to a scene. And he would be back soon enough, his spot on his side of the bed not yet even cold to the touch.

"V?" he said. "You with me here?" And I was. Because there were so many possible explanations.

The bears, somewhere. Elsewhere. Doped on honey and all that meat and hibernating deep. Metabolic rates dropped low. Breathing slow, bodies gone cold. Torpor. It was winter after all.

I wanted to go to the beach and see. I wanted to scour the brush where they found her body. For clues, for proof. Those sticks and thorns scraping every exposed part of me. I'd take off my coat, roll up my sleeves, a martyr. Let them at me. Let them have more of my body. My tights, torn, the thorns lodging everywhere. I wanted abrasions, contusions, really bad black-and-blues. I wanted to go hands and knees, face close to the dirt, mouth close enough to eat it, looking. For a hair of hers, for a necklace, a bracelet, a ring, one of her long cigarettes. Something of her person. Verona. I could have found her myself. I could have saved her if, instead of drinking too much with this very same man, we had chosen instead to drive to the beach to watch that black water heave and pull. I could have seen her running, flash of bright hair against the night. I could have gotten out of his truck and opened my arms to her. Called her name and opened my arms to her. The ripped strap of her camisole flapping. Missing one shoe. Her bag, gone. But still, in my arms, finally. Our chests pounding, hearts smacking at each other, back and forth. Ripe, bursting, throbbing with life, still, both of us. Our bodies cooling at the same rate in the winter night. Our bodies, starting at the same temperature, cooling, slowly, together. Her bones the same as mine, lining up, the same as when I held her hand at that party. Same, same, same. I could have ushered her into the car and petted her hair and positioned her in front of the heating vents, let's warm up, let's kill this chill, and around us, all around us— it would seem to be in our heads it was so loud—the crackle of the police radio as he called it in, as he called for backup. For help. To save us.

So I asked him to take me to the beach.

CHAPTER THIRTY-ONE

He was late to his three thirty, but not by much. And plus, that's what people expected from him, from Chief Declan Brady. But we sat at the beach, on the ocean side. We over-shot where the bodies had been found and then did a Uturn and made our way back east until he turned off the parkway and stopped the car. Cut the engine. We sat like that for a minute, quiet. Watching the water. It shimmered in the sun. It was still very sunny. Then I got out.

Did not scour. Did not search. Did not wail into the dirt, tears falling and mixing to make some earthy poultice of my guilt. *I'm sorry, I'm sorry, I'm so, so sorry. There is no reason it should have been you.* Say this, chanting, chant it, palms together, place your forehead to the ground, Hail Mary for good measure. Weep, for God's sake. Cry for her. I did. I do. Later. Over and over. *It could have been me, but instead it was you.*

We got out and I had to take off my heels because I was sinking right in. The sand was freezing, even through my tights. But we walked down to the shoreline anyway. It was windy and the water was rough. The chop and churn had left froth everywhere. A recent storm had brought up a lot of seaweed. I went closer than he did. We weren't holding hands. I went all the way up to the water line until I couldn't go anymore, and stopped. The bottoms of my feet burned with the cold. They had become wet. They were becoming numb.

I turned around to say something but he was yards behind me, ten or fifteen, watching. Watching me, not the water. He had his hands on his hips. I smiled. I waved. And I think I saw pleasure in his face. I think I saw happiness, my making him happy. And then I had to look away from him. Because I wanted nothing but the expanse of the ocean, its glare, shards of light. It was all I could take. The cold sand. The gulls, their spirals, the smack of the shells they dropped to break.

All that brush behind me, to the left and right, encircling: a shawl, a crown, an embrace. That brush wanted to pull me in. That brush, wind whipping through, that brush pulsed. Four of them, five now, ten, a thousand. I should be there too, with them. No. No. Stop, there are no more, they are all gone. Saved. Found. She is found.

I wanted nothing. Let me have nothing. I wanted to see nothing. I wanted to breathe, only to breathe. That air. The beginning of my life. I wanted to do something specific so that I would never forget what it felt like. Pinch the inside of my wrist, leave a mark that I could keep pinching, ad infinitum. Get a tattoo: a black dot, a new moon, the letter V. So small you almost couldn't see. You'd really have to be looking. On the tip of a finger, in the bend of an elbow. So small, only I would know. Only someone who knew every inch of my bare body would know.

I forgot what I had turned around to say to him. Maybe something about how rough it was, how bright, I don't know. Maybe it was something like that. But to this day I do not remember. Because it was overshadowed. It was the perfect time for him to do it. So private. Not a soul. The light. The sea. The wind. It was all so perfect.

CHAPTER THIRTY-TWO

They almost sang it. As though robed, all altos, extolling the virtues of a husband, a home. They went in turn.

Rebecca: "Congratulations! I'm so happy to see you so happy! I knew you would find The One!"

Laura, a countermelody nudging in, starting low and swelling up: "Now your real life can begin, now you leave your past behind, now you have the joy we have."

My mother, at last, with the role she was born to play, with the finale: "I had real concerns, I will admit it now, Virginia, but you made it."

When all of this was over, the girls nagged me for pictures from different angles. *A video would be even better*, Laura texted. *We just want to see that sparkle*. Wink face, smiling face, crying/laughing face.

I obliged. A three-second video of my fingers moving, opening and closing, come hither in the winter sun, shooting out shivers of light. A stranger's hand. Another woman's hand. A hand with a ring.

You made it.

CHAPTER THIRTY-THREE

It always ends with a wedding. Short engagement, of course. We were not young. We were not in a position to spend the time and post the pictures of ourselves sampling cake—a plate of eight slices, a rainbow's range of white icings—and choosing amuse-bouches and which sparkling cocktail upon entrance, and guipure or Chantilly, and gardenias—no, white tea roses—no, gardenias, and a song. "*At Last*," he had suggested. *Really?* I said. I said, *Who even are you?* We chose all these things, but we did it quickly, quietly. We did it from brochures and websites. We did it in time for the June date we were able to get only because someone else's wedding had fallen through, broken up. But we stepped right in to fill it, ignoring the omen, thankful the stars had finally aligned.

I'll tell you: June 18, sunny and eighty-one degrees, not a cloud in the sky.

My mother fussed with everything. With the dress's hem, with the angle of the veil, with my hair—a chignon, expertly mussed and low on my neck.

Deck kept himself hidden. All that morning I didn't see him. I almost expected him to disappear, to have never existed, to be something I made up entirely. Imagined, like so many other things. But he texted me at noon: *I cannot wait.* Complete with the period, and I would have parsed it, that period, I would have dissected, sliced, and studied it had I had the time. Had I any longer cared. *I love you madly,* I wrote back, and the words looked hollow and fake, silly, even though I left off the period to convey a certain spontaneity, a certain wildness. Something feral still left. The *madly* a nod at our shared dark, a nudge, an elbow, remember, *remember*? It didn't look that way after I sent it, but that had been my intention.

At two, I stood in the living room, my face close to the glass of the sliding door of that house on the water. Pete's house, of course. The caterers in the kitchen joked. I heard the roll of a bar cart, the rattle of glass bottles. The clangs while they set up the trays. Their sighs. I heard the jangle of silverware.

I watched the people outside, twenty people, small party, all seated, their backs to me, not yet too hot. Most had flutes of the juice and champagne mixture we had chosen. The door was thick, so I couldn't hear them, but so many were turned toward each other, smiling. The judge was waiting at the front, scrolling through his phone. And there was the ocean, in front of them all, its depths warming in the early summer sun. Its depths.

But no Deck yet. He was running late, missing cufflink, mismatched socks. Or nervous. Or ill. He was vomiting in the white bathroom upstairs, grasping the towel rod that we had, that I had—I could run up there and help him, pull him up, promise him that nothing was going to change, that it would still be just the two of us, the same as it had always been. Always, I promise you, always and forever, the end.

I would promise him that I was a good person, I am—you know that—an understanding person. Vows. I thought of our vows. I did not move. Maybe he was gone, then. Just gone. *Out on the road.* On *pressing business.* Dealing with something that *just came up.* Inscrutable as usual. But what can you do? I had tried. I had known love.

But no. Five after two he came up the side steps. Dark blue suit, baby-blue tie. Blue, blue, blue. Like that first day I'd seen him, his blue filling the room. Something borrowed, something blue. Something borrowed was gold and filigree, tucked inside the band of my underwear, pressing its delicate metal into my flesh. A relic from another life. An ex's, now mine. My body gave it a warm home. Deck was calm, ever unruffled. He shook hands with the judge and smoothed back his hair and assumed a stance that said *waiting.* That said *ready and waiting.*

Somehow the door slid open for me—the birds, a princess, a caterer—and then everyone turned around. We had chosen a violinist for the ceremony, and she started playing that song, but the breeze quickly took it away, pulled it back toward the bay side, yanking, toward the brush, toward where they'd all been found, toward more women, maybe, as of yet unfound. And maybe I belonged there with them, waiting silent and still for the name of the guilty—one bad man; several bad men separately; several bad men working together, a grouped evil—though we may never know. It is years later and we still do not know. They continue to investigate, though they have no leads. Detective Ford had nothing, in the end. It was not Denny Casey. And the tips kept coming in; they keep coming in. Husbands, teachers, boyfriends, cops, fathers, priests, clerks, attorneys, doctors, sons. The truth will come out. It will lay itself bare. On anniversaries, reporters set themselves against the backdrop of that brush: thorny, beckoning.

My wedding music still circles through those thorns somewhere.

My violin.

My wedding music. On my wedding day I could hear only strains of that violin. That song. I can never remember the name of it, the song they play at weddings, but it was that one. The bits that registered rang through me, a plucked string. I smiled at our guests. I started to walk toward him.

He did not cry as he looked at me. He did not well up. His bottom lip did not tremble, but neither did mine. He smiled. He half nodded. He took me in. I looked at his face. I looked and I looked and I saw him—I finally saw him—my future husband. I saw everything. I saw a good man. I saw as much as you could see of another person and that felt right to me, and I thought: I did this. I made this happen. Now everything can start over because I decided that I love you.

ACKNOWLEDGMENTS

Thank you to my agent, Maria Whelan. You are tireless and determined and so smart and I would be lost without you.

Thank you to Toni Kirkpatrick for taking a chance on this book and for seeing a place for it in the world.

Thank you to the entire Crooked Lane team: Matthew Martz, Doug White, Rebecca Nelson, Dulce Botello, Melissa Rechter, Madeline Rathle, Holly Ingraham, Molly McLaughlin, Hannah Pierdolla, and Jess Verdi. And thank you to Heather VenHuizen for the gorgeous cover design.

Thank you to everyone at Stony Brook Southampton and to Roger Rosenblatt, especially, for introducing me to such a warm and welcoming community.

Thank you to Meg Wolitzer for suggesting such a perfect title.

Thank you to Susan Scarf Merrell for years (and years) of advice and hand-holding. You are one of the most generous people I know.

Thank you to my sister and my girlfriends for being there. Always.

Thank you to my parents for encouraging me to follow this wild dream. I only wish my father were here to see.

ACKNOWLEDGMENTS

Thank you to Tom for your unwavering support and your patience and your belief in me, even and especially when I was at my most difficult. It's been a long road.

And to Giacomo, thank you. Thank you for absolutely everything. You have taught me so much more than I have taught you. You are my light.